Sworn to Protect

SWORN TO PROTECT

Rescue Ops Book 1

DIANA GARDIN

FOREVER
YOURS

New York Boston

Copyright © 2017 by Diana Gardin
Excerpt from *Promise to Defend* copyright © 2017 by Diana Gardin
Cover design by Elizabeth Turner
Cover copyright © 2017 by Hachette Book Group, Inc.

Forever Yours
Hachette Book Group
1290 Avenue of the Americas, New York, NY 10104
forever-romance.com
twitter.com/foreverromance

First published as an ebook and as a print on demand: June 2017

Forever Yours is an imprint of Grand Central Publishing. The Forever Yours name and logo are trademarks of Hachette Book Group, Inc.

The publisher is not responsible for websites (or their content) that are not owned by the publisher.

The Hachette Speakers Bureau provides a wide range of authors for speaking events. To find out more, go to www.hachettespeakersbureau.com or call (866) 376-6591.

ISBNs: 978-1-4555-7153-6 (ebook), 978-1-4555-7154-3 (POD trade edition)

To the Dolls, for being the very best reader group there is. I hope you love Jeremy and Rayne's story: This one's for you!

Acknowledgments

First of all, I'd like to thank my Lord and Savior Jesus Christ, who gave me the desire and skill to write. Through Him I can do all things!

My family is always there for me when I put down my computer and unplug from all things writing. I'm so thankful they're along for this ride with me.

Thank you to my agent, Stacey Donaghy. You are more than an agent: You are my friend, and I'm so very thankful to have found you. I am even more thankful that you're always on my side.

To my fabulous editor on *Sworn to Protect*, Lexi Smail: Working with you is such an enlightening experience. Your thoughts and ideas on the world of NES are invaluable, and your expertise when it comes to how to make a story take off is something I could never trade. Thank you for everything!

To the team at Forever Romance: you are all such a well-oiled machine. From editing, to copyediting, to cover design and all of the other inner workings I don't even get to see, you are all fabulous and I'm lucky to be a part of it all. Thank you for your efforts on my behalf!

To my favorite sounding board and the girl who has become one of my very best friends, Sybil Bartel: I don't know how it happened, but you're like the other half of my writing brain. You're there at all hours of the day and night, whether I need to get an idea out, or I'm completely out of them. I only hope I help you as much as you help me! Love you, girl.

To the very best group of writers a girl could ever ask for, the NAC: Ara, Meredith, Kate, Bindu, Sophia, Laura, Missy, Jessica, Amanda, Jamie, Marie, and Marnee—you are my very best source of sanity. Without you, this business would have ended me long ago! Love y'all!

To the bloggers who have supported me throughout this journey: There are too many of you to name, but you know who you are. You have read every single book, given me great reviews, and shared my work with as many people as you can. I couldn't do any of this without your help and your enthusiasm. A thousand thank-yous.

And last but never least, to the readers who find their way to Wilmington, North Carolina, to hang out with the sexy men of Night Eagle Security and the women who are strong enough to love them. I hope you fall in love with this world as much as I have, because without you I'd be nothing. <3

Prologue

RAYNE

My heels click on the polished marble floors as I hurry from the inner office back to my desk in the outer suite. The air, chilly in the late evening hour, feels extra frosty as it filters through my silk sleeveless blouse. I throw a glance back over my shoulder, my eyes scanning the empty hallway behind me for any sign of him.

Just because I don't see him doesn't mean he isn't close. And getting closer.

A sound echoes somewhere in the giant building, close enough that it ricochets through my body like a gunshot. I jump, my heart leaping into my throat as my pulse skyrockets.

I go still, listening.

The sound of insistent footsteps pounding on the same marble I just traversed spurs me into moving again. I skid to a stop at the end of the hallway, looking down the intersecting hall in both directions.

Which way? Which way?

Going for the exit would be the long way. The elevator is two halls away, and my movements can be tracked on any security camera. Especially when my boss, who started this multi-million-dollar tech corporation, is the man I'm running from now.

Oh, my God. I need to get home. I need to get to Decker.

Thinking of my sweet boy triggers a new surge of adrenaline inside me, and I leap forward, choosing to head right, toward the stairs. At least if I'm in the stairwell, I can hear anything coming above me or below me. All I'll have to do is get down fourteen floors to the lobby, and then I'm free.

Free. Free. Free.

Kicking off my shoes, I grasp them in one hand and break into a run. Crossing the short distance to the large double doors marked STAIRS, I push through them and allow them to latch silently behind me. Sucking in a deep breath, I start down the steps.

One flight at a time, Rayne. You can do this. You have *to do this.*

If Wagner Horton takes time to scan the security footage, that's even better for me. That gives me time to get out of this damn building, and get to my kid. The heel of my palm pounds against my head as I hurry downward. Over and over again. As if I could thump away the memory of the sight that got me into this mess in the first place.

Just work, the same work I've done every day for the past eight months. Only this time, being Wagner Horton's executive assistant gave me access to information I never wanted and wasn't supposed to see.

A sound from somewhere above me jars me back into awareness, back to the here and now. Step by step, I rush down the stairs. When I'm crossing the threshold to the seventh floor, the stairwell door below me opens and closes.

I freeze, holding my breath.

"Rayne? I know you're here."

Wagner's voice has never, ever scared me.

Until now.

I mean, he's a tech geek turned billionaire. I never considered him to be dangerous. But the look in his eyes tonight when he discovered me in the building after hours, working late…I shudder, remembering.

I close my eyes, willing him to *just go away*.

Silence from one floor below me.

Brrrrrrrrrrng.

In my pocket, my cell phone rings.

Wagner's laugh floats toward me. "There you are."

The sound of his feet pounding up the stairs mingles with the quiet thump of my bare feet turning and heading up one more floor. Moving faster than I've moved ever, I throw myself through the eighth-floor stairwell door and into the hallway.

The only option I have now is to hide, or to get to the elevator before he gets to me.

I choose the elevator. Sprinting around the corner and into the hall where those heavenly golden doors lay waiting for me.

"Come, on, come on, dammit!" Stabbing at the button repeatedly, I glance over my shoulder again and again.

The elevator doors slide open as Wagner rounds the corner all the way down the hall.

"Rayne!" he screams.

The desperate sound reaches into my chest and squeezes my heart, stuttering the beats.

Frantic, I push the CLOSE button over and over again, jabbing it with such violence I'm sure to feel the pain later.

OhmyGodohmyGodohmyGod.

Please…close! Close!

My voice is silent as I yell at the elevator doors. They begin to slide shut and I sag against the back wall of the box, letting out the breath I'd been holding

And then Wagner appears, looming *right there*.

With a yelp, I press against the back wall of the elevator.

His face is a mask of hatred and fury. He goes to stick a hand between the doors, but it's too late. The doors slide shut.

With my heart in my throat, I ride the eight floors down to the parking garage. I know for a fact that, since only one elevator goes up to our offices, Wagner would have had to take the stairs. I have a decent head start, but I run anyway as soon as the elevator opens.

Straight to my car.

Police. I need to go to the police.

But the memory of a photo I saw on the wall in Wagner's office every day for eight months flashes in my brain. It's a picture of him and the chief of the Phoenix police department, smiling and shaking hands for the camera after Wagner's money built the department a brand-new, state-of-the-art headquarters.

I've never thought that having a chief of police in your pocket was a real thing, but that picture sends me reeling.

There's no way I'm going there. Not until I know who I can trust.

Yanking the door open and thanking the heavens for key fobs, I start the thing and peel out of my spot. Pressing the car's Bluetooth button, I order the vehicle to call my babysitter.

"Payton? Yeah, I'm leaving work now. I don't have time to explain, but I need you to grab Decker, get in your car, and drive to the airport. Don't hesitate, Payton. Do it *now*."

I'll mourn the loss of my belongings later. Maybe I can send for them.

But right now? I have to get out of Phoenix. Maybe forever. I know now that what I saw was important.

Maybe important enough for him to kill me.

I'm going to have to do the one thing I *never* wanted to do.

For the first time in nearly nine years, it's time for my son and me to go home.

1

JEREMY

When my fellow team member Grisham Abbot strolls into the Night Eagle Security conference room a few minutes after I do, I lean back in my big, leather chair.

The seriousness and tension of the undercover mission I just led siphons off me, being replaced by the relaxed comfort of being home.

It's like I'm two different Jeremy Teagues: the one who kicks ass during a security or black ops mission or the laid-back jokester I tend to be when I'm not working. Sometimes they get in each other's way.

Sometimes they fight for supremacy.

Grisham eyes me, one hand shoving through his short blond hair as he comes to a stop across the table beside his usual seat. "You recover from whatever it is you think you saw at the airport this morning?"

Inhaling, I try not to flip back to that moment in the airport. But the memory creeps in anyway, regardless of how hard I try to fight it...

We're just passing under the decorative model of a single-engine plane hanging overhead into the baggage claim area when a mane of long, raven hair catches my eye. My stomach flips, my muscles tighten, and my back teeth grind together.

Fucking hell. That hair.

She turns, her profile facing me, and everything inside me stills.

My steps stutter to a stop, and I'm pretty sure the air in my lungs does, too. Everything around me, the airport crowd, the noise, fades away, and it's like I'm staring through a tunnel of mist and fog and the only thing I can see at the end of it is her.

Because, swear on my dog, it's her.

I'd scoured the airport after that, my head swiveling left and right, my eyes roving. Searching.

There'd been rows of taxis lined up in front of the terminal, and that ghost could have disappeared into any one of them.

Or I could have just been losing my fucking mind. More likely.

Because I exorcised that ghost a long time ago. I don't need it to start haunting me again.

I snap back to the here and now as Grisham begins to lower himself into his chair. I ignore his question and lean forward. "Let's grab a beer after we debrief." I lift my brows, hoping he'll accept the invitation. I'm still feeling the need to unwind, let loose a little after our op.

He stares at me like I've lost my mind. "Man, I've been away from my fiancée for almost a week. There's no way in hell I'm going anywhere but home after we give Jacob the rundown."

I feign a heavy sigh, but I knew his answer before he'd said it.

"Whipped," I mutter.

"Damn right." Grisham's statement comes with a proud smile.

Jacob Owen strides into the room. "Let's debrief, gentlemen." His tone is wry as he sends me a pointed stare.

He leans over the low, rectangular table where, as a team, we use painstaking research to plan our missions. Clasping his hands together, he looks at Grisham and me in turn, holding our gazes as he assesses our reaction. His blue eyes, webbed with lines that are the only indicator of his middle age, stop on me.

"First black ops government contract. First time leading a Night Eagle mission. A lot of firsts for you in the last few weeks, and for the firm. Right, Brains?"

I nod my head and hold steady under his scrutiny. I'd give my left nut for Jacob Owen, pretty sure the whole team would. Adjusting to normal life again after Special Forces is difficult. For some of us, it's impossible. But Jacob gets it. And when he brings one of us into the fold at Night Eagle Security, we thrive.

Finally, he speaks again, this time addressing both Grisham and me. "You did good, boys."

Letting out a breath, I lean back in my seat and listen while Jacob fires questions at us about the intel we received that will bring down not just the Miami part of the arms ring, but the South American branch as well. He informs us that in a few months' time, we'll be leaving for Costa Rica on a second mission to first infiltrate, and then help the CIA eliminate, this nasty operation for good.

When our debriefing comes to an end, Jacob shakes both of our hands and glances at Grisham.

"Ghost," he barks.

Grisham "Ghost" Abbot leans forward, his elbows connecting with his knees as he locks eyes with his future father-in-law. The ex-SEAL earned his nickname with his uncanny ability to sneak up on enemy forces in the field. Grisham Abbot is the strategist of our group. He's a planner, an analyzer by nature, and that skill works to our advantage when it comes to nailing down the nitty-gritty details of a potential operation.

"Sir."

"Get home to my daughter. She's missed you." Jacob's lips twitch.

As we leave Jacob's office, I want to pump my fist in the air. I want to shout "Hell Yeah" now that I know for a fact that we're going black ops again.

I've been with NES for a little over a year. In that time, we've specialized in personal security for clients who can afford to pay the price for the best protection out there. In the past six months or so, Jacob has been in talks with some government agencies. His connections there have asked us multiple times to protect foreign dignitaries, their families, and other important international people who are working or vacationing close by, and we've excelled at every single one of those assignments.

This last mission, sending us to infiltrate the illegal arms organization in Miami, was not only the first time I've taken the lead on an op, but also the first time we've had an official "black ops" contract with Uncle Sam as a private contractor.

Deep cover, secret mission…everything that comes with it is my element. I fucking love it. The reason they call me Brains is because I have an obsession with techy gadgets for the field. I have a whole room dedicated to storing all of the tools and equipment we may need for a mission or an assignment, and I love stocking it up and keeping it up-to-date with everything current in the world of tech and gear. This job is in my blood, and I could never imagine doing anything different.

My adrenaline is still pumping from everything we accomplished, and I know when I get back to my house, the first thing I'll need to do is run.

Grisham and I file out the metal sliding door into the lobby.

Ronin "Swagger" Shaw claps me on the back as soon as the office door is closed. "Nice, guys. Heard you kicked some ass." I accept congratulations from the man who's been my teammate and best friend for years. First the army, then the police academy, then NES after we met Jacob while working on a kidnapping case.

Dare "Wheels" Conners, our other teammate and the man who can drive anything out there like a goddamn stuntman, follows suit with a fist bump.

When I'm in this office, in my city, with my people, I'm home. There're no surprises, no unexpected bullshit the way there is when I'm on a mission. It's how I like it.

And it feels good to be home again.

But as I'm back in North Carolina, weaving through the Wilmington streets on my drive home, my brain drifts back to long, black hair, flawless, olive skin, and the endless sea of blue eyes I once almost drowned in.

It couldn't have been her.

2

RAYNE

The cab pulls up to a cute Colonial-style home with a manicured yard. Bright flowers dot the mulch-hugged beds, and the house is a crisp white, gleaming against the backdrop of the afternoon sun. Black shutters and a red front door complete the picture-perfect look. It's my first time seeing the place, but the perfection is less than shocking. My sister's home is right out of a magazine. I wouldn't expect anything less.

It's a far cry from my tiny little Mediterranean I'd been renting in Phoenix. The scrubby landscape there meant no flowers or bright green grass, even though my tastes are a lot more eclectic than my sister's.

The Uber driver drops us off in the driveway and gives us a wave before heading back down the street.

My son, Decker, and I stare up at the house. There's resignation on my face, while his holds nothing but eight-year-old curiosity.

"So this is where Aunt Olive lives?"

I nod, rolling my lips between my teeth. "Yup."

Neither of us moves toward the house.

"Did you live here when you were little, Mom?" Decker is staring at the house like it's a possibility Captain America lives inside.

Shaking my head, I put my arm around him and squeeze. "No, sweetie. Mommy and Aunt Olive lived at a different house in Wilmington when we were growing up."

The house where I lived with your grandparents, who I haven't spoken to since I got pregnant with you.

"And," I remind him, "your aunt is in Europe for a few more months for work. She said we could stay here as long as we want."

He glances at me, and I melt the way I do every single time I look at him. The kid is beautiful. An olive complexion that matches mine, but with hair a shade lighter. He keeps it long, the ends touching his collar, and his locks are thick and lustrous. His deep-set eyes are the most beautiful shade of jade green. Like his father's. When I stare into them, it takes me back to the best and worst time in my life. His thick, long lashes brush his cheeks as he glances down.

"I'm gonna miss my friends."

Getting down on my knees on the cement so that I can face him at eye level, I offer him a soft smile. "I know, baby. And I'm sorry about that. You're going to make new friends here, I promise. And you're gonna love the beach."

His expression brightens. "Yeah? Can I learn how to surf?"

Closing my eyes briefly, I mutter a curse.

"Mom…you said a bad word. You gotta put a quarter in the jar."

Standing, I circle an arm around his shoulders and pull him toward the house. "See baby? The more things change, the more they stay the same."

Putting in the automatic door code, I let Decker and I into the garage and then the house.

The house is pristine. I don't see a speck of dirt or dust anywhere, and I know for a fact I won't be able to keep up the standard of living Olive does. We've always been so different. It's glaringly obvious when I'm in her house.

"Whoa," whispers Decker, his eyes wide. "Mom? I think we're gonna get it dirty in here."

Patting his back, I nod. "Yeah, Deck. I'm pretty sure you're right."

A couple hours later finds us settled in, Decker in a guest room upstairs and me in my sister's master bedroom. The sitter brought Decker a few things from home but I left with nothing, so I borrow some of Olive's clothes. Evening has fallen, and as there's no food in the house with Olive being out of the country, I decide to delay grocery shopping for a day and take Decker out for pizza.

Using Olive's car, I drive us the short distance into downtown Wilmington. It's a straight shot into downtown from Olive's suburban neighborhood, and Decker's face is glued to the passenger-side window the entire time. The surroundings are familiar to me, but I realize he's never even left Phoenix. All the green, the salty-sea smell, the beachy vibe…it must feel to him like we're in a foreign country.

"What do you think?" I ask him as we idle at a red light.

He turns to me, dimples showing up deep in his cheeks as he grins. "Awesome!"

Smiling, I ruffle his hair. High praise from an eight-year-old.

For the first time since I arrived at the airport back in Phoenix, I take a deep breath and don't feel like my world is caving in. Putting half a country between me and Wagner Horton gives me a sense of security that I crave. But deep down inside, I know the illusion of safety is just that—an illusion. Wagner, despite the lapse in technological creativity he's been experiencing of late, is a genius.

Maybe everything will be okay. Maybe Decker and I can be safe here. Wagner has no idea that I'm from Wilmington; he doesn't know where I'd run. I can change my name back. I can disappear, as far as he's concerned. I'll stick to the plan. No credit cards until my new last name is official. New phone, already purchased at the airport. And just in case I have to run again? I have my emergency stash of cash.

I shiver. I don't want him to find me.

I can't even fathom what it all means, what he'll do to keep his secret buried.

"Let's eat there!"

Decker's shout alerts me, and as I pull into the parking lot I eye the vibrant sign of my favorite restaurant as a teenager. There were a lot of memories made at Vinny's…especially memories with Jeremy. Of course this is where Deck would choose to have dinner.

"Come on," I say with a smile, pulling him with me into the restaurant.

Fragrant, spicy air meets us, and immediately my mouth waters. Decker and I haven't eaten since lunch during our layover in New Orleans, and I know his little tummy must be grumbling same as mine.

The hostess seats us and I peruse the menu while Decker stares around us with curious eyes. Leaning over toward him, I poke his belly.

"Pizza is the same here as it is in Arizona, baby."

He grins. "Good. Can't mess up pizza."

"Nope."

After we order, Decker points to the small section of arcade games the restaurant houses in a corner. He opens his mouth, but I wave him on with a smile before he asks.

"Go. I'll come get you when the pizza gets here."

The smile stays on my face as I watch him race over. He immediately jumps into a pinball game with another little boy who looks about his age, only that little boy is at Vinny's with his mother and his father.

Pain stings my chest as I watch the happy couple with their baby daughter and allow myself to wish, just for a second, that I could have given that kind of life to Decker.

Pulling out my phone, I reread Olive's text:

I told my friend Berkeley to expect a call from you. She works with me at the design firm. Her husband might have a job lead for you. ☺

Lord knows I need a job lead. My meager savings, excluding my emergency stash, won't hold Decker and me for long.

I'm starting a new life here in Wilmington, trying to erase the old, painful memories this town still holds for me. Eating pizza at my favorite restaurant with my son and finding a new job is a really good start.

Maybe I can make this work.

God, I hope so.

My phone vibrates in my hands, and I glance down at it to see a Phoenix area code.

My hopeful smile disappears. The blood rushes downward, leaving my face and pooling somewhere by my feet. I don't recognize the number as Wagner's, but I know…I just *know* before I open the text.

When I do, I drop the phone, both hands clapping over my mouth.

I will find you bitch. You fucked with the wrong guy.

The tenuous feeling of security from just a moment ago vanishes, leaving me cold and scared and lonely.

What the hell am I going to do?

The unexpected knock on the door on Saturday afternoon practically gives me an ever-loving heart attack. The riotous *thump-thump-thump* in my chest causes me to rest a hand there while I stare toward the entryway. From my spot at the kitchen sink, washing up the dishes from breakfast and lunch, I have a clear view to the front hall.

Before I can decide what to do, Decker comes skidding down the hardwood hallway from his room. He glances at me and then at the door.

"I'll get it!" he yells.

"No, Deck! Stop!"

The frantic panic in my voice halts him. He pivots, a slow and wary movement and look s at me expectantly. "Mom?"

Wiping my hands on a towel, I hurry forward. Very aware that I'm in a pair of Olive's workout pants and a faded tank top, my hair in a messy bun on top of my head, I grab his shoulders and lean down so we're at eye level.

"Sorry, sweetie. I just…we don't know anyone here yet, and I'd rather you not answer the door by yourself. Okay?"

I plaster a bright smile on my face and hope my too-smart kid falls for it.

He eyes me, a shadow of doubt in his eyes. "Okay."

Who would be knocking on the door? I don't know anyone here. Not anymore.

I take a deep breath and pull the front door open, Decker hovering beside me.

A tall, gorgeous woman with dark brown skin and oodles of braided hair cascading down around her shoulders stands on the front porch with a sunny smile. She's holding a basket in her hands, and there's a little boy who looks to be about Decker's age standing beside her. She looks perfect and trendy in light-blue, ripped-up jeans, heeled sandals, and a flowing white top.

I try really, really hard not to feel like a hot mess, but let's just be honest, shall we?

"Hey, there." Her smile is contagious. "I'm Macy, and I live next door. Olive called me this morning, asking me to stop in and check on you."

All the tension leaves me with a relieved sigh, and I step back from the door to let them both inside.

"Oh, my gosh! It's so nice to meet you, Macy. I'm Rayne Alexander, and this is my son, Decker."

Macy smiles at Decker. "Decker, your aunt told me all about you. This is my little man, Julius."

Julius shoots his mom an annoyed glance, probably due to the "little man" comment, and he eyes Decker. "I go by Jay." Another pointed glance for Macy. "I got a hoop. You ball?"

Decker looks at me, pleading in his eyes. I nod, smiling. Glancing at Macy, I ask. "Just out front?"

With a wide smile, she assures me. "Right in our driveway."

"Go ahead." I land a pat on Decker's back before he runs out the front door with Julius.

Ushering Macy down the hall and into the great room off the kitchen and dining area, I grab the basket she offers.

"Thank you so much for bringing us…" I lift the towel lining the basket and grin. "Muffins! Delicious. If I'd known you were coming by, I would have chosen *not* to look like Cinderella."

She laughs, waving a dismissive hand. "Girl, please. Just between you and me, I only dressed like this to come over here to put on a good impression. I'm a stay-at-home mom. I *live* in yoga pants."

That's the moment I decide I might adore Macy.

"Drink?" I ask her, walking over to the cabinet where Olive keeps the glasses.

She glances at her phone. "Damn. Too early for wine. Just water then. I'll only stay a minute, I know you're settling in."

Macy makes herself at home on one of the brightly printed chairs in the great room while I get her water. All at once it hits me: I didn't have a single girlfriend while I was in Phoenix. I was a single mother at eighteen in a brand-new city. I was trying to support Decker and myself. So I didn't exactly go out looking for friends. And I definitely wasn't dating.

Handing Macy her water, she thanks me, and I sit down on the couch adjacent to her. It's the only comfortable piece of furniture in the large room. But, of course, it's white.

Gesturing to the couch, I offer Macy a wry look. "I'm pretty sure that by the time Olive comes back, this white couch is gonna be stained with orange juice or maybe there'll be a fruit snack stuck to it somewhere."

Macy's laugh is booming and buoyant. Just like she is. "Yeah…Olive's place isn't exactly kid-friendly."

Shaking my head, I sadly eye all the pretty pieces around the room. "Definitely not. She's a fabulous aunt to Decker, though. We never got to see her much when we lived in Phoenix…she got out maybe every couple of years. But they love each other."

Macy nods, eyeing me over the rim of her water glass. "You know what? I'm just gonna say what I'm thinking. When Olive told me she had a sister staying at her house with an eight-year-old son, I just thought you'd be in your thirties, like me.

"But clearly"—she looks me up and down—"I assumed wrong. You're young and gorgeous. Now I'm gonna have to take an extra class at the gym to make sure I'm keeping up with you."

Laughing, I pull my feet up underneath me. It's so easy talking to Macy, but I don't want to give her my whole sob story. "I had Decker when I was eighteen."

Macy nods. "Gotcha. And I'm going to assume, since you're staying with Olive, that his father's not in the picture."

Something inside me shifts, crawling deeper into my soul to try and hide my feelings about Decker's father. The only time I ever think of him is late at night, when I can't sleep. That's the time I allow thoughts of him to drift in, and the longing and aching I feel whenever I see a whole family together is fleeting.

"Decker and I do just fine on our own." My smile is tight, but not because I'm irritated with Macy's curiosity.

I just try to avoid thinking of him at all costs.

Her eyes soften at the corners, melting into puddles of chocolate. "I bet you do."

We share a smile, and I have to admit that even though Macy probably doesn't understand any of what I've been through, she's a sympathetic soul.

"Will Decker be going to the local elementary school?"

Nodding, I bite my lip. "I feel so bad about throwing him into school like that. But the sooner he gets into school and starts making friends, the better. And a week from this Monday's the first day of school, so that's even better." At least that's what I told Decker, and I'm hoping he loves it. "He's an easy kid, I think he'll do fine."

After a beat, I add, "And I'm starting my new job this Monday. So I need him to be in school."

First thing this morning, I called the friend that Olive works with, Berkeley, and spoke with her husband, Dare. He said they've been using temps as assistants at the place where he works, and that I should come in on Monday because they'd just lost one. I told him that that'd be perfect, because my old job in Phoenix was as an executive assistant. He told me he'd call his boss for me and that I should show up at the address he gave me on Monday morning.

Dare and Berkeley both seemed so sweet, and I almost cried with the relief of having a new way to support Decker and myself.

Macy places her glass down on a little round side table beside her chair, sure to slide a coaster underneath it first. She must know Olive well. "You know what? I drive Julius to school and pick him up every day. I can do the same for Decker, if you'd like."

I think my eyes bug out a little as I stare at her. The thought of putting Decker on a bus in this town, even though it's my hometown, scares the life out of me. Especially after the threatening text message I received last night.

"Macy…there's no way I can impose on you like that."

She shakes her head. "It's not an imposition. You live next door. And I can keep him at my house after school until you get home from work. Moms have to help each other out."

Leaning forward, I grab her hands and squeeze them. I don't care if I don't know her very well. I might kiss her. "I don't know what to say…thank you so much! I'll start giving you weekly gas money."

Macy starts to protest, but I lift a hand to cut her off. "And, anytime you want to have a date night with your husband, you let me know. I'll keep Julius."

Macy beams, reminding me again that she might just be the sweetest person I've ever met. "Deal. What are you doing with Decker this week when you start work?"

Shrugging, I try to exhale the stress I've been feeling trying to get everything in line. "I'm not sure yet."

"Well, now you do. I take Julius to the Boys' Club during the day; he likes to play ball with other kids and hang out. I can keep Decker with us, and he can go too. Is that okay with you?"

Maybe Macy doesn't realize that I've just designated her an actual angel, but in my book, she definitely is. "Thank you so much, Macy."

Leaning back on the couch, all the air goes out of me as the reality of today hits me. I found a job and a babysitter for Decker.

And maybe a new friend.

"So what's your new job going to be?" asks Macy.

I lift one shoulder in a half-shrug. "Well, I'll be an assistant. A friend of my sister's from the design firm…her husband works for a security company or something like that. So I think they probably install alarms or something."

I should probably get them to install one at Olive's house. A little extra security would go a long way for me right now.

3

JEREMY

Come on, Night. Last mile." My feet dig into the sand as I enter the final stretch of my six-mile run.

The midnight-black Cane Corso grunts, his blocky head bobbing as he puts on a burst of speed. Little devil always gets competitive on the last mile. At 110 pounds, Night is a blue-eyed mass of solid canine muscle. He wants to beat me every time. With a chuckle, I put on the burners, keeping up with him as we sprint along the beach. Doesn't matter how bad my lungs burn, how tingly my leg muscle become, my dog will not beat me on a run. Ever.

The early Monday morning surf brushes over my bare feet as they kick up clumps of packed sand, and I glance out over the horizon. The morning is dawning clear and bright, and knowing I have the whole day ahead of me to do what I want is invigorating.

Ghost and I returned from Miami on Friday, and the general rule around the office is that we take the next workday off after a mission completion. So today is all mine, and I have plans to do some training exercises with Night, grocery shop, and head out on my boat.

Perfect day off.

I drop Night off at home and rinse off in the shower before setting off to the health foods market. The only one in Wilmington is about fifteen minutes away from my house in the downtown area, but it's worth the drive. Cooking is what I love to do when I'm not training or sneaking around undercover, and buying the best farm-to-table ingredients has become kind of an obsession for me.

On a Monday morning, just a week before the kids will be heading back to school, the market is packed with frazzled moms getting ready to prepare school lunches and meals for busy families. Not many dudes shopping in this store, but that's okay with me.

I scan each aisle, grabbing items from the shelves and bins and throwing them into my cart, checking them off my list as I go.

White Asparagus, check.

Lemons, check.

Whole-grain hoagie rolls, check.

My eyes drift to the long, bare legs of the woman beside me in the bread aisle. She bends over a bin, rummaging through it, searching for the bread she wants. Her denim cutoffs, already short enough for her ripe, round cheeks to peek out from underneath, calls me to attention. I swallow, a slow grin curling over my mouth.

I'm about to open my mouth to speak to her when a Nerf

football lands in my cart. Snapping my mouth shut, I grab the small yellow ball and study it. I search the aisle, and it clicks into place when a small boy jogs toward me, his face glowing with mischief and excitement.

"Sorry, mister," he says with a grin.

Little monster isn't sorry! I can't hide my own grin as I grip the soft ball and raise my arm.

"Catch," I say before tossing the ball in his direction.

It spirals in the air, arcing toward him, but it's a little high. The kid jumps, reaching for it. He snatches it out of the air.

"Nice!" I push my cart over to where the kid landed. "Good catch."

His dark hair falls into his eyes, eyes that are just as startling a shade of green as mine are, and he pats the ball with his other hand as he smiles up at me.

Cute kid.

"Dude!" he exclaims. "Do you play football? That was a perfect pass."

His eyes are alight as he sizes me up. He takes in my height and build, which come from constant training exercises at Night Eagle and the daily runs on the beach. There's interest in the kid's eyes, like he's hoping I'll tell him I play for the Carolina Panthers or something.

"Played in high school a little bit, kid." It's partially true. I did play football in high school here in Wilmington, but it was more than just a little bit.

I lived and breathed the sport. Thought pro ball would be the path my life would take me down until that fateful day during my senior year when everything changed. My whole life as I knew it became a lie, and the only thing I wanted to do when I graduated was leave it all behind. Joining the army did that for me, it gave me the escape I needed.

The kid's eyes light up. "Cool. You were lucky. My mom won't let me play."

Staring down at him, I offer my most sympathetic smile. "I'm sure she's just trying to look out for you."

Glancing around the store, I see that the kid's still alone in the aisle. "So where is your mom?"

A twitch of concern pulls at me. I'm not really a "kid" guy because I haven't been around them much. But I don't want this one to end up on the evening news.

The kid grins. "I'm here with a friend. Gotta go!"

He lifts a hand in a wave, turns, and is gone, disappearing around the corner to another aisle, and I'm left by myself in the bread aisle.

No cutoffs girl to keep me company, either.

That's a bummer.

Pushing my cart through the store, I finish my grocery shopping and leave the health foods market.

But as I'm loading up my Land Cruiser with grocery bags the full force of the meeting with that little boy, a complete stranger to me, barrels into me. A flashback of me, begging my grandfather as a little boy to come outside and play football with me. My grandfather, refusing every single time because he was too busy running an empire to play with the grandson he was saddled with. Me, wishing every single night that instead of being raised by my grandfather, I could have been raised by a dad who loved me, and wanted to play with me. Me wishing that my parents hadn't died in a plane crash when I was only three years old.

I haven't thought about any of that for years. The discipline of the Rangers helped me learn to block it out, and the force of the swirling thoughts resurfacing now is almost enough to bring me to my knees.

I sink into the driver's seat of my car, staring blankly ahead of me.

Damn. I haven't thought about any of that in so long. Why now?

I wish, more than anything at that moment, I had an answer to that question.

I spend the rest of Monday afternoon out on my boat. Right behind my job and Night, the *Havoc* is my third love. I bought the twenty-two-foot Moomba when I retired from the army. The boat, just like the historical house I bought and renovated, fulfills an emptiness in me I've never been ready to address. So, for now, I let the adventure the boat brings fill me up.

I bring Grisham with me, and we take turns driving the boat while the other wakeboards. Before I knew Grisham as well as I do now, I would have assumed the prosthetic foot he earned when his Humvee was bombed in Syria a few years ago would have limited him. But he never lets it slow him down. The dude is a natural in the water, and he's still damn fast on land. When I finally come off the water for the last time, wet, limbs heavy with exertion, but grinning my face off, I grab my phone and check it. The boat floats gently in the ocean surf, the shade from the dock cover making my screen bright.

I let out a chuckle when I read Ronin's message, and Grisham glances at me as he's loading his towel into a bag.

"What?"

I point to my phone. "It's Swagger." A wide grin spreads across my face. "Says there's a new chick working the desk at the office. Says she's fine."

"Oh, shit. You two gonna do this again?" He leans against the leather seat, crossing his arms across his chest. A cocky-ass grin spreads across his face.

"I don't know what you're talking about." I get ready to step off the boat, pointedly pretending I don't know what he's getting at.

"Yeah...right. You're coming from behind, though. I wonder if Ronin has proposed yet." Grisham's having a hard time keeping his laughter at bay, his eyes narrowing as he tries to keep a straight face.

I hop to the dock, turning back to face him as I shake my head. "Don't be jealous just because we're still single and you're about to be on lockdown."

Grisham groans, jumping down with his bag on his shoulder. "You two are idiots."

I glance off into the distance. "Wonder if I can get him to send me a pic."

Grisham snorts, heading down the dock. "Sure. Ask him to. That way she'll think of him as a perv, and the road is paved for you tomorrow when we get back to work."

My mouth forms a slow smile, admiring Grisham's genius.

"That idea is the best one you've ever had, Ghost."

His expression turns to disbelief. "I was kidding, you asshole!"

Grabbing my towel and wrapping it around my shoulders, I grab the straps of my duffle and follow my teammate off the *Havoc*. "Still a damn good idea."

As we stroll to our cars, Grisham shoots me a glance. "Seriously, though. Not a good idea. Dare told me this girl knows Berkeley somehow. So she probably isn't up for grabs. Not for you, anyway."

I raise an offended eyebrow. "What's that supposed to mean?"

Grisham opens the door to his Jeep, throwing his stuff in before glancing back at me. "It means you like to love 'em and leave 'em, and she's not the type. Plus we have to work with her."

I brush him off. "All the assistants the boss has hired have been temporary. He can't trust anyone since the incident with Kyle, and…"

I trail off when Grisham's eyes darken and his face turns scarlet. It doesn't matter that almost a year has gone by since his now the psycho assistant who used to work at Night Eagle attacked his fiancée. The dude is in prison now, but the thought of him sends Grisham into a rage.

"Don't mention his name to me, Brains."

I hold up both hands in surrender. "Yeah, man. I'm sorry. What I meant to say was…assistants are always from a temp agency. This one won't be any different."

Grisham's face returns to its normal color. "Yeah. Maybe.

All I know is that Dare says she's a friend. So you know what that means."

Sighing heavily, I open the door to the Land Cruiser. "Yeah. It means I can't touch her. But…at least Swagger can't, either."

The next morning I drive past the brick, nondescript building where Night Eagle is housed, pull into the lot at the end of the block, and get out of my car. Arriving at the same time that I am, Ronin calls out to me.

"Man, today is gonna suck for you. I beat you to meeting the new girl yesterday, who's *hot*, and I definitely won her over."

Grinding to a halt, I face him. "Bullshit."

His grin falters for just a second, and that's all the time it takes for me to turn around and saunter toward the office.

When I pull the door open, the black-haired girl behind the desk in the lobby has her head down, studying something in a manila folder.

But her hair…so black it's almost blue. Long, thick, and flowing down around her shoulders. The first thought that flies through my head is the rules. I don't surround myself with raven-haired women. They fuck with my head.

And those shoulders…exposed to me because of her sleeveless shirt, I can see that they're slim and delicately curved, like the tantalizing line of her neck.

"Fuck me," I mutter. That hair, that slim, lithe frame…
So similar.

"Hey, Rayne." Ronin's blown in the door behind me, and he greets the woman sitting at the desk by name.

A name that punches awareness through my system hard

enough to make my knees buckle. With one hand, I grab onto the doorframe to hold myself up.

And then she glances up, a smile on her face that evaporates when she locks eyes with me.

No.

Eyes the color of the sky just before morning, the darkest, and truest blue. Eyes that, once they lock on me, widen with recognition and…what? Disbelief? Definitely that. But there's also a note of longing, and then they narrow with what can only be contempt.

She pushes up from her desk, sending the folder with papers in it flying, and takes two quick steps backward. She bumps into the wall behind her, her body jerking to a stop.

It's a body that hasn't changed much in the nine years since I've seen it. She's still tall, long, and lean. But the changes that have occurred, they're sending my own body into over-drive faster than my mind can catch up to what's happening. Lush, shapely hips flow outward at her waist, making the tight black skirt she's wearing look as if it's painted on. There's a hot flush forming on her cheeks, flowing down to her chest, turning her olive skin dusky. My eyes follow the flush of color, falling into the valley between her perfectly swollen tits.

It's exactly the same as the girl I last saw when I was eighteen. Only now…*holy hell.* The girl I knew is a woman. The most gorgeous woman I've ever seen.

I'm frozen in the doorway, Ronin giving me a shove so he can get around me. Standing beside me, he glances from Rayne, to me, and back again.

Her mouth opens and closes twice before she finds her voice. "Jeremy."

I take a step forward, and then another one, stopping when every visible muscle in her body tenses at my approach.

"So, you two know each other?" Ronin sounds amused.

This can't be happening. I don't want to see her right now...I can't handle it. She's not supposed to be here.

I'm. Not. Prepared. For. This.

But my body isn't responding the way my brain is. I can't force my feet to walk away from the woman who haunts my dreams. Nor can I turn my eyes from the face of the person I once loved.

My heart rate kicks up, pounding like it's fighting to break free from my chest. My stomach twists like I'm gonna be sick, the taste of the breakfast I cooked this morning coming back up my throat in a sour bile. My whole body breaks into a sweat, the same way it did when I ran six miles on the beach this morning.

When her name grinds out of my mouth, it sounds like I've been swallowing razor blades.

"Rayne?"

4

RAYNE

Oh God.

My name has never sounded like that. Not since...since *him.*

Jeremy Teague stands before me, looking so much like the boy I used to know. With several *significant* changes.

He's always been tall enough to fit me underneath the crook of his arm, for my head to fall against his chest when we were snugged up on the couch. And now that height is all filled out with...muscle. Lots and lots of muscle. Big, broad shoulders. Brawny biceps with scrolling tattoos swirling around the sinewy muscles. Sexy-as-sin, corded forearms that look as if he could pick me up and toss me over his shoulder on a whim.

The boy I left had his golden-brown hair cut in an almost-buzz. But this man standing before me has his long locks pulled up into the sexiest man-bun I've ever seen.

I'm not even the kind of woman who likes man-buns!

And I'm for damn sure that underneath that tight gray

T-shirt, there's drool-worthy, washboard abs and rock-hard pecs just waiting to be stroked.

Closing my eyes, I curse, "Damn it straight to hell."

When I open them again, Jeremy Teague is still standing there, now staring at me with a wide-eyed, shocked look. Ronin, who I met yesterday, stands beside him, watching the both of us with an amused grin.

Ronin is super handsome. Really, all the Night Eagle guys are.

But standing beside Jeremy now, Ronin's chocolate brown hair curls and stunning green eyes don't hold a candle to Jeremy.

Where Ronin's eyes are clear, bright green, Jeremy's carry depth of color like I've never seen. I remember staring into those eyes over and over again. They're jade with golden and chocolate flecks swimming throughout, and they change color with his mood.

Right now, they're the darkest hunter.

I turn accusing eyes on Ronin, because there's nowhere else for my anger to go right now. I don't dare meet Jeremy's gaze. I might never be able to climb back out again.

"When you guys told me I'd meet 'Jeremy' today, I didn't know you were talking about Jeremy Teague."

Truthfully, the first name jarred me down to my soul. But what are the odds? I didn't even allow myself to consider...

Unless...Olive! Could she have known that Jeremy worked here? Of course she could have. She told me she's been around all of the Night Eagle guys before during group hangouts.

Ronin places both hands in the air, like he's protecting

himself from the raw venom in my tone. "Hey. How were we supposed to know you two—?" He glances at Jeremy. "What *is* the deal with you? Did you guys date or something?"

This is too much. A harsh laugh barks out of my mouth before I can stop it, and then I'm snatching my phone off my desk and storming for the door.

The door currently blocked by one big ol' Jeremy Teague.

He guesses my intended target and jumps out of my way. I brush past them both and enter the code that opens the solid metal Night Eagle door. Then I'm out into the burning Wilmington sunshine, and sucking in gulps of fresh, salty air.

The first thing I do when I'm across the street and facing the boardwalk is collapse onto a sidewalk bench, placing my head between my knees. The buzzing in my ears turns to a roar, and I don't recognize the sounds coming from me. Heaving, gasping sobs wrack my body.

Dammit! Shit! Fuck!

Why didn't I prepare myself for this? I knew damn well that returning to my hometown meant returning to the place where Jeremy used to live. But I never thought, after all these years, I'd just run into him this way. I thought I'd have plenty of time to prepare myself for a potential meeting.

I'm not on Facebook or any other social media sites. When I left town all those years ago, I never looked back. I changed my name, taking my grandmother's maiden name as soon as I settled in with her. In Phoenix, I was known as Rayne Matheson. Other than my sister, I kept in touch with no one, not even my parents. They retired in the mountains of Asheville, so I knew I wouldn't have any unwanted reunions with the family who basically abandoned me so many years ago.

I never bothered to ask Olive, but I assumed Jeremy had left this town a long time ago. He was destined for football greatness. I never thought he'd still be *living* here.

But Olive did.

Sitting up so suddenly I see stars dancing across my vision, I stab Olive's contact information and place the cell to my ear.

When she answers, I skip the pleasantries.

"Did you know?"

My sister must hear the utter pain staining my voice, because her tone is soft and empathetic when she responds.

"Oh, honey. You saw Jeremy?"

Laughing, a joyless sound if I ever heard one, I practically scream into my phone. "Answer the question! Did you *know*? And you put me in that situation?"

Olive is quiet for a moment before she answers. I spend the moment watching a seagull as it picks at a discarded paper cup on the sidewalk beside my bench. "That he worked at Night Eagle? Yes, I knew."

The fight goes out of me then. I list to the side, my eyes closing in my agony. "Olive…how could you do this to me? Does he know?"

"Sweetie, he knows nothing. I swear. When I first ran into him, he didn't even realize at first that I'm the same Olive he knew as his girlfriend's little sister back in high school. I mean, he wouldn't though, would he? I'm over a hundred pounds lighter." She laughs, a nervous titter that lets me know she's sorry. "But when he realized, he did corner me, ask about you. I refused to answer any of his questions, telling him that I no longer kept in contact with you since you'd left. And God, I've tried my damnedest to stay away from him since then. I haven't talked to him about you or Decker, Rayne. I swear it. But I know that everything happens for a reason. You're back in Wilmington. You've brought Decker home. Jeremy lives here now. You can't just keep on going the way you have been. Things were bound to change. He's not the same kid you left all those years ago."

I remain stubbornly silent.

"And he's kind of a badass now, if you haven't noticed. He can protect you."

Sitting up straight, my eyes fly open. "What makes you think I need protecting?"

I haven't told Olive the reason for my quick departure from Phoenix. She's my sister, so she was there for me when I told her I needed a place to stay. But I didn't want to put her in danger by giving her any extra information. Had she been at her house in Wilmington when this all happened, I don't know that I would have put her into the middle of all this.

Olive sighs. "You have your secrets, Rayne, but I'm your sister. I know you. Your voice, the night you called…you need help. I can't be there right now, but Jeremy can. Don't close yourself off to him."

"You know what his grandparents did, Olive. What *he* did."

Her weary sigh drifts across the line. "Yeah, I know. But you never really knew for sure how involved he was."

"I gotta go, Olive." I'm suddenly too tired and too angry to be having this conversation. My head is throbbing just behind my eyes, the beginnings of the mother of all migraines.

"I love you. Always. Call me when you're ready to talk, Rayne."

I end the call, staring out at the waves crashing against the sand in the distance. I promised Decker that today after work when I pick him up from Macy's house, I would take him to the beach.

His very first beach visit.

And now I feel like I might be splitting apart.

Maybe coming back here was a mistake.

5

JEREMY

The sound of the big metal Night Eagle door slamming shut snaps me out of the makeshift trance I'd been in since I saw Rayne sitting in the place that I love.

My place.

The first thing I do after she walks out is slam my palms against the wall beside me. The sharp slap of stinging pain that results feels *good*. Leaving my hands where they landed, I lean against the wall, my nose nearly touching it. I concentrate on inhaling and exhaling. Remembering how to breathe is a task right now.

"So," says Swagger, startling me.

In the seconds that it took for me to register Rayne Alexander was actually here in my space, I forgot Ronin was a witness to the reunion.

"Obviously I don't have to introduce you to the new hot assistant."

Turning on him, an animalistic roar builds in my chest.

Ronin holds his ground, staring at me with his head cocked to one side. His eyes search mine, and I can see his mind busy assessing exactly what he's seeing. Too late, I shutter my expression. It's hard, though. Seeing Rayne has ripped open a wound that healed a long time ago.

Or maybe it never really healed. Maybe the stiches just ripped loose.

I feel like it. Like there's an jagged, gaping hole right where everyone can see it.

Ronin sighs, turning away from me and heading back to the hallway where we all have offices. "Find her. Boss Man and the rest of us figured out after one day with her that she's the best assistant we've ever had. You scare her away, and I have a feeling Boss Man might send *your* ass packing."

When he disappears, I'm left staring around an empty front lobby.

I don't want to go find her. I don't want to have this conversation. Nine years ago, my life completely changed. It was a sudden series of events that occurred my senior year of high school that changed everything. Losing her altered the trajectory of my life in ways I still can't comprehend. But it also made me the man I am now. I don't want any of that to change. My mind tells me that I need to close myself in my office and try my damnedest to forget that Rayne Alexander just reentered my life. But my heart won't allow it. I have to find out why…*all* the reasons why.

I'll never sleep again until I do.

With a sigh so heavy I can feel it in my bones, I push through the heavy Night Eagle door and out into the bright coastal sunshine. I glance right, then left, seeing no sign of her. My eyes narrowed against the glare of the sun, I search the quiet street.

Night Eagle is located on a block in the upscale Wrightsville Beach area. The building is out of the way of the trendy shops and restaurants, sitting along a side street that ends at the ocean. I close my eyes, listening to the tugging in my chest as it pulls me toward the sea.

I find her on a bench at the boardwalk, looking out onto the crashing waves. My breath catches in my throat at the sight of her. I had to teach myself how to function without her daily presence in my life, and it took changing everything about the way I lived to do it. She was a fixture at my side in high school, cheering me on during all my football games, snuggled up on the couch with me in my grandparents' basement most nights. We were attached at the hip, until one day we weren't.

Forcing one foot in front of the other, I walk toward her.

As if she can sense me coming, she glances up. Her face pales, but she doesn't look away. She watches me until I'm sitting on the bench right beside her.

Finding every ounce of strength I have, I scan her face. She's only twenty-six, so there're no lines around her eyes or her mouth. But the youthful glow she had when we were teenagers is gone, replaced by wisdom I'm not sure she should have been able to earn by this age. Her sapphire eyes glitter with awareness as she returns my gaze; her tongue darts out to lick her plump lips. My gaze stays locked there, watching as it glides along the top lip and then the bottom. In response, my cock twitches in my jeans and my blood heats in my veins.

"Fuck me," I mutter, for the second time since seeing Rayne again.

"Fucked is the perfect word for this situation."

Reeling back, I stare at her. "You never used to cuss when we were kids."

Rolling her eyes, she shifts so that her body is facing away from me. "Yeah. Things change, Jeremy."

We sit in silence for a few moments, both of us keeping our own thoughts to ourselves. I don't know where to start. Ask her why she left? Why she never told me she wanted to go, or why she didn't want to be with me anymore? Ask her why she changed the plans we had made for our future without even considering me?

Instead, I start with something so much simpler. "Where have you been?"

She doesn't look at me when she answers. "Phoenix. My grandmother lived there. She helped us—me—when I needed to leave Wilmington. She passed away a little over a year ago, though."

I'm silent for a minute, just taking in the fact that she's been living halfway across the country. And she never said a word. "I'm sorry. About your grandmother."

She nods. "Thanks."

"So it was just that easy for you? Leaving, I mean? I never heard a word from you. Not even an e-mail. You just disappeared." The venom I'm trying so hard to keep out of my voice leaks through, soaking my words with animosity.

When I was eighteen and hurting from the sting of the loss of her, I couldn't do much. But when I had the connections I needed to find her, I searched. I really did, but I never found a trace of Rayne Alexander anywhere.

The anger rolling around inside me is real. She abandoned me. I can't forget that. And seeing her flawless face and perfect body again isn't going to change that.

Her eyes flash a darker blue as she glares at me. "I don't owe you any explanations, Jeremy. If you really wanted to know why I left, you would have made different choices."

Incredible. She's the one who left me, but I'm the one who's supposed to feel guilty?

The hostility between us sizzles, stemming from suffering copious amounts of pain. I'm not sure where her pain comes from, exactly, but it's there. It's written in her eyes and it's in the slight tremble of her voice. What made her up and leave Wilmington so suddenly all those years ago? Was it something I did or said? The thought is crazy. An eighteen-year-old girl doesn't just up and leave her hometown before she even finishes high school over hurt feelings.

But on the surface, there's something else simmering between us. The way my body reacts to hers, like I'm pulled toward her on a tether. No matter how many years have passed, the underlying current of attraction is still there.

Fuck. Fuck. *Fuck.*

Turning to her, my voice is low and dangerous. "What are you talking about? I looked for you. I wanted an explanation."

She blinks.

"Is there any reason you would have been really damn hard to find, Rayne?" Measured, steady, my words are weapons as my stare burns into hers.

Her eyes close briefly, and she doesn't speak.

I wait.

"I…I changed my name." The words fall off her lips in a whisper.

Pushing up from the bench, I pace away. I shove my hands through my hair, trying to chase away all the inappropriate thoughts suddenly flooding my brain. This isn't just some girl I'm attracted to. And it's not how this is gonna go down.

It's time to get ahold of all those thoughts and emotions before they fuck me sideways.

"I have a question."

Her voice is so quiet I almost don't hear her over the crashing of the waves on the shore beyond us.

Stopping midpace, my arms drop to my side and our gazes lock.

"What do you want to know?"

She gestures back toward Night Eagle and then toward me. "What…what happened to you? I never thought you'd be working for a security company. I mean…installing alarm systems is great and all. But it's not exactly what I pictured when I thought about your life."

"You thought about my life?" I blurt the question out before I can stop myself.

Rayne's cheeks blush a dusky rose. "Of course I did, Jeremy."

I plop back onto the bench beside her. "There's a lot about Night Eagle you probably don't know after just one day of working there. We don't install alarm systems. Every man in that building is ex-Special Forces. Including me."

Her jaw goes slack as she returns my stare. "As in, military Special Forces?"

I hold her gaze. "Yup."

I want to laugh when she starts to splutter, but my heart won't let me. "But…but…I thought you would go to college and play football? I assumed you'd be on some NFL team by now."

Confusion has placed an adorable little wrinkle in the center of her forehead. Without thinking, my finger darts out and traces it. Her eyes widen at my touch, and I watch in fascination as her pupils dilate and her breathing hitches. Her chest rises and falls more quickly as the rate of her breathing increases, and my eyes drop to the perfect swells of her breasts peeking out at the vee of her shirt.

But she doesn't move to pull away from my touch. Not even a millimeter.

So I'm not the only one who's still affected here.

There's no wedding ring on her finger. There could be a boyfriend, but as far as I know, I'm not stepping on anyone's toes by touching her. She could—

And there! That's why I can't do this. Being around her again is making my mind go crazy, thinking things I have no business thinking.

"Like you said, Rayne," I whisper, still drowning in those sapphire depths. "Things change."

Between us, her phone emits a startling ring. An inkling of fear flickers in her eyes just before she glances away from me and down at her phone. I drop my finger but don't move back. It's like I can't move away from her now that I'm close again.

Glancing down at her phone, her expression falls. Catching a glimpse of the screen, I see that it's a blocked number.

Fear? What does she have to be afraid of?

She glances up at me again, shuttering her expression for my benefit. But it was there. There's something out there that she's scared of.

Is she running from something?

"Rayne? Who was on the phone?"

"No one." Her answer is quick and automatic, a response she's programmed herself into saying.

She frowns, assessing me. She doesn't know that I've spent the last eight years of my life training and working so that I can keep the people around me safe.

I know absolutely nothing about Rayne Alexander's life now that she's all grown up. And I'm still furious with her. But if there's someone out there she's afraid of, I'll make damn sure that fear is eliminated.

6

RAYNE

He never played college or professional football?

The question bounces around in my mind, creating more questions. Why didn't he follow through with his dream? Wasn't that the whole reason he and I didn't work out all those years ago?

And why would he have tried to look for me? Was it that his football glory days were done and he finally realized what a mistake he'd made? Well, if he'd had his way, it would have been too late. And that thought just sends a heated fire running through me. It almost seemed like Jeremy thought he had a reason to be angry with *me*.

None of what happened back then was my fault. It was all his and his horrible grandparents.

"We have a few new clients. I'd like you to add all of their information to the spreadsheet I showed you earlier. And I need flights and travel itinerary for the two men I'm sending to South America next week on a mission. Can you handle that?"

When Jacob Owen talks, I listen. I've noticed that's the case with anyone he's speaking to. Today's my second day of work, and I've already learned that he's the ultimate alpha of Night Eagle, and that he's a little gruff and scary when he talks. Giving him a pleasant smile, I nod my head.

"Yes, Mr. Owen. That's no problem at all." The word *mission* sparks my attention, though I try not to let Mr. Owen know it.

I know that the men working at Night Eagle are ex-military, but from some of the snippets of conversation I've heard and some of the documents I've handled that I'm not "cleared" to read, I can attest to the fact that their black ops careers are definitely not behind them.

And Jeremy, the man who used to be the boy I loved, fits right into all of it. I can't help but follow him with my eyes when he walks by. There's a predatory confidence to the way he moves that draws my attention. Hell, it'd draw any woman's attention. It's hot. In a raw, primal, animalistic way that makes me want to undo one more button on my top. Which pisses me off. I refuse to feel anything for that man.

As soon as I returned to my desk after my talk with Jeremy, I slid Decker's framed photo off my desk and hid it in my drawer. I'm going to have to deal with it eventually, but now isn't the time for Jeremy to find out that I have a son.

Above all else, I've always protected Decker from anyone who might hurt him, who might not love him.

The blocked call on my phone earlier hasn't left my mind.

I've pushed it far away into the depths, but now that the day is winding down and my work is about done, it's creeping back into my thoughts.

I have another brand-new cell phone number. *There's no way Wagner Horton could have my new number.*

The little voice inside my head laughs, mocking me. *If Wagner Horton wants your number, he'll find a way to get your number.*

And if he does have my number that means he thinks he can find me. Suddenly, I'm so very happy I kept the area code a Phoenix one, and that I withdrew cash to pay for Decker and my plane tickets to Wilmington. I can't hide from Wagner forever, but maybe if I can figure out exactly what he did, I can tip off the proper authorities to his crime.

My phone is in my hands, and I'm turning it over and over again as I ponder. I don't even notice Jeremy standing beside my desk, and when he clears his throat, I jump like I've been poked with a stick.

His eyebrows lift as he glances from my phone to me and back again. "Everything okay?"

Nodding, I place my phone in my purse and shut down the computer. "Fine. I'm just getting ready to head home."

Jeremy leans against my desk, and when he folds his arms the muscles on his biceps flex. I can't help it when my eyes stray there, tracing the inky lines of the tattoos swirling around his muscles.

"When did you get those?" I ask.

Dammit. My voice betrays me every time I speak to Jeremy. It's still surreal that he's standing here in front of me like this.

Glancing down at his arms, his deep voice caresses me when he answers. "After I made Ranger battalion. Maybe someday I'll tell you what they mean."

Oh. It's unexpected, how much I want to know that story. I used to know all his stories.

As I stand, I give him an awkward wave. "Well, bye. Guess I'll see you tomorrow."

A struggle happens right before me on his face. The warring emotions chase one another until finally, he holds a hand out toward the door.

"I'm going to walk you to your car." His tone is grudging.

I'm so taken aback by this that I just take him in for a second. His rigid stance, his irritated expression...everything about him says he doesn't *want* to walk me to my car, but he feels he *has* to.

I can't even help it when my eyes roll skyward. "Oh, really, Jeremy? How the hell have I made it from my place of employment to my car for the past nine years? Are you *really* going to walk me?"

I stare at him, arms folded, my stance identical to his.

"I'm walking you to your car, Rayne. Maybe I haven't been there for the past nine years to do it, and maybe someone else has been doing it instead. I don't give a shit. All I know is that I'm here now, and I'm walking you to your damn car. Understood?"

A tingle of pleasure that I'll never admit to ripples through me, heating me up from the inside out.

I think of Wagner, and the relief I feel at having this big, muscly man walk me to my car is immediate.

"Understood."

A few minutes later, we're heading toward my sister's car. Jeremy nods toward it as I pull out my keys.

"This is you?"

"It's Olive's. Mine is still in Phoenix." *Along with most of the things I own.* But I keep that thought to myself.

Jeremy quirks a brow. "Yeah? Are you planning on staying in Wilmington?"

I shrug. "For now."

Jeremy clears his throat. "So, Olive…she works with Berkeley now, huh? We've seen each other a few times a barbecues, and I went on a trip to Georgia with her not too long ago. I recognized her pretty quickly, even though she looks a hell of a lot different now than she did in high school."

Smirking, I nod. "Yeah, like she's a redhead now. And she's lost a lot of weight, too. She's been through a lot."

We both have.

"She was pretty tight-lipped when I asked her about you. Said she hadn't been in touch. I'm guessing that's not actually the case, is it?" He only needs to take one look at my face for his answer.

Curiosity gets the better of me, pushing me to ask questions I know I shouldn't. "What would you have said to her if she'd been willing to talk to you?"

A tendril of resentment, a feeling that I've buried way down deep in reference to Jeremy, unfurls inside of me. If he'd chosen differently all those years ago, if all the promises he made to me had been true, he wouldn't have had to ask my sister about me.

He'd know firsthand.

We stop walking beside Olive's little luxury coupe, a car that I've been having an interesting time trying to cram myself, Decker, and all our stuff into anytime we need to go somewhere.

"Hell, I don't know." Jeremy takes a deep breath. "Back then, I was young and stupid enough to think we were it. Forever. And then you left…took me a long time to bounce back from that, Rayne. A long damn time."

Something inside me, a piece of me I thought had been healed a long time ago, fissures open. My voice breaks on my next question. "How are your grandparents, Jeremy?"

His expression darkens, his green eyes going all stormy and cool. When Jeremy and I were together, he had a strained relationship with his grandparents. But since he lost his parents at such a young age, they were all he had.

They're the reason I knew, all those years ago, I had to leave Wilmington without a backward glance.

But, looking at his expression now, the first-ever tingle of doubt shoots through me about that decision.

"I haven't spoken to them in years, Rayne. I cut them out of my life right before I enlisted."

He's searching my gaze, looking for any reason I could have for asking that question.

"I…I didn't know."

Jeremy opens my car door and waits for me to climb inside. Just before he shuts it, he leans in the slightest bit and looks me in the eye. "Yeah. There's a lot you don't know about my life after you left, Rayne. And I have a feeling it's the same way for me with you."

7

JEREMY

By Friday, Rayne and I greet each other when we arrive at Night Eagle in the morning. We're polite when we bump into each other in the lounge grabbing coffee or heating up lunch. On Wednesday, when the guys went out for lunch she refused to come. It put a pain in my chest, leaving her alone at her desk while we went out to eat. I'm not sure why, I know I'm not responsible for her. But it did. And I walk her to her car at the end of every day.

It's killing me. The fact that I can't stop thinking about why she left me all those years ago. How could she have just walked away from everything we had? Was it all in my head? Maybe she wasn't as serious about me back then as I was about her. Maybe she never saw a future with me. Fuck. Just thinking about it makes me want to hit something.

I'm going to ask her. But I haven't found the right time. As it is, she's skittish as hell around me, and I don't want to make that worse.

We haven't spoken about the past or our feelings or whatever the natural, combustible attraction that seems to sizzle between us is. So far, it's working for us.

At least that's what I tell myself when my body pulls me toward her desk whether I want to go or not. And the way I physically react when I see her twirl a piece of that black, black hair around her finger while she's staring at something on her computer screen.

I've been comparing *this* Rayne to the one I knew in high school. To the one I knew *intimately*. The differences are subtle, but they're there. The way she carries herself is the biggest variation. In high school, she was a quiet girl. She was always gorgeous, but she had no clue how much. I was the outgoing one, pulling her to sit with me and the other football players at lunch. Dragging her to parties with the most popular kids in school—the ones she couldn't care less about. She was happy just to be with me, but I knew she didn't want to do half of the things I did.

But not this Rayne. This Rayne is quick to offer a helping hand or a smile to one of the guys. Every time I hear it I want to punch the man who made it happen. It's insane, because these guys are like my brothers. But dammit if I'm not pissed every single time they make her light up. Her laugh is the best thing I've ever heard. It's big and boisterous, and sometimes she laughs so hard she starts to hiccup.

And then there's her sailor's mouth.

The girl never uttered a curse word back then. Her family was very religious, attending Catholic church every Wednesday night and Sunday morning. She didn't dare utter a curse word back then. But now? Now she curses just as well as we do, and that's saying a whole damn lot.

I can't figure out the thing that makes her the *most* different, though. Can't pinpoint the cause, can't quite put my finger on exactly what it is that makes her seem even warmer, more loving, more thoughtful than she was before. She was always a sweet, kind girl. It's what made me fall for her in the first place. But now it's like that sweetness has been amplified. And it's in direct conflict with her dirty mouth, which just makes me want to know more. It makes me want a lot of things I know I shouldn't, that I *can't* have.

Even when I tell it not to, my body reacts to her. Every time she pulls her lip between her teeth. Every time her midnight blue eyes meet mine and smolder with some unseen emotion. Every single time I see a peek of the perky breasts that were really nice in high school, but are just spectacular now.

And I'm having a more difficult time every day hiding the way my stomach clenches when she checks her phone with that look of fear on her face.

It's at one of these times that I don't fight the pull and stalk toward her desk. Snatching the phone from her hand, I read the text that put the disturbed expression in her eyes.

"Jeremy! What the fuck?"

Ignoring her pissed-off shout, my eyes narrow and my teeth clamp shut when I read the words on her screen.

You can't hide forever. I will find you. And I will take what's mine.

Rage explodes inside me. Glancing around the lobby, where Grisham and Dare are acting like they're not listening to us, but who are clearly paying attention, I grasp her by the elbow and tow her and the phone down the hallway and into the lounge.

Tossing her phone onto a countertop, I spin her around until she's pressed against the nearest wall. I cage her in with my arms, leaning forward while taking deep breaths to try and control my temper.

"Tell me about that text, Rayne. Tell me now." The words are gritted out through my teeth.

"It's none of your—"

"Dammit, Rayne! If you tell me it's none of my business I'm probably gonna break something. I know that I shouldn't care, shouldn't want to know. But I do! Okay? If someone is threatening you like this, then I need to know about it. I just *do.*"

She clamps her mouth shut, staring back at me with stubborn fear in her eyes. While I'm watching, a lone tear escapes and rolls down her cheek. She's too mulish to wipe it away, so it just keeps falling while I trace its track with my gaze.

"Fuck me." The curse is muttered from me while I use a thumb to wipe the tear away.

"Rayne…I know it's been a long time. You don't know the man I am now. But there's no way in hell I can watch you keep getting these texts—see the fear in your eyes when you read them—and not do something about it. You're working in an office full of guys that can take out whoever this is. But you have to trust me enough to let me help you."

She sniffs. "I don't trust anyone, Jer."

Jer. The nickname rocks me, sending me reeling into the past where her plump lips would utter that name on a sigh while I kissed the sweetest spot in the world—the hollow right above her collarbone.

Blinking, I shake off the image and dip my head a little. "I know. What I don't know is *why*. What happened to you?"

Her mouth stays firmly closed.

"You think I'm gonna let this go, Rayne?"

She just stares up at me, a war going on in her eyes. It's like she wants to tell me what's happening, but something inside won't let her. She doesn't want me to get close.

I'm suddenly aware of the fact that we're only inches apart. I can smell her. The fresh, slightly sweet scent of something floral washes over me, mixed with the hint of spice that is just Rayne. *This* Rayne.

"I just want to help you," I whisper, before letting my thumb roam over her soft skin.

One hand is still braced against the wall while my thumb sweeps a path across her cheekbone, and even though I'm fighting the lust bubbling up inside me, my cock swells in my jeans. Taunting me. Forcing me to think about what she'd look like now if she were lying naked under me. All that gorgeous black hair splayed out on the pillows, my name falling from her lips while I please her.

Whether I'm willing to admit it or not, that's still a deep, dark desire inside me. Pleasing her. And I don't want to just please her. No, I want to possess her, to own her. Because a long time ago, I did. But she slipped through my fingers, and I was left wondering how the hell I lost her.

The urge to close the last remaining inches between us and kiss her is intolerable. Like she can read my thoughts, her pupils dilate and her chest rises and falls with a heavy breath.

It takes all my strength, but I push back from the wall and back away, not going far but putting some distance between us.

Much needed distance.

But I keep her in my sights. I'm waiting.

Taking a deep, shuddering sigh, she hangs her head. "There's someone in Phoenix…a guy I used to work for."

My body goes rigid with where this story might be going. Rayne with another guy? Of course there were other guys, it's been over nine fucking years.

She shakes her head quickly. "Not like that. He was just my boss."

I try not to be relieved, and fail. "And?"

"And he's looking for me."

That's all she gives me. Taking a step forward, I fold my arms across my chest.

"Why, Rayne? If you two weren't…why would he be looking for you? And why don't you want him to find you?"

She grabs her phone off the counter, clutching it to her chest like protection.

Come on, Rayne. Trust me. Tell me. Why are you so scared?

"I, uh, didn't give him any notice when I left. I got a bad feeling about him and just took off. There're loose ends back there."

Shaking my head slowly, I assess her. Her stiff posture, the way she isn't looking me in the eye.

She's lying.

"Do you want me to find him?"

Startling, she finally looks up at me. "Can you do that?"

With a shrug, I shoot her a small smile. "You really don't get who we are and what we do here, do you?"

She returns my smile with a shaky one of her own. "Um…well, I guess you don't need to find him. I know his name and where he lives. I just don't want him to find me."

I inhale sharply. "Are you scared he'll hurt you?"

I can see with her reluctance that it goes against every ounce of independent strength she has to admit it, but finally she nods.

I hiss out a breath through my teeth. "Give me his name, Rayne. We'll keep an eye on him to make sure he doesn't get anywhere near you."

Stark relief scrawls across her features. "Really? Thanks Jeremy."

Nodding, I move toward the door and beckon that she come with me. "It's not a problem. But today's Friday, and I don't want to go the weekend without being able to let you know what I find out. Why don't you give me your number so I can update you?"

She nods, handing me her phone. I plug my number in and send myself a quick text while she turns off her computer and gathers her stuff. When I hand her back the phone, she offers me a small smile.

"Thanks. For this. I mean….you didn't have t—"

"I want to." My interruption has her looking at me with a new expression in her eyes. It's not quite trust, but it's something closer to it.

Progress.

When she's ready to go, I lead her out of the building and walk her to her car. Before she gets in, she turns to me and throws her arms around my neck.

Stooping so she can reach me, something warm and liquid melts inside me. She whispers in my ear, and a shiver crawls down my back as a result.

"Thank you." Her voice trembles, going so soft it's barely a whisper against my skin. Her arms squeeze tightly around my neck, but the pressure is welcome.

I can't answer her. It might be because of the lump that finds its way inside my throat, but I gently push her into her car and close her door. She stares at me for a few seconds, just watching me with an unreadable expression on her face. It feels like she's summing me up or evaluating me. But for what? For whether or not I'll be able to protect her when she needs it?

I've started parking right beside her every morning when I arrive, so I unlock the Land Cruiser with my key fob and climb into the truck while she reverses and pulls out of her parking spot. I watch, still thinking about the way her body felt pressed up against mine, when she pulls out into the street.

It's because I'm watching that I notice the dark sedan start up and pull out two cars behind her.

It shouldn't have gotten my attention; it normally wouldn't be a big deal.

But something feels *wrong*, and with what she just told me about the guy she's afraid of from Phoenix, I immediately start the Land Cruiser and pull out after them.

Years spent first as an enlisted soldier, then as a member of

Special Forces, then as a part of the elite team at Night Eagle, my instincts have been sharpened. Right now, my nose is telling me that something stinks.

The little silver coupe weaves in and out of busy five o'clock traffic. I'm following, always two or three cars behind her sedan tail. I'm waiting, waiting to see if the other car will drop off, make a turn, anything to prove to me he's not following Rayne.

But he stays with her, making unease in my gut grow into urgency.

"Okay, asshole. You want to follow her? You get to deal with me, too." I grit my teeth, gripping the steering wheel so hard my knuckles are white.

I've seen the other guys deal with personal cases. The assistant who used to work for Night Eagle stalked Grisham's fiancée, Greta. Grisham was a machine when he found out, bent on keeping his girl safe from a psychopath. I was on the force when I first met Dare. His girlfriend, Berkeley, had been kidnapped. He wasn't going to stop hunting the man who took her, not until she was back in his arms again.

Maybe Rayne and I aren't like them.…We're not together. And I'm not…shit, I don't know. I'm not responsible for her. But this feeling inside me, watching someone follow her home, it's an overwhelming sense of protectiveness. Like I'd fight my way through any obstacle to make sure she's safe.

After fifteen minutes, Rayne pulls into a residential subdivision. Winding through the neat, manicured streets lined with live oaks and cookie-cutter houses, Rayne's brake lights flash and her right signal begins to blink.

There's one car separating her and her tail, who I'm now directly behind. Anger boils in my blood when I see the bright red of the sedan's brakes.

Not today, motherfucker.

When Rayne pulls into the driveway of a white two-story, I gun my engine, swing out from behind the sedan, and pull out beside him. Staring the driver down through my passenger side window, I jerk my chin forward, indicating he should keep going.

If he wants to keep breathing today, he will.

I want to get my hands on him, and I want it to happen now. I want to know who he is and what he's doing following Rayne home from work. But I noted his license plate, and that'll have to be enough for now.

Rayne's the priority.

I pull into the driveway right behind Rayne. She's already climbing out of the coupe, and as I jump out of the Land Cruiser I can read the shock on her face.

"Jeremy? What are you—?"

The sedan's engine revs as it continues down the block, and Rayne's question is cut off as she stares after it. Her face drains of color and she drops her purse on the ground.

"Oh God, Jeremy—was that…was he…?" Her hands float up to tug on the ends of her hair.

Striding forward, I wrap her in my arms, turning her to face the house. I scan the street, searching in both directions for any sign of the sedan or any other suspicious-looking vehicles in the area. The street seems clear, but I can't shake the anxiety in my stomach.

Too close. Too close. What if I hadn't seen the sedan pull out behind her? What if I hadn't been able to follow her home?

The thought sends an oily finger of fear curling around my stomach.

"Rayne? What just happened?"

A woman's voice, from the house next-door, has my head swiveling in that direction.

And then two little boys bound out of the house behind her, their excited chatter lighting up the world around them.

The little boy with dark hair and green eyes? Him, I recognize. He's the same kid with the Nerf football at the grocery story on Monday.

I feel rather than see Rayne tense up beside me. I turn to her, ready to ask her what danger she just perceived, when the dark-haired little boy jumps onto the driveway with both feet slamming onto the ground. With an athletic swivel, he bounds toward Rayne with an excited gleam in his eyes.

"Whoa, that car just screeched away like the movies! We were watching from the window!"

Rayne turns to me, her eyes wide and full of something I can't comprehend. I glance down at the kid again, and then back up at Rayne. There's nothing in my mind that sets off alarm bells, nothing that alerts me to anything amiss. I'm about to open my mouth and ask her what's wrong, when the kid pipes up again.

"Hey, I know you. Saw you at the store. You're the football player!"

Glancing down at him, I shoot him a smile. He's a pretty damn cute kid with all that dark hair and those striking green eyes.

And then he turns those eyes, full of adoration and curiosity, onto Rayne.

"Mom? Is he your friend?"

Mom? Wait…what? The fuck?

The bottom drops out from under me and I'm freefalling, the terrifying sensation you get when you've jumped but your chute doesn't open right away. Everything I thought I knew about my life and this woman shifts, tilts, changes…

And my world splinters apart.

8

WAGNER

She ran from me. And that's not part of the deal.

I've wanted Rayne Matheson from the moment she was hired as my assistant. I can remember how urgent that need was, right from the very beginning. I spent months grooming her, training her. Teaching exactly how to please me at work. And my...she was a receptive student.

The hours I spent, imagining how well she would learn to please me in the bedroom. And how delightfully delicious it would be to punish her when she made a mistake. Just the thought of it sends a raging need straight to my cock, and an irritated growl leaves my throat.

Rayne Matheson. Come to find out it's not even her real name. She changed it when she moved to Phoenix as an eighteen-year-old pregnant girl, hoping to escape her past. Escape it she did, until it ran her down. My deal is set. And the best part of the bargain?

Gaining Rayne for my very own.

Chasing her across the country wasn't part of the plan, but it's something I'll gladly do if it means I can have her all to myself when the paperwork is signed and the prize is delivered.

Leaning my head back against the first-class leather seat, I close my eyes and wait for my anticipated landing in Wilmington.

Sometime later, I'm strolling through the despicable little airport in the coastal town I've never before visited. After gathering my luggage from baggage claim, I pull my cell phone out of my pocket and check it as I head for the exit.

Three missed calls from the investigator. This is either very good news, and I'll have a lot less work to do than I expected, or it's bad news.

Pushing the SEND button to return the call, I wait as it rings.

"Hello?"

Clearing my throat, I spot my driver holding up a sign with my name on it and veer off in his direction. "Mr. O'Shea? I see I have several missed calls. Good news or bad?"

My tone indicates that I'll tolerate nothing less than the former.

"Sir. I followed her home from work this evening. It took me some time to figure out where she was working. But once I had her true last name and made the connection with her sister to the coworker, I found out that she's found employment at a security company in town. After work, I followed her home."

My hopes soar. "This is good! Send me the address, and I'll have the car take me straight there. This can all be sorted out tonight!"

O'Shea clears his throat. "Well…"

My hope is quickly replaced with rage. "Well, *what?*"

"Someone spotted the tail. I wasn't expecting him…I think it was one of the men who work for the security company. He was following me and cut me off at her home. I had to leave, but I'm guessing that they know I was following her, and that they'll take action accordingly."

As I climb into the Town Car idling at the curb in front of the airport, I pinch the bridge of my nose. I suck in deep lungfuls of air, trying to calm my temper before I explode.

"You stupid son of a bitch. Aren't you a professional? How could you have been discovered?" My voice is deadly calm, hiding the fact that if Kevin O'Shea were in my presence right now, I'd have him by the throat.

"He seems…trained. He knew what to look for. He knew how to cut me off before I could pause in front of her home. I'm sorry, sir. But I promise you, I will continue to gather information on Miss Alexander."

Pulling the phone away from my ear, I stare at it for a moment. When I'm ready to speak again, my voice is nothing but a whisper.

"You're damn right you will. Rayne Alexander belongs to me. You'll will do whatever it takes. Do you understand me?"

I can practically hear Kevin O'Shea's gulp from across the line. "Yes, sir. I do."

Hanging up the phone, I relax while the driver hired by my new business partner chauffeurs me to my hotel.

I don't know who the new player is, the one who saved Rayne from my private investigator's prying eyes, but I will not be thwarted.

She will be mine.

9

RAYNE

*N*o. *No. No.*

It's not supposed to happen this way.

I grip Decker's hand in mine, probably a little too tightly. Without glancing at Jeremy, because I'm delaying that as long as possible, I tow Deck back to Macy.

"Sweetheart, will you stay at Jay's house for just a little bit longer?" I turn to Macy with a pleading glance. "Be over to get him in a few minutes?"

Her eyes flick from Jeremy to me, down to Decker, and back to me.

"Go ahead boys. You can help me make individual pizzas for dinner."

Decker and Jay high-five. Jay immediately turns and heads back for his house, but Decker turns back toward me. His face is full of concern. "Mom? Everything okay?"

My gut clenches, and my eyes fill with tears that I will not shed in front of my son. Clearing my throat, I nod and offer him a bright smile. "Yep. Just need to talk to my friend from work for a few minutes. Then I'll be right over."

He glances toward Jeremy, unsure. But he finally turns and follows Jay back into the house.

Macy eyes at me, folding her arms across her chest. Keeping her voice low, so Jeremy won't hear, she addresses me. "Do you need anything? Want me to call anyone?"

I shake my head. "No, please don't. It's not what you think, Macy. This is…I know and trust Jeremy. I promise you that's the truth."

She scrutinizes me. Whatever she's searching for, she must have found, because she reaches out and squeezes my shoulder. "I can keep Decker as long as you want me to."

I squeeze back, giving her a grateful smile. Even though smiling is the very last thing I feel like doing at this moment.

"Thank you, Macy."

With one last warning glance at Jeremy, she heads inside after the boys.

Slowly, I turn to face him. The look on his face almost brings me to my knees.

He's staring at Macy's house, following the path Decker took with his eyes. I can almost see the wheels in his brain turning, turning, turning. His face is ghost-white, and he's repeatedly running his hands through his hair.

"Jeremy?"

When he turns his gaze on me, there's so much torment in his eyes I need to look away. I *want* to look away, but I can't. I'm tethered to that gaze, whether I want to be or not. He takes a step closer to me, and I plead with my eyes.

"Jeremy—"

He holds up one finger, walking until we're closer. "You have a son?"

The words are broken. Like he swallowed shards of glass before he spoke them. My tears spill out, running down my face. I don't bother to wipe them. Inside my chest, my heart constricts, squeezing tighter and tighter until I know it must be failing.

Because Jeremy's is.

"Yes." The word falls out on a sob.

Jeremy's teeth clench together and his hands ball into fists. His eyes, sometimes the color of a calm green pasture, turn into a torrential storm.

"How old is he?" The words are like bullets, each one slamming into me with brute force.

"Jer—" I choke on the word, unable to get it out.

Jeremy's voice rises. *"How old is he?"*

"Eight!" I scream. "He's eight, Jeremy. He was born exactly seven months after I left you."

Knowing I need to escape the look in his eyes, I turn and flee. I run for my house, but I don't bother to close and lock the door. I know, without a doubt, that Jeremy would knock it down right now.

And after hearing what he said about his grandparents, I had been thinking about how involved Jeremy was. But seeing his reaction right now slices me open: I made a mistake. He had no clue what they, along with my own parents, did to me all those years ago. He was a victim of their cruelty, of their insistent need to control everything, just like I was.

But I didn't know. They fed me lies.

Sitting on the couch, I'm finally swiping at the streaming tears, staring at the door when Jeremy walks through it.

He's like a hurricane, filling up the room with his presence. His energy swirls all around me, pressing in from all sides. But I keep my eyes glued to my hands, which are folded in my lap.

He doesn't sit beside me.

Instead, he paces the room. His footsteps heavy and thudding against the hardwood floors. When he speaks, his voice is stronger than it was outside, but it's so full of anger and turmoil that I rock backward, like I've been punched.

"I have a son? God, Rayne...*I have a son?*"

The silence between us grows, stretches, distorts.

Finally, I look up at him. I look him straight in the eye, because he deserves that. "Yes, Jeremy. You have a son. He's...he's my whole world. And he's amazing."

All the air leaves him in one breath. His body sags as he crouches on the ground, one hand brushing the hardwood planks while his forehead rests against the other palm. His eyes are squeezed shut.

I wait. My limbs are frozen, my eyes never leaving his face. The air in the room grows thick, heavy, almost oppressive as I wait for his response.

Finally, he looks up at me, falling back onto his butt and pulling his knees up. The emotion in his eyes is devastating.

"What did I ever do to you?" His voice is trembling with his heartbreak.

"Nothing!" I swipe at my eyes.

"Then why would you keep this from me? My *son*? Why would you take off all those years ago without saying a thing?"

Unable to help myself any longer, I rise from the couch and make my way across the living room to where he sits. Crouching down beside him, I reach out and stroke the side of his face with my hand. He flinches but doesn't pull completely away. The hurt in his eyes slices through me, threatening to cut me down altogether.

"I'm so, so sorry, Jeremy. I made a mistake…I should have talked to you. I thought you didn't want me, or us." I indicate myself and toward the home next-door, where Decker is staying with Macy and Jay.

His expression turns to a mask of bewilderment. "Why the hell would you think that?"

Sighing, I know I'm not ready to tell him this story. But it's not about me anymore. Because of my choice not to trust him all those years ago, my son has missed out on eight years with his father.

And Jeremy has missed vital time with his son.

I retreat back to the couch, and Jeremy follows me. When I sit down, he perches beside me, his intent gaze watching me, waiting.

"When I got pregnant senior year, I was so scared, Jeremy. I didn't know what you would think. I thought maybe you'd think I was trapping you here in Wilmington with me, when I knew you wanted a future in football anywhere but here."

His gaze is laser-focused on me. "You meant more to me then than any football career."

I take a shuddering breath. "I had *hoped* you'd feel that way, and I was going to tell you no matter what. But I told my parents first."

He winces, because Jeremy knew my parents back then. Strict, iron-fisted Catholics, my pregnancy devastated them.

"They were so ashamed of me, Jer." I glance down at my hands, all that shame and the feeling of abandonment washing over me again like I'm back there in that time.

I suck in a sharp gasp when Jeremy's big, warm hand covers mine. He squeezes gently, encouraging me to go on. But if I look at him right now, I'll lose it. So I stare at our hands and continue with my story.

"They went to your grandparents. The adults talked it out, made decisions without either you or me. Your grandparents insisted that we let them tell you, and that everyone would make a decision accordingly after that.

"It was right before winter break, and my parents took Olive and me on vacation to the mountains, remember? Well, they sat me down and told me that your grandparents had called and told them you didn't want to have anything to do with me or the baby. That it would ruin your future, and it wasn't what you wanted."

Now I glance at him. His eyes are wide, disbelieving.

"I swear to you on all that is holy, they never told me, Rayne. *They never told me.*"

I nod, sending him a small, sad smile. "I starting wondering about that when I spoke to you the other day. I finally realized that maybe everything wasn't as it seemed then."

He pulls our joined hands to his mouth, just resting them there. He squeezes his eyes shut for a moment, and I just wait, watching him. Finally, he opens them and squeezes my hand again.

"Keep going, Rayne. What happened next? You never came back from that trip. Why?"

The urgency in his voice is strong; the desperation in his gaze signals he needs to know the ending of this story more than anything else in the world right now.

"My parents told me they were taking me to a doctor's office for a prenatal checkup."

My voice breaks on the last word, and Jeremy brings my hand to his lips. He holds my hand in both of his, holding me steady when I'm trying my hardest not to fall apart.

"Only it wasn't a doctor's office. It was an abortion clinic. They'd accepted money from your grandparents to have the baby aborted, and extra cash to boot. I was so devastated, Jeremy. So hurt and scared and...alone."

Tears roll down my face as I remember how I felt that day all those years ago. Finally, I thought my parents were going to be there for me during this ordeal, that they were going to support me. I'd already decided I was going to keep our baby. It was part of me and part of Jeremy, and I wanted that.

Sniffing, I wipe my eyes. My voice is filled with irate venom. "Devout Catholics, my ass. Their daughter creates one scandal, and they're willing to go against their beliefs. Ironic, huh?"

When I glance up at Jeremy, his eyes are brimming with his own unshed tears. He grabs the back of my head and pulls me in until our foreheads are touching.

"I wish I could have been there for you. I *would have* been there for you." His whispered words work as a healing balm, soothing the scar tissue left from years of hurt and anger.

"But I didn't know that. I'd been told that you wanted nothing to do with our baby, and that broke me, Jeremy. Even after I'd given birth, the thought of finding you and introducing you to our son after you'd rejected us once... I just couldn't go through that again."

We locked eyes, and the pain swimming in his mirrored the ache I felt down to my soul.

"I left that clinic and never looked back. I ran, Jeremy. I ran and my grandmother got me to Phoenix. I've never spoken to my parents since, but Olive is in Decker's life."

Jeremy pulls back, a small smile crossing his face for the first time. "Decker? That's his name?"

Unexpected shyness blossoms inside me, and I nod. "Decker James."

He tests out his son's name for the first time. "Decker James."

As I stare at him it once again dawns on me just how hard it was doing it all without Jeremy. Believing what they wanted me to believe, that he didn't love me. That he didn't want our baby. It wrecked me in so many ways, changed who I am inside. I couldn't recover from that rejection, not just for me but for my child, so I had to bury it deep and keep moving forward.

But it was always there. And knowing that it wasn't true slices me open.

We're both silent for a few minutes, lost in our thoughts. But our hands remain linked, and when Jeremy speaks again his voice has lost the desperate edge from before.

"What have you told him about me?"

I meet his gaze. "Just that he was born out of love, but not all moms and dads live together. I told him that I didn't know where you lived, and so far he's been okay with that."

Jeremy nods, his expression thoughtful and anxious. "I want to meet him, Rayne. I want him to know who I am to him."

Standing, I walk to the living room window and glance out at the nearly dark street. A shiver creeps down my back when I remember what almost happened on that street less than an hour ago.

I've had Decker all to myself since he was born. It's been my sole responsibility to care for him, love him, and raise him. I've never had to share that task, and I never felt like I was lacking. It's been a joy to raise him, even though doing it alone was hard at times.

Learning to share him with Jeremy is going to be a challenge.

But I've never run from one of those, and I *want* Jeremy in Decker's life.

Nodding, I turn to face Jeremy again, folding my arms across my chest. "You can meet him. I'm not sure I'm ready to tell him you're his father yet, though. Maybe we can ease him into that after you two have gotten comfortable with each other?"

Jeremy's face falls a little, but he nods. "Yeah. If that's what you think is best, Rayne."

He stands up and comes toward me, an unreadable expression on his face.

Wonder? Awe?

Why would he be looking at me that way?

"I can't believe you've been raising our son alone all this

time." He stops when he's standing just in front of me. His arms reach out like he wants to pull me in close, but he stops himself, shoving his hands through his hair and turning away from me instead. The wonder dissipates and a tortured expression takes its place, a flash of pain chased by venomous anger.

"How have you been doing it all alone? Where does my son go when you're at work? Is he happy? God…I don't even know what he's like." He shakes his head, a strand of his hair falling into his face.

Uncrossing my arms, I use my hands to punctuate my words. "He's happy. And healthy. I had my grandmother to help when Decker was a baby and a toddler, but she passed away about a year ago. I've been doing it the way most single mothers do…he's been my whole world for his entire life. Neither of us has known anything different." I spread my arms wide at the last.

Jeremy throws his head back, a frustrated groan ripping from his throat. "It didn't have to be that way for you, Rayne!" His voice rises a notch, but his anger doesn't intimidate me. It *devastates* me.

"I would have been there!" Pacing away from me, his long legs stride with purpose toward the window. "I never would have let the girl I loved raise our son alone. Never!"

A fresh wave of tears prickle my eyes. "I…I was crushed when I thought you didn't want our baby. If you didn't want that part of us, you didn't want me, either. As soon as I found out I was pregnant, he was a part of me. We were a package deal. And the way your grandparents talked…they were so adamant that there was no way you would want us. I shouldn't have believed it…but I was young, and scared, and my parents' betrayal made me feel so alone. I didn't know what to do…so I ran."

A shiver shakes me, and I wrap my arms around myself again. Tears soak my cheeks, and when Jeremy turns to face me, his eyes flashing, he takes one look at me before the anger on his face relaxes into sorrow.

"I feel robbed, Rayne. Time with my son…with my family…was fucking stolen from me. I don't know what to do with that."

I nod. I'm wrung out, drained, exhaustion setting into me from the top of my head to the tips of my toes. And the pure, unadulterated sadness seeps in, right down to my marrow. "I don't, either."

We stare at one another, the silence stretching, twisting, reaching between us. And I find myself second-guessing every choice I ever made. I know I did what I thought was best for Decker and me at the time, but the pain in Jeremy's eyes, the sorrow written in every move he makes, tears me apart. I wish I had believed in him. I wish I had believed in us. Where would we be right now if I had?

Finally, I step toward him. My voice is nothing but a hoarse whisper. "But we're here now. And so are you. We can make this—your relationship with Decker—right."

His gaze deepens, and I nearly fall into the wilderness of his eyes. "Yeah…I plan on it."

His voice is full of finality, of determination. The confidence in it makes me quake just a little bit.

A car door slams outside, a noise that normally wouldn't

have phased me. But Jeremy's gaze flicks to the window, and his body goes rigid. He closes his eyes briefly.

"Fuck. This has been…incredible. Finding out about him. But we can't forget that something really, really bad could have happened tonight if I hadn't followed you home."

I pull my arms in tighter to my chest, fighting the urge to quiver. "Who do you think that was, Jeremy?"

The sinking feeling in my gut tells me I already know the answer to that question.

His eyes cloud over. "I don't know. I'm gonna head back to the office to run his plate, but I don't want to leave you…and Decker…alone."

Understanding dawns on me. "My friend Macy, from next-door. Her husband travels a lot for work, and she and her son are alone a lot. I'll ask her if we can stay over."

Jeremy looks skeptical. "How well do you know her?"

My mouth twitches. His protectiveness is…attractive. More than attractive.

Sexy as hell.

"She and Olive have been neighbors for a while now. Olive trusts her, and so do I. She watches Decker while I'm at work."

Jeremy narrows his gaze. "No…that's not gonna work for me. I need to know that you and Decker are safe. I want to check you into a hotel. Just for the night, until I can do some digging."

I eye him. "You really think we need to?"

He nods, and I don't even consider arguing with him. There's no question in my mind that Jeremy has Decker and my best interests at heart, and if he says we shouldn't stay here tonight then I'm going to go with that.

"I'll pack our things." Turning away from him, I head for the stairs. But Jeremy's voice, deep and sure, makes me pause.

"We're not done talking about this, Rayne. I want to know more about…what it's been like for you. I want to know everything."

He wants to know what it's been like for me?

Oh, God. My heart squeezes in my chest, a dangerous feeling that I haven't had in years spreading through my insides like warm chocolate syrup. Jeremy cares, and not just about his son.

About me.

Maybe he never stopped.

10

JEREMY

My brain is on overload.

I have a son, and everything I used to think about the way Rayne left me all those years ago was wrong. She left because she thought I was a part of my grandparents' disgusting plan to end our child's life.

My contempt for them, which I thought couldn't be any stronger, grows.

What if they had succeeded? What if Rayne had been forced to abort my baby, if she hadn't been strong enough to resist them the way she had? I can't begin to imagine the kind of horror that would come from doing something like that against your will. She might have never recovered.

As it was, she left thinking I didn't want her. Didn't want our baby. The thought sends rage boiling through my blood, but if I allow myself to focus on that right now, it will consume me. It'll drag me down to depths I might not be able to climb back out of, and that's not an option.

Right now, the mother of my child needs me to figure out who was tailing her tonight.

She's scared; I can see it in her eyes when she talked about her boss. That asshole knows where she works, and where she lives. It's only a matter of time. If he's allowed to continue to hunt her, he'll get what he came for.

And I'll die before I let that happen.

Punching the code into the high-security door at Night Eagle, I pass through the entrance and head back toward my office. The light turns on automatically when I enter, and I pull out my leather chair and sit, switching my computer on and waiting for it to boot.

Decker. My son's name is Decker. And if his mom's in trouble, he's in trouble. That's reason enough to want to help them.

No reason to evaluate the burning need I have to protect them, like they're *both* mine.

While I wait for the computer screen to flash on, I place a call to Jacob Owen. If a member of his team is at the office after hours, he wants to know about it, and why. I fill him in quickly, letting him know I'll keep him updated and ask for it if I need his assistance.

A surge of adrenaline courses through me when the computer is up and running. This, I excel at. Computers are my thing, in addition to my Special Forces training. My skills in computer science are what got me here. It's what I got my degree in when I completed undergraduate studies while I was in the military.

Through the military, I learned a few tricks that weren't a part of my coursework.

Flexing my fingers, I dive in. *First things first.* Using Night Eagle's secure, untraceable network, I log into the DMV Web site, quickly typing in the license plate from the car following Rayne. Just the thought of his audacity, the fact that he thought he'd get away with following my girl...following *Rayne*...with the intent to harm her is enough to reignite my fury. Swallowing down the rage, I study the screen.

There's a photo and a name: Kevin O'Shea. Grabbing my phone, I log his address. I might need to pay him a visit later. Closing down the DMV's system, I use the best search device known to man: Google.

He comes up as a private investigator.

Okay. So Kevin O'Shea wasn't working on his own, and maybe his intent wasn't to hurt Rayne tonight.

Relief, the purest form I've felt in a long time, settles over me. Now that I know the danger to her isn't immediate, the muscles in my body relax. I hadn't realized I was still holding that much tension, but I was. And I still have work to do.

My phone buzzes on the desk, alerting me to an incoming call. Rayne's name scrolls across the screen, causing my heart to thump in a wild rhythm in my chest.

"Rayne? What's wrong?" My voice is low, urgent when I answer.

"Hey, Jeremy. No, nothing's wrong. I just wanted to...check in. Decker is out for the night...he was excited about the hotel so it took him awhile to get to sleep."

Her voice sounds deeper, more gravelly with tiredness, and I can't believe how the sound of it makes me picture her sounding like that as I lay beside her.

I release the tension with a sigh. "That's good, Rayne."

It's also good to hear her voice on the other end of my phone. But that, I keep to myself.

"Did you find anything out?"

Leaning back in my chair, I study Kevin O'Shea's face on my computer screen. "Yeah. Turns out the guy following you was a private eye. Maybe not dangerous, because it means the person who hired him probably isn't close. But I'm still glad I was there. Didn't want him camping out watching you and Decker."

She sucks in a breath. "It freaks me out, you know? That he knew where I worked, and now where I live. He was watching me."

Yeah, I don't like it either. Not a bit. But my job isn't to scare her further. It's to comfort her. And now that she has me on her side, she needs to know I'll never let anything happen to her.

"Hey, don't worry about that now. You're safe. I'm gonna check a few more things out here before I go home, but I was thinking…do you and Decker want to hang out with me tomorrow?"

Being that tomorrow's Saturday, I can kill two birds with one stone. I can spend some time with my son for the first time, and also keep an eye on Rayne to make sure O'Shea isn't still tailing her. Or worse, that her old boss hasn't arrived in town before I have a chance to get the team on top of tracking him.

I want to make sure he stays as far away from her as possible, preferably right where he belongs: in Phoenix.

There's a pause, and then she answers. "You want to spend the day with me and an eight-year-old?"

There's a smile in her voice, and it tugs on something so deep down inside me. Something I didn't know was there before. "I'm gonna admit something to you, Rayne...it's a secret, so don't tell anyone."

Her soft chuckle warms me, heats my blood. "What?"

"My Saturdays aren't usually all that exciting. Just me and Night, unless the guys and their girls are having a barbecue."

She chuckles again. "You don't say? Who's Night?"

"My dog. Can you guys be ready by nine? I'll pick you up at Olive's. Wear your swimsuits, but bring clothes to change for later in the day."

Silence across the line, and I realize I'm holding my breath waiting for her response.

Come on, Rayne. Let me have this.

She sighs. "Hell, Jeremy. I never could say no to you. We'll be ready at nine."

I pump my fist in the air, but over the phone, I say, "Cool. See you then, Rayne."

"Good night, Jeremy."

Good night, Jeremy. I'll be damned if I'm not gonna fall asleep dreaming about the day when she says those words from right next to me, in my bed.

When I pull the Land Cruiser into Olive's driveway the next morning my heart rate picks up in my chest the way it kicks in during the middle of a run. It feels like I'm getting ready to face an enemy of the state with nothing but my good looks as a weapon.

You can do this, Teague. He's an eight-year-old kid. Not scary.

She's a beautiful, sexy woman who just happens to also be your baby mama. Not scary.

Damn scary.

As my ineffectual pep talk comes to a close, the front door flies open and Decker comes barreling out onto the walk.

Ready or not. This is happening.

I jump out of my SUV, strolling toward him as he comes to a stop right in front of me. Looking up at me, he folds his arms.

With none of his exuberance from seconds ago, he scowls. "Are you my mom's boyfriend now?"

Holy…I'm fucked.

Glancing toward the house, I see that Rayne is nowhere to be found. With a sigh that I barely keep hidden, I squat down so I'm at Decker's eye level. My own green eyes stare back at me, unblinking.

Damn. He's the perfect mix of me and Rayne…

"Whatcha lookin' at?" Decker snaps me back to the here and now.

"Yeah, so…hey, dude. I'm not your mom's boyfriend. If I was, would that be a problem?"

Decker studies me for a minute before he shakes his head. "No, it's just that she's never had one before. I wanted to know why she picked you."

It takes a whole hell of a lot of strength not to fall backward on my ass with that statement. She's never had one before?

Instead, I school my features and give my son a smile. "There's gotta be a first time for everything, right? Let's make a deal, right here, right now. If I decide it's time to make your mom my girlfriend, and I think that's what she wants too, I'll ask you first."

The kid smiles. He's missing a tooth, one of his canines on the bottom. It's fucking cute. I didn't notice it before. How many lost teeth have I missed?

He holds out his hand, and I grab it in mine so we can shake.

"Deal."

That's when Rayne decides to make her appearance, and as I stand back up again and glance at her, it's another *I'm fucked* moment.

She's wearing a filmy black cover-up, hanging down to about midthigh. Her toned legs go on for miles. Miles. Black, strappy sandals slap the ground when she walks, and as she approaches I can see her toes are painted cherry red.

Might as well be fuck-me red.

My eyes travel back up those long, tan legs to discover that the cover-up doesn't leave much to the imagination. I can make out the outline of a bright red bikini underneath, and all I want to do in that moment is pull the thin material covering her right off so I can feast my eyes on what's underneath.

Her long, dark hair is piled up on top of her head in a messy knot, and when I finally scan her face I realize she's wearing huge dark sunglasses.

Stunning. Earth-shattering.

Today's gonna be a hell of a lot more difficult than I thought. What was I thinking, inviting her to do something where she'd be in a bikini, before I've even had the chance to acclimate myself to her presence in my life?

Her brows lift above the glasses. "Do I pass inspection?"

Clearing my throat, I nod and reach out to open the back door for Decker. "You look…you gotta know how you look, Rayne."

Decker's glance passes between me and his mother. He grins. "She's pretty, right?"

I grin at him. "Yeah, dude. She's real pretty."

Rayne reaches Decker, puts her arm around his shoulders, and pulls him to her side. "Decker, this is the guy from work I told you about. My friend Jeremy. Jeremy, this is my son…" She looks up at me, and I can read the emotional look in her eyes. It says, *our son.*

"…Decker," she finishes.

"It's real nice to meet you, Decker. You like boats?"

Decker nods, his eyes filling with excitement. "I've never been on a boat. Is that what we're doing today?"

"Yup. You think you can handle being my first mate?"

Rayne gives me a smile over Decker's head, and man…that feels so damn good. Pride fills me up, threating to burst out of me any second.

My family.

"What's a first mate?" Decker asks as he climbs into the backseat.

I shoot him a grin right before I close his door. "I'll tell you when we get there."

Following Rayne around to the passenger side, I open her door for her, wait for her to climb in, and inhale her heady scent. It's stronger today, maybe because it's accented by her lotion or her sunblock or *something.* Everything about her threatens to rule me, make me forget what I'm doing.

After closing her door, I jog around to the driver's side and start the car. Twisting around to make sure Decker's buckled up, the nerves inside me flare up again.

Rayne's hand lands on mine on the gearshift. "First time driving with a kid in the backseat?"

Glancing at her, I wince. "Am I that obvious?"

She glances back at Decker, who has a handheld video game device in his hands and is deep into whatever game he's playing.

"It's precious cargo, but you'll be fine. You're ex-Special Forces for God's sake." She grins, and I return it.

"Yeah. I got this."

"You got this." She agrees and lets go of my hand.

Immediately, I miss it. I want her hand there. It belongs there. It's such a weird feeling. I haven't had this kind of reaction to any woman since....well, since *her*.

I was so sure I'd moved forward. Without Rayne.

But maybe I was wrong.

11

RAYNE

W hoa! Your boat is so cool!"

Decker's enthralled shout should make me happy. It should make me smile, seeing him, with pure elation, looking at the black and red boat bobbing on the gently rollicking water.

Instead, all of my limbs are trembling. When I look at the boat, I see a death trap about to swallow my son whole. I'm not the least bit scared for myself; I grew up in Wilmington. I've been on my share of boats in my life.

But Decker's never been on one.

I've always kept him close. Maybe a little too close, too safe, too protected. But he's absolutely everything to me. He has been since he took his first breath.

And he's all that I have.

Decker glances at me, and I can't hide the panic in my eyes as hard as I try.

"Isn't it cool, Mom?"

My attempt to form words fails miserably, and Jeremy's

sharp gaze lands on me. I look at him helplessly, trying to convey with my eyes what I can't say with my words. Finally, feeling ridiculous, because how could he possibly understand, I look down at the wooden dock where the three of us stand.

"Hey, Deck."

The nickname rolls off Jeremy's tongue like he's been using it Decker's whole life. It warms me, makes something I can't quite comprehend begin to stir in my chest. In my soul.

Jeremy's face goes very serious as he places his hands on my son's shoulders and leans so he can look him in the eye. "See that drink machine over there? I have a cooler on the boat I wanna stock, but I didn't know what you'd like. Go check it out and then come let me know what you want, yeah? Make sure you pick some out for your mom, too."

My ovaries threaten to explode as Decker meets Jeremy's gaze with a solemn one of his own and nods, like the assignment he's just been given is life-or-death.

As soon as Decker's out of earshot, Jeremy rounds on me. "What's wrong?"

Shaking my head, I glance away to study the wooden decking.

"Rayne. Don't do that. I need to know, so I can fix it." His tone is stern.

Meeting his eyes, I roll my lips between my teeth. To my utter horror, my eyes well up. *Shit and damn.*

Jeremy's eyes widen, and he takes a step closer. He pluck's my chin in his hand with his thumb and forefinger.

"Tell me." He breathes heavily.

Glancing at Decker to be sure he's still busy picking out

drinks, I let my words tumble over one another. "We don't do stuff like this, Jer. Stuff where he can get…hurt. You know? I protect him. He's everything to me."

When the words are expelled from my lungs in a rush, I snap my mouth shut and wait for his reaction. There's no doubt he thinks I'm ridiculous, that I've been smothering our son to death.

Understanding washes through his expression. His green eyes soften at the corners, his mouth kicking up on one side. "He's here, Rayne. He's here and he's awesome, and that's because of you. You've been keeping him safe this whole time on your own. I get it. But I'll never let anything happen to him. On my life, I promise you that. You are *both* safe with me."

He holds me, staring into my eyes until I know without a doubt his promise is true. Decker comes running back up to us just as I nod.

"Sprite! I want Sprite! And my mom usually drinks wine, but there's none in that machine, so she wants Coke."

Decker turns his big, serious eyes on me. "Right, Mom?"

Jeremy's lips twitch. "Wine, huh?"

I fold my arms over my chest. "What? It's not like I go out…ever. I drink wine on the couch while I watch irresistible reality TV. And *Scandal*."

Jeremy's eyes cloud over. "You don't go out?"

I wave my hand around. "Coke sounds good, baby."

Jeremy studies me. "Well, you can have your wine with dinner tonight."

I lift my brow. "Dinner?"

With a secretive grin, he jogs over to the machine and starts gathering cans of soda. When his arms are full, he marches back toward us and hops nimbly onto the boat to put them in the cooler under the bench at the back. When he jumps back onto the pier, he shows Decker how to step from the pier onto the boat.

I watch, my breath hitching as my son copies his dad, looking athletic and limber. I never realized how naturally gifted he is. When Jeremy reaches out for me, I place my hand in his and step onto the speedboat.

Jeremy fits Decker with a life vest, which settles some of the nerves threatening to choke me, and leads him to the chair right beside the driver's seat.

"This is where my first mate needs to sit. I'll untie us from the pier and then I'm gonna show you how we drive this baby."

I've never seen Decker's face so lit with pure joy. It calms me, washing away the remainder of my fear because he's just so damn *happy*. And he doesn't even know yet that the guy spending time with him, showing him how to do things, is his father.

I push my lips out in my best exaggerated pout. "What am I supposed to do while you two men drive this thing?"

Jeremy glances over at me. Decker elbows him like they're in cahoots. Jeremy's eyes are sparkling, the corners crinkling as his face shows that he's just as happy as our son. "You can sit back and relax. I'm guessing it's not something you do a lot of."

Hmph. Didn't I just tell him I usually use wine and my couch to relax?

Scanning the boat's deck, I note that there are comfy-looking seating benches all around the edge. I choose an L-shaped corner and put my bright, paisley beach bag down. From be-hind me, I half-listen in with a smile on my face while Jeremy explains the engine controls to Decker. When the growling engine purrs to life, the slight, salty wind rustles my hair as Jeremy guides the boat out of the slip. The marina where Jeremy keeps his boat is located on the Intracoastal Waterway, not the oceanfront. So Decker lets out a whoop as the boat picks up a bit of speed and curves around the peninsula and out into open water.

With a little sigh, still facing the sea, I close my eyes and allow myself to enjoy it. I used to adore the ocean. Jeremy's grandfather had a boat, and as soon as Jeremy was old enough to drive, he'd take me out on it. It was a safe place for me, a blissfully happy place.

I lost my virginity to Jeremy on that boat. We most likely conceived Decker on that boat.

My cheeks flush as I remember, and the heat creeping through my body drives me to remove my cover-up. Pulling the gauzy material over my head, I pull a tube of sunscreen out of my bag. With my Greek heritage and olive complexion, my skin doesn't burn easily. But I protect myself when I'm going to be basking in the sun.

"Decker," I call, turning to face them.

Jeremy glances in my direction as Decker tears his eyes away from the water. His cheeks are flushed, his eyes bright and full of…life. It's the happiest I've seen my son in a long time, and my heart skips just looking at him.

"Aw, Mom. Can you put it on me really fast?" Decker's spied the sunscreen tube in my hands.

Jeremy, on the other hand…his gaze never makes it to my hands. His eyes are roving hungrily up and down my body, which is now clad only in my new red bikini. The slow slide of his gaze on my skin leaves it even more heated and flushed than it was before, and my face is on fire. But I can't look away from him as he studies me like he's learning a new subject for the very first time.

My body is definitely different from the last time he saw me.

When he finally meets my gaze there's a fire in his eyes that steals my breath.

He wants me? The thought hits me hard, slamming into my awareness and causing my nipples to harden and tighten, and liquid heat to coil deep within my belly.

Feeling like I'm too wide-open and exposed, and not just on the outside, I whirl away from Jeremy and drop one knee to the bench. I concentrate on slathering Decker with sunscreen like I haven't completed this task a thousand times.

But Jeremy's gaze doesn't leave me. I can feel it more now that I'm not looking than I did when I couldn't tear my eyes away. He's stroking me softly with nothing more than a look.

And it becomes painfully clear just how long it's been since I've been with a man. Since anyone's touched me, made me feel…anything.

I've been a mom zombie. Is it possible that Jeremy, the one man I thought I'd never have another chance with, never even thought I *wanted* another chance with, could be the one to bring me back to life?

Decker's soon covered and back at the helm with Jeremy, who then pulls his gaze off me and back onto the water. He's in his element as he points out landmarks on the coastline for Decker. Lying back on the bench, I close my eyes and listen to the smooth whir of the engine and the even smoother sound of Jeremy's voice. It coats me, pouring over my limbs and deep into my bones.

When the sound of the engine begins to soften, I sit up and check our surroundings. Jeremy is pulling into a little cove, one I recognize, that harbors a tiny, secluded beach. My stomach flutters, and I can't help the grin that threatens to split my face in two.

"It's our cove," I murmur to myself.

When I glance at Jeremy, his eyes are on mine. The expression in them sends a pang of longing slicing through me. It's sharp and thorough, lancing me with a tumult of emotions I'm not prepared or equipped to handle. It aches, and it heals all at the same time. I can't swallow around the lump that rises in my throat. Jeremy looks as if he's going through the same thing as he holds my gaze, the bittersweet memories bombarding him all at once, too.

"You remember." It's not even a question; he's already seen the recognition in my expression.

I nod anyway, letting him know that I can't forget this place and what it meant to us.

"Remember what?" Decker looks from me to Jeremy and back again.

I can't rip my eyes away from Jeremy, and he's still holding mine when he answers Decker. "Well, I don't just know your mom from work, Deck. We actually knew each other when your mom lived here a long time ago. And this spot? This little cove is a place where your mom and I used to hang out when we were teenagers."

Clearing my throat, I drop my eyes to Decker and give him a bright smile. "Yep!"

Decker grins. "Cool."

But Jeremy's not done. "Yeah. I'm pretty sure this is the exact spot I taught your mom to swim. Gave her lessons one summer. She was pretty terrible."

My mouth falls open. "Bastard!"

Decker jabs a finger in my direction. "Swear jar!"

Jeremy's lips stretch into a wide grin. "Yeah, Rayne. Swear jar."

My eyes narrow. "Okay. You two want to gang up on me? Fine. But I was not a terrible swimmer. I'd just never had lessons before."

Decker's lips purse to one side as he evaluates me. "But you grew up at the beach."

Laughing, Jeremy finishes the path he started on, leading the speedboat into the cove and dropping anchor in shallow water.

"Are we stopping here?" asks Decker.

Jeremy, not looking at me, nods. "Yeah, buddy. Thought we could play on the beach for a bit, drink some sodas and hang out. Then when we get hungry, we'll turn around and head back to the marina to grab lunch."

Decker's grin is huge. "Awesome."

Jeremy rustles his hair and my heart grows two sizes.

The way he's looking at him?

It's the way a father looks when he loves his son.

Taking a deep breath, I follow Decker off the boat and into the water, where the three of us wade toward the beach. When I glance behind me, I see that Jeremy's got a football in his hand.

"Football?" My tone is quizzical.

Jeremy inclines his head toward Decker. "I think I remember that this dude likes to toss a ball around."

He and Decker exchange a knowing glance, like they have some kind of inside joke that I don't know about.

"How could you possibly know that?" I'm aghast, looking back and forth between the two of them and wondering how they already have an inside joke.

Jeremy offers me a quick explanation of how the two met in the grocery store on my first day of work, when Decker tagged along with Macy and Jay, and I marvel at how fate nearly brought the two together.

I settle on the beach, pulling my knees up to my chest, while Jeremy directs Decker to run a route in order to catch the football.

I've never allowed Decker to play football, or any contact sport for that matter. But football, especially, just brings up too many memories from high school. I would attend every single one of Jeremy's games, and he was truly a star. I can see the natural athleticism in Decker, I know he gets it from Jeremy. But watching Decker on a football field would shred me.

But now, as I observe the pure joy in their faces as they throw the ball back and forth, Decker running on his little legs to catch each pass Jeremy tosses him, I have a feeling I'm not going to be able to keep him from the sport much longer.

That damn lump is back in my throat. I look away and brush the tears from my eyes before they fall, not wanting Jeremy and Decker to read my emotions right there on my face.

After blinking several times, the sight of both of them approaching grabs my immediate attention.

"What's wrong?" My voice is urgent as I stand, brushing sand off my butt. "Is Decker hurt?"

Jeremy, eyes soft, lays a hand on my shoulder, allowing it to slide down my arm. His touch, even one this slight, sends a fiery tingle arcing along my skin. Trying not to shiver, I meet his gorgeous green gaze.

"No, he's fine. We're having fun. We just decided it's time for you to join in."

"Yeah!" Decker shouts. "Come on, Mom! Both of us against Jeremy. We can take him down, right?"

Renewed energy fills me, and I give Decker a firm nod. "You're damn right we can."

Decker giggles, pointing at me. "Swear jar!"

"Dammit," I mutter and turn to glare at Jeremy as he gives an outright belly laugh.

Jeremy eyes me but speaks to Decker. "Your mom has some trouble keeping her mouth clean, huh?"

Decker rolls his eyes. "Always. She's the only mom I know who cusses in front of a little kid like me!"

Glowering, I throw my hands up. "No mom is perfect, Decker!"

His face grows serious as he reaches for my hand. "You are. You're perfect for me, Mom."

His little fingers curl around my hand and squeeze, and so does my heart.

This kid!

Glancing at Jeremy, I can see that his eyes are locked on where Decker and my hands are joined. When he glances back up at me, his eyes shine with wonder.

"Think you're right about that, Deck." His voice is velvety soft. "Pretty perfect."

12

JEREMY

Oh, boy.

I watch with amusement as Decker and Rayne set up for a play on our makeshift field.

I don't think I've ever played with a kid like this before. Especially not a kid and his mom. Never dated a single mom, never cared to. It just never seemed like my idea of fun.

But I can't remember the last time I've enjoyed a Saturday morning so much. Maybe it's because I'm not just hanging out with a woman and her son. It's so much more...I'm putting time in with *Rayne* and *my son*. We're coming up on lunchtime, and the hours with these two have just flown by. Rayne is sexy as hell in her bikini, drawing me in with all sorts of crazy thoughts about what I want to do with that body. Things I never did to her the first time around. Tricks I've learned about how to please a woman that I'm *dying* to use on her.

God. She's stunning; all dark-golden skin, thick black hair, and navy blue eyes. Throw a red bikini on top of all that? It's the perfect picture. And when I look at both of them together, the little boy who loves to play and laugh and run, standing beside this beautiful woman…it's the picture of perfection. The kind of perfect I thought I'd lost. When she walked away, I'd sealed myself off from the hope that one day I'd have this.

But now I desperately crave it.

I want them in my life. Both of them.

"Hut!" Decker calls, hiking the ball backward.

Rayne catches it—*that's my girl*—and trots backward, her big blue eyes zeroing in on me. *Just like I taught her.*

I stalk her like a predator as she scopes out a path to get past me.

It won't happen.

I fake right, and she takes the bait. Dashing toward my left, she squeals in surprise when I'm right back in her path after my fake-out. I grab her around the waist, feeling the supple pull of her skin and the heady, heavenly scent of her, and we both go down.

Making sure I fall first, I hit the sand, holding on to her to break her fall as she slides down on top of me. She giggles as I roll her, hovering above her and staring down into her face alight with laughter and sunshine.

Goddamn. Beautiful.

She stops laughing, her smile fading slowly as she takes in the seriousness of my gaze, her plump pink bottom lip disappearing between her teeth. My cock twitches in my trunks, eager to get to his target.

Decker laughs behind us. "Good try, Mom. Jeremy faked you out, though."

Clearing my throat, I get to my feet and pull Rayne up with me. We both brush sand off our bodies, but my eyes are on her hands, not mine.

"He's sneaky." Rayne's voice carries a note of teasing as she jabs an elbow into my side.

"Hey," I protest, lifting my hands into the air. "This is football. It was my job to sack the QB."

Her lips puff out in a pout that I want to kiss away. *What's wrong with me? I'm not some horny teenager. I'm standing in front of my kid. I'm a man in control of my dick. Come on, Teague.*

"Again!" Decker's excitement is contagious, and Rayne and I both agree to keep playing.

Ten plays later, we're all out of breath and ready to head back to the boat. Once we're back onboard, Rayne settles Decker on a seat with a soda, and he leans back to take in the wake as we drive.

I indicate that she should come sit next to me, and she obliges, perching on the seat at my right.

"Thank you for today." Her voice lifts to be heard over the roar of the engine, and I glance at her to see her studying me. I want so badly to ask her what she's thinking, but I'm pretty sure we haven't made it there yet. We're still getting to know each other again, and I'm well aware of the fact that she doesn't completely trust me.

"It's been the best day I've had in a really long time. He's…" I glance over my shoulder at our son, who's staring out at the waves like there's no place he'd rather be. My heart swells to a size I didn't know was possible, stretching to accommodate the instant love I feel for Decker.

"Look," she begins.

The serious tone of her voice makes my ears perk. "Yeah?"

She takes a deep breath, and my own breathing hitches. I'm not going to like what she's about to say, that much is clear.

"I don't expect anything from you, Jeremy. I've been doing this by myself for eight years, and if you don't think you have room in your life for Decker, I'd like for you to just tell me now. He already adores you, and I don't want to dangle you in front of him just to rip you away."

She says the words like she actually believes I'd cut and run after spending the day with her and my son.

Anger bubbles up inside me, threatening to spill over. But I'm dealing with Rayne here, not a target. She's the mother of my son, and she's coming from a place of protection for our child and probably for herself. I reach over and take her hand in mine. It's not something I planned to do, but I need to be touching her when I say what's on my mind.

"Rayne. From this day on, I want to be part of his life. I want to protect him, teach him, and watch him grow. I want to teach him every single thing there is to know about being a good man. I swear to you, I want this. I want him. I always would have."

I purposely omit the growing feelings swirling around inside me for her, because this is about Decker. And she needs to know that now that I have him, there's no turning back.

He's my son.

Her eyes are glossy and full of emotion. Her bottom lip quivers, and my stomach tightens. My hand squeezes hers, but what I really want to do is pull her into my arms. Maybe we'll get to the point where I'm the guy who can do that for her, but we're not there yet.

My grandparents robbed me of more than I ever could have imagined. I thought all they robbed me of was my respect for them, and the future I thought I'd have. But they stole my family from me, and I don't know how I'm going to deal with the resulting rage.

It's the last thing I want to do, but I know it has to happen. At some point, I'm going to have to pay them a visit, let them know that I know what they did. That no matter how old and frail they are now, I can't forgive this.

Not this.

Rayne wipes her eyes, and I clear my throat. "And did I hear you thank me for 'today'? Today isn't over yet, darlin'."

She lifts one perfectly arched brow. "Oh? What else do you have in mind, Mr. Teague?"

The Moomba cuts effortlessly through the waves, bouncing every so often as we glide toward the ICW. The sun has bronzed Rayne's skin to a sexy caramel, and I'm aching to taste it…to taste her. I want to know all the ways she's different, now that she's all grown up.

And all the ways she's still the girl I fell in love with as a teenager.

"We're going to grab lunch out here near the beach, and then I would really like you and Decker to come to my place tonight for dinner."

Her eyes widen in shock. "Jeremy…that's spending the entire day together. I can't monopolize your time like that. It's Saturday, I'm sure you have things to do tonight."

She's talking about dating. She thinks I'd want to hang out with some chick over her and Decker? Wrong.

Holding her gaze, I shake my head. "I don't have plans, Rayne. But I want to. Say you'll come over."

She hesitates, glancing back at Decker. Finally, she relents. "Okay. What can I bring?"

I toss her an amused glance. "What can you make?"

She blushes, the faint red stain creeping into her cheeks slowly. "I mean…I can make stuff."

Grinning, I guide the boat around the peninsula toward the marina. "Yeah? You can? Tell me what's on your list of specialties."

Her blush deepens.

Decker walks up beside her. "Specialties?"

I glance at him, aiming a wicked grin and inclining my head toward Rayne. "I just invited you guys over to my house for dinner. I'm trying to find out what your mom cooks."

Decker laughs. "Cooks? She makes peanut butter and jelly pretty good. And coffee."

Swallowing my chuckle, I shake my head. "It's okay, cooking is kind of what I do."

Rayne huffs.

This time, my chuckle slips out. "Hey, Deck…how long do you think it'll take before your mom lets me teach you how to wakeboard?"

Decker's eyes are wide and hopeful. "Really?"

When I glance at Rayne, she's gone slightly green and her eyes are wide. Easing the Moomba into my slip, I give her a reassuring smile. "We'll take our time with that. But I'll get you both on a board at some point."

She gulps.

Scanning my wide-open great room, staring into the kitchen, my raw nerves force me to view my place in a whole new light. When I bought the Craftsman and remodeled it, I was newly out of the army and putting down roots in my hometown. Bachelor roots. I redid the house, knocking down walls and redoing the old hardwood floors, shining up the woodwork and adding paint to the walls. I hired a contractor to redo the kitchen, and everything in here gleams.

But is it good enough for a family?

I'm jumping ahead a few steps; I know that. Me and Rayne…we haven't said anything about starting back up again. We haven't even glossed over the subject. There might not be anything left there to build on. Even as that thought crosses my mind, I know it's not true. We have a foundation, all right. We have chemistry, maybe more than we did as teenagers. The way my insides spark just from looking at her, the way my cock responds to her touch or her nearness…that's no accident. There's definitely something there.

There's a soft knock at the door, followed by a more insistent pounding that jacks my heart rate up to stressed-the-fuck-out. Beside the big brick fireplace, Night lifts his head and barks. It's deep and meant as a warning for me. My fingers snap toward him.

"Night. Stay."

I cross the great room into the front hall in just a few strides, flinging open the door to a smiling and bouncing Decker and a wary-looking Rayne.

I study her as I usher them in, shutting the door behind me. Her face is drained of color, and though she offers me a weak smile, it's just that: weak. Holding my hand up to Decker to halt him, I release a low whistle.

Night comes trotting into the entryway, his nails clicking on the hardwood floors. Rayne tenses beside me, so I grab her hand. My other rests on Decker's shoulder.

"Whoa! You have a dog! He's huge! He's so cool." Decker's appreciation for Night sends warm vibrations throughout my body.

Giving Rayne's hand a quick, reassuring squeeze, I kneel beside Decker. "He's friendly, buddy. But you need to show him right away that you're the boss. Here…" Holding his hand, I flip it palm-up and direct it toward Night, who ambles forward and sniffs.

Decker chuckles while Night greedily pushes his big blocky head against his hand. "Is he your guard dog?"

I glance toward Rayne. "He can be. He acts on my command. He's really well trained. Watch."

Standing, I snap my fingers again and Night is at full attention. Bending my arm at the elbow and pulling it toward me, I leave it in an L-shaped position. Without a word from me, Night sits. I hold my hand out in a "halt" signal and back into the great room. Night follows me with his eyes, but his haunches stay rooted to the floor. Finally, when I'm standing by the fireplace I use a calm and commanding tone my dog is used to. "Come, Night."

Night immediately trots over to stand beside me. Pulling a treat out of my pocket, I hold it out and let him take it from my hand.

"Awesome!" Decker exclaims. "He's the best dog ever!"

I can't help the beaming pride that radiates off of me. This kid is so impressive. Night is a 110-pound hulk of muscle and mayhem, intimidating to grown men. But Decker is staring at him with adoration in his eyes, like my dog is just a playful pup. "That's just the start of what he can do. But you should know that once he gets to know you, he'll protect you no matter what."

Decker nods gravely, like I've just divulged a top clearance-level secret. Pointing toward Night's basket of toys beside the fireplace hearth, I nudge Decker in that direction. "His favorite is his rope."

As Decker lunges for the rope, Night's tail wagging happily beside him; I cross back to the front door where Rayne still stands.

"You're not afraid of dogs, are you?" I ask her in a low tone.

She shakes her head, glancing at the door. "N-no."

Unable to keep from touching her, I rest my hands on her shoulders and peer into her face. "What's wrong, darlin'?"

She glances at the door again. "I don't know, Jeremy. As we walked from the car to the front of the house, I just felt like... I don't know." She shakes her head, frustration showing clearly in her features. "This creepy feeling came over me, like someone was watching me."

I'm filled with cold, slithering dread as I move her away from the door. A sick feeling settles in my gut at the thought of her and Decker being watched walking to my front door. Every protective instinct I have jumps into gear, and I give her a push toward the great room where Decker and a playfully growling Night are tugging on the frayed, colorful rope.

"Stay with Decker," I instruct her in a firm voice. "I'll be right back."

Striding to the entryway table, I slide open the drawer and retrieve my revolver. Making a mental note that I'm not going to be able to keep it there anymore, now that Decker will be a fixture at my house, I place my hand on the doorknob.

Rayne's voice rises an octave. "What are you going to do?"

Glancing at her, I incline my head in Decker's direction. "Shhh. Don't wanna scare him, Rayne. I'm just gonna check things out, OK? I'll be back in a minute. Go over there, with Night and Deck."

Nodding with eyes full of apprehension, she obeys.

Good girl.

Soundlessly, I open the front door and slip outside into the balmy night.

The lighted front walk leads straight down to the sidewalk in front of the house. There's a driveway to my right, leading around to the detached two-car garage, but as I scan the yard, I see nothing out of the ordinary. Keeping my weapon lowered but gripped securely in both hands, I move with a quickness down the front steps and into the grass beside the front walk.

I trust Rayne's instincts. They're what ensured our son entered the world safe and sound. I don't know what she went through back in Phoenix—I'm counting on the fact she'll trust me enough soon to fill me in. I still think there's something she's not telling me. But one thing's for sure: she's scared. And she has a reason to be. If her hackles rose out here on my turf, I'm gonna make damn sure whoever spooked her never does it again.

Sticking close to the front shrubbery and the shadows that cling there, I skirt my way to the corner of the house. Glancing around it to the side yard, I note nothing of interest there. The neighbor's house is dark, probably out for the evening.

From my vantage point, there in the shrouded darkness of the yard, I scan the street again. I'm looking for anything that shouldn't be there: a lurking stranger, a car that doesn't belong, anything out of the ordinary would have me heading in that direction. The street seems clear until my eyes land on a lone figure walking at a slouched clip from behind the house directly across the street.

Every muscle inside me goes still as I watch the person. He's dressed in dark clothing, and he's too far away for me to see the direction of his gaze. When he makes it to the sidewalk on the other side of the road, he suddenly stops, and his gaze rivets toward my house.

"Motherfucker." The curse is a whispered murmur, but his head whips in my direction anyway.

Stepping out of the shadows, I call out. "Stop right there, asshole."

He freezes, a baseball cap pulled low over his face, right before he breaks into a sprint. Muttering a curse, I holster my gun in the back of my jeans and take off after him.

My body goes into autopilot. My shoes eat first grass, then pavement, and my gaze zeroes in on the suspect. His arms pump by his sides like he's running from the Devil, and the way I'm feeling right now, it's probably a good assumption.

I'm gaining on him, the rage burning through my veins and giving me the adrenaline rush that I don't even need to outrun this guy. I push my legs faster, willing myself to end this *now.*

But then the bastard cuts a hard right, veering into the yard beside him. When I follow, I watch him disappear over a wooden fence. Then I hear the sound of the German shepherd who lives there barking like a mad hound.

Stopping, I suck in a deep breath and watch, but the man I was pursuing doesn't return to the street.

Guess he decided to take his chances with the dog. Fuck!

I could go after him. But I don't move. *Goddammit.* As much as I want to chase the fucker down and find out who he is and what he wants with Rayne, I know in my gut that leaving them right now would be a mistake.

As the man I want so badly to lock in a room and use every single interrogation method I've ever learned on him flees, something very clearly slides into place in my brain.

I have a family.

No matter what happens, it's my job to protect them.

There's no way I'm letting Rayne and Decker out of my sight until this game of cat and mouse is over.

13

RAYNE

When Jeremy steps back in his front door, he holds a finger to his lips and points to his gun. Inclining his head toward Decker, I understand. He doesn't want our son to see his gun, and he won't be putting it back in the drawer where it was before. He disappears around a corner, and when he comes back his hands are empty.

I release a breath I've been holding since the second he walked out the door. I tried to smile for Decker, helping him play with the big, sweet dog, but my mind was outside with the man who insists on protecting me at every turn.

Why does he do it?

He's a good man; that much is clear. But is that what drives him when it comes to my situation? I haven't told him everything about it, yet he throws himself in front of me at every turn, every time he thinks there's a threat. Is it just his protective nature?

The last thing I want to do is jump to conclusions when it comes to Jeremy. I don't want to assume that just because he wants our son in his life he wants me, too. I don't want to force him into having some kind of twisted relationship with me in order to spend time with our son.

I would never force him to do anything he didn't want to do.

But does he know that? Is he protecting me out of some sort of obligation to the mother of his child? Or is it something more?

All of these questions are turning over and over in my mind, rippling like flags in a strong gust of wind, as Jeremy stops in the front hall and beckons me to join him.

With one last pat for Night, I glide toward him, pulled by my connection to him as much as by my desire to find out what happened outside.

"Did you see anyone?" My voice trembles slightly; I'm almost afraid of the answer. One private investigator following me on behalf of Wagner Horton was one thing. But feeling like I'm being shadowed wherever I go, like it's not safe for Decker and I to leave the house…it's unthinkable. Unbearable.

Jeremy's expression is guarded as he watches me. "There was a man out there, Rayne. Watching. I think."

My heart thumps harder in my chest, pounding out a distinct rhythm of fear. "You think?"

A frustrated noise rumbles in Jeremy's throat as he drives a hand through his hair, hanging loose now around his shoulders. "He ran when I called out. I chased him for a few blocks, then I lost him. And then the thought of you and Decker in here alone…"

He didn't finish his sentence. He didn't have to. He didn't want to leave us. Something inside my chest grows warm and melty at the thought.

Wrapping my arms around myself just to keep them busy, I chew on my bottom lip as anxiety sucker punches me. "I never should have dragged you into this. I can handle Wagner, I just need time. I can go to the authorities as soon as I have proof of what he did." I trail off as his expression darkens, growing more intense.

The air between us suddenly crackles as the air around us pulls taut. It's like Jeremy's presence is sucking the air right out of the room.

He takes a step closer, crowding me. "You didn't drag me into shit, Rayne. I'm where I want to be. And this is where I want you and Decker to be. You're not leaving here tonight."

I open my mouth to protest. "We can't…I mean we're not your responsibility—"

With another ferocious growl, he pulls me around the corner into a nook beside the entryway. Out of Decker's sight, he presses me against the wall next to a locked cabinet. I don't have time to think or react. Everything about Jeremy overpowers me, but it doesn't elicit fear. Instead, my thighs clench together as my lips part with a rush of air. My breath comes in pants as his pupils widen.

Then he claims my lips.

And *oh God,* this isn't the same boy I kissed so many times in high school.

This kiss is fierce; it's relentless. One hand is braced against the wall, the other slides down my side and wraps tightly around me, pulling me against his hard, hard body. His mouth works against mine, insisting, his tongue darting out to lick the seam of my lips, coaxing me none-too-gently to open for him. With a needy moan, I do, because all of the blood in my body is leaving my head and rushing straight to my throbbing core. His tongue meets mine, tangling and dancing and twisting, and it's so sensual, so erotic, that I can't get enough.

My hands slide up his chest, under his shirt, and there's a low rumble of sound deep in his throat that reverberates through my whole body. His muscles, so sinewy and strong, twitch beneath my fingers. It's like my body is in tune with his, a perfect synchronization that promises utter and complete pleasure with our connection.

Tearing his lips away from mine only long enough to trail soft, fluttering kisses over my jaw, his voice is hungry. *"Rayne."*

My name, from this man's mouth? It's soul shaking. And the way his lips are so reverent now against my skin…like he's worshipping me. I shiver in his arms, at his complete mercy.

I'm broken from the trance of Jeremy's kiss by the cackle of laughter from the other side of the wall as Decker plays with Night. The dog's soft, chuffing bark lets me know that Decker is safe with him, and my heart is full of conflicting emotions I can't handle or control right now.

Pushing away from Jeremy, I slide out from between him and the wall.

I glance away from him, but his finger catches me under the chin and I look up into his earnest expression.

"I want you here." The statement is simple fact. "I want both of you here. But more than that, right now, I need you here. I need to keep you both safe. Let me."

I nod. There's no turning him down. At least not right now.

Jeremy catches my hand as I turn away, yanking me back to him. I stare up into his stormy gaze.

"That kiss? I meant it. We're not running away from it…just postponing it for later. Yeah?"

A rush of heat makes me want to fan myself, but I swallow it and offer him a sultry smile. I'm pretty sure that right now, sultry is all I have in me. My knees are weak from that kiss.

I salute him, trying to find a lifeline of humor before I crack open and show him everything I'm feeling inside. "Roger that."

The surprised gleam in his eyes is what I see before I whirl around and head back toward Decker.

He's barely even noticed my absence. With shining eyes, he glances up and beams at me. "Watch this, Mom!"

Backing up from a sitting Night, he holds a nearly shredded tennis ball in his hand. "Night…catch!" Then, he tosses the ball in an arc into the air. Night leaps up from his spot, twisting his body and catching the ball in his mouth.

He's surprising agile for such a big dog.

"That's awesome, sweetie!" It really is.

"Atta boy, Night." Jeremy's come up behind me, his proximity causing my body to crave his closeness again. A flashback of his mouth against mine, his hand on me courses through my mind, and I shut my eyes, trying to dispel it.

It's been a week. A week since Jeremy stepped back into my life.

This is too fast.

My head spinning, I rub my temples.

"Hey, Deck," Jeremy calls as he steps up beside me. "We're grilling out. Want to help me get the grill going?"

Decker shoots me an incredulous glance. "Can I?'

I ruffle his hair with a smile. "Guess so."

His answering smile almost breaks my heart.

As they walk into the kitchen and the set of double French doors leading to the backyard, Jeremy glances back at me. His expression is a complete match to Decker's.

Happy. Content. Fulfilled.

My God. Look at what they've brought into each other's lives already. It's like they've been missing the other one all along.

My eyes fill, and a sudden urge to sob nearly takes over.

"Jeremy?" I call.

He turns, his gaze sharp. Taking in my face, he moves to come back to me. But I shake my head with vigor.

"Bathroom?" I squeak.

He gestures, and without another word I find the powder room and lock myself inside. The guilt is eating me alive, one tiny bite at a time, and I'm overwhelmed with the cluster of emotions. I'm sad for the time they've lost together. Hell, I'm sad for the time that *I've* lost with Jeremy. Seeing him and Decker together just cements the fact that he would have been there, would have been a great father all along. But I'm also so damned happy that their bond is coming so naturally to both of them. The stress of all the emotions, combined with the fear that Wagner will eventually catch up with me, is too much to handle.

I lean against the bathroom door, and my knees give out on me. Sliding down the door, I bury my head in my arms.

And I cry.

When I enter the backyard through the French doors, Jeremy is standing beside an enormous gas grill on a stone patio, and Decker is playing in the manicured backyard with Night. I watch the dog and Deck frolicking around for a second, my heart lifting when Decker rolls onto the ground exactly the same way the dog does, laughing wildly while Night licks his face.

Jeremy glances up as I approach. "I've never seen Night take like this to someone before. It's amazing."

I gesture toward the platter of chicken breasts, covered in spices and seasoning, sitting beside the grill. "What can I do?"

Jeremy chuckles. "I got this, darlin'. You wanna tell me what just happened in there?"

I offer him an apologetic smile. "Not really?"

He frowns. Using a pair of tongs, he picks up the chicken pieces and places each one on the sizzling grill. "I thought after we eat we can go out and get anything you and Decker need for the night. Then tomorrow I can go with you back to Olive's place to get some stuff for the week."

I nod absently, watching Decker play with Night. Then I startle, glancing at Jeremy again. His profile is striking in the dusk, handsome and strong. "Wait, what? We can't stay here, Jer."

He meets my gaze with a steady one of his own. "Why not?"

I put a hand on his arm. "Because this is moving too fast for me. And it'll confuse Decker. We'll stay the night, but we're going home tomorrow."

Jeremy sighs. "Yeah, I get that, Rayne. I don't want to rush Deck. But, God…this is so damn hard. I just want him to know that I'm his dad, you know? I missed enough time. I also want to be there for you both until we're sure you're safe. And being with him feels right."

I nod, because I can see that. The two of them together…it *is* right. Sliding my hand down his arm, I intertwine our fingers together. I want to comfort him, to reassure him that I'm not going anywhere, and that neither is Decker. We have time. "I think…I think he's going to be happy when he finds out, Jer. Really happy."

His eyes blaze. There's so much emotion there, shining through the green and gold. "Yeah?"

"Yeah."

His expression clouds over "Listen, if you expect me to let you go home tomorrow—and I still don't know if I'm comfortable with that—you need to tell me everything. Tell me what happened in Phoenix with your boss. Tell me the real reason he's got eyes on you. Everything, Rayne."

My stomach jumps with anxiety. But I know he's right. He's trying to protect me, but he doesn't know the whole story.

Can I tell him what I saw? I really want to tell someone…the secret is eating me alive.

Can I trust him?

14

JEREMY

I'm standing out in the hallway, my arms folded across my chest, when Rayne steps out of the guest room upstairs. She finds me there, offers a small smile, and pulls the door nearly shut behind her.

"Thought you were downstairs." Her voice is soft.

I push off the wall and extend my hand. Warmth radiates up my arm and into my chest when she takes it.

"Wanted to be here, you know…in case you needed me." The admission seems so trite when I say it aloud. She's been tucking Decker in for eight years. What would she need me for?

But Rayne doesn't act like what I said was idiotic. Instead, her fingers curl a little more tightly around mine as we head downstairs. She glances down at our hands and then up at me. The question in her eyes is clear.

What are we doing?

I veer straight for the couch and pull her down beside me.

Night lifts his head and chuffs to acknowledge our sudden appearance. Then he rests his head back on his paws, lounging comfortably on his bed beside the fireplace.

Rayne sits, the weight of a stressed-out, scared single mom on her shoulders. She's beautiful, stunning, gorgeous…but the weary way she holds her elegant body and the taut line of her mouth makes me want to punch something.

Or lift all that weight and place it on my capable shoulders. Hasn't she been carrying it alone for long enough?

I point toward the stairs. "He's the best kid, Rayne. You did so good."

Her mouth immediately transforms into the smile I'm craving. "He is, right? God, I got lucky with him, Jer. Being a single mom…it's hard, you know? Especially when it happens at eighteen and you're not the least bit ready for it. My grams helped me a lot, giving me a place to live rent free and watching Decker so I could get an associate's degree. But it's still the hardest job on earth."

She's taken her long, silky hair down from the knot she had it in earlier, and it tumbles around her shoulders in irresistible waves. Her hair…it's always been her signature. At least for me. It's something I could never forget. I lift a piece now and let it fall through my fingers.

"I'm sorry I wasn't there." My voice has dropped low; the words are hard to expel. "But damn, I wish you'd come to me before you ran." I can't hide the exasperation in my voice. I'm trying so hard not to be angry, because what's done is done.

She looks me in the eye, her gaze steady and full of meaning. "I know you are. It wasn't your fault. I know that now. I wish…I wish I had trusted what we had. I wish I'd come to you no matter what your grandparents said."

I wish she had, too. But somehow, we're both going to have to try to let go of the past and move forward from here.

What that means for us? I don't know yet. But I want to find out.

"Hey. There were times that I was there, though. Remember when you had that big photography project due on Monday, and I convinced you to come to my football game on a Friday night?"

Her lips twist in a smile that's half-annoyed, half-amused. "Yes. How could I forget? I was sitting there in the stands, cheering you on, while simultaneously thinking that I needed to have a twenty-seven photo story done by Monday morning. Complete with essay."

I chuckle, scrubbing one hand over my face. "Yeah. But what happened the next day?"

She stares into the distance, remembering. And now her smile is fully genuine. "You took me out on the boat Saturday. We stayed out for hours, and you pointed out things I could use for my project. I took the photos, you drove the boat, and now that I think about it, it was one of my favorite days. You came through for me."

I lean forward, turning to face her head-on. "I want to come through for you again."

She's quiet, her hands worrying the hem of her shirt while her bottom lip disappears into her mouth.

"Tell me, Rayne. Tell me everything. I want to know the whole truth about what happened in Phoenix, with your boss."

After she hesitates for what feels like an eternity, she finally starts talking. And as the story pours out of her, she draws her knees to her chest, like holding them there can keep the asshole ex-boss of hers out of her life. I'm listening with rapt attention, cataloguing details about Horton that I can't find online. Like the fact that he got lucky when his small-time tech company blew up, but that he's not the guru behind all of his software. He has a team of computer geeks who keep him relevant. If it weren't for them, Wagner Horton of Horton Tech would be all washed up.

"My last night there...I was working late. Wagner wasn't expecting me to be there. I saw something." Her voice trembles, and I lean forward, staring into her eyes.

"What'd you see?" The hair on the back of my neck stands at attention, and my instincts are telling me her next sentence is going to be vital.

Rayne's voice drops to a whisper, like someone other than me is going to hear her. "I discovered documentation proving that Wagner Horton is stealing technology from another company. His biggest rival, to be exact: Prednar, Inc. He's getting ready to roll out the next new tech that will change the way people communicate, but it's not his idea. It was Prednar's, and he used corporate espionage to steal it and claim it as his own."

Her revelation makes my insides feel like they're being hollowed out. If what she's saying is true, and I believe it is, then she has something on Horton that he would never, ever want to go public. People have killed for less. A lot less.

Fuck! I want to hit something, but I focus on Rayne. Her

midnight blue eyes are brimming, like she's holding back tears. She knows exactly how serious this is.

"You're sure?"

She bobs her head. "Jeremy, I've been over and over this in my brain. Every possible scenario. But I know what I saw can't be explained any other way. He's a tech thief. And he's going to profit big-time off of what he stole."

She's got a point. "Tech companies have all kinds of crazy spyware in place so their new software and designs don't get hacked. Wagner shouldn't have been able to get in. Maybe he had help."

She leans forward. "You mean, like someone on the inside at Prednar was helping him?"

Nodding, I rub my chin.

"Yeah. You don't have proof, do you? Nothing to show the authorities that can end this?" I raise a hopeful brow.

There's a hesitation. She glances down at her knees, still pulled tight against her chest. "What I saw was a code...it was encrypted in the Horton Tech software. But it had the ir-refutable Prednar logo incorporated in a way that couldn't be erased. He kept it, I'm guessing, in case anyone on his team needs to check the code against what they're working on. It was a file I was never supposed to see."

"Can you show it to me?" Adrenaline pumps through my blood, because codes? That's something I can work with. I'm nowhere near the top of the hacker game, but with help I know I can get what we need.

"I would, but I can't log on to the network unless I'm inside the Horton Tech system."

Smirking, I shake my head. "That can be arranged, darlin'."

She narrows her eyes at me. "When did computers become your superpower?"

I lift one shoulder as her hair catches my attention again. When she moves, a rush of floral-scented sweetness washes over me and I'm pulled into this fantasy where neither of us is wearing anything but that scent. Despite the fact that we're discussing a serious and possibly dangerous subject matter, my body responds to her closeness the way it has a habit of doing. The rhythm of my heart becomes rapid and irregular, my eyes become laser-focused on her lips, and my cock goes hard, making my jeans uncomfortably tight.

Shifting in my seat, I lift one shoulder in a shrug. "After."

After a career-ending shoulder injury, after my grandfather showed how little he cared about my well-being, after you left, after everything changed.

She studies me, scooting closer on the couch. Now with her legs tucked underneath her, she reaches out and traces a line with her index finger around the scar at my hairline. It's small, and faint, but it's definitely there.

"After what, Jer?" Her voice is the softest blanket, one I want to wrap around myself and burrow into.

I don't think about this topic. I don't talk about it. I've built a suit of armor around myself in the years since it happened, turning to constant lightheartedness to get me through. Humor helps me remember that I can trust the people around me, that they're not all shameless traitors the way my grandfather was.

No one's ever had a reason to ask me what happened back then. Until now.

Shuddering, I fight for a lame attempt at a joke. "After I lost the three most important things in my life: football, my grandparents, and you. But hey…they say change is good, right?"

Her expression softens, but she doesn't crack a smile.

Right. Because she knew me Before. *Everybody else in my life got there* After. *She's not gonna let me hide behind a joke or a prank. Not Rayne.*

I grab her hand, the one that was tracing my scar, and hold on to it like it's the only thing keeping me afloat.

"Jeremy," she whispers. "You said that you cut ties with your grandparents after high school ended. But you didn't even know what they did to me. Tell me what they did to you."

Her eyes are dark pools of pleading, and a sigh escapes me because I know I'm going to tell her everything.

"It was March of senior year, and I was in spring training. Remember how we used to lift weights and run plays without pads in the spring?" I sit back on the couch, pulling Rayne with me. With a breath's hesitation, she snuggles in under my shoulder, and *damn*. It feels fan-fucking-tastic. Like she never left.

"It happened so fast, Rayne. One second, I'm standing there, throwing a pass. We're goofing around, just playin'. And then the next, I'm lying on the ground looking up at the sky, knowing that something really bad just happened to me. I felt it…it wasn't just the pain. There was this feeling of finality that let me know everything was about to change."

The soft exhale beneath me pulls my attention, and I glance down at Rayne. She peers up at me with pain-filled eyes. The sight of them makes me want to comfort her, even though I know that pain is empathetic. She feels it on my behalf.

"Oh, Jeremy," she whispers. "I'm so sorry. Football was everything to you."

Releasing a grim chuckle, I bend down and press my lips to her hair. The contact induces a chain reaction in my body that starts in my lips and travels south. She's going to become like a drug to me, that much is obvious. Inhaling, I pull her a little closer just because I can.

"It never should have been, though, right? Seems like loving it so much made me blind to what was really important."

Her quiet sigh is absorbed into my chest. "Maybe not. But it meant so much to you."

"Yeah, it did, sweetheart. It did. But it's what happened after that that was the final straw. I knew my scholarship was done. There was going to be surgery. And then recovery. And then months of rehab. No Division One school was going to wait around for that. So my grandfather tried to sign a deal with the Devil."

Moving so quickly it causes Night to raise his head in alarm, she sits up and stares at me. "What are you talking about?"

Holding her gaze, I caress her hand gently in both of mine. Now that I know what my grandparents did to her, she's not going to handle any of their actions well.

"I mean he hired a doctor whose medical license was revoked for questionable practices, experimenting on patients with drugs that weren't legal yet. The doctor was going to give me something for my arm that would possibly eliminate the need for surgery. My grandfather wanted to cover up the whole thing, keep the university who'd offered me a scholarship out of the loop."

Her eyes grow wide, her hand tightening its hold on mine. "That's crazy."

I nod grimly. "Damn crazy. All he wanted to do was make sure I made it to the NFL. He didn't care that this potential treatment was untested and could be dangerous for me. And my grandmother? She just went along with whatever he said. I had no one looking out for my best interests back then. Nobody but me."

I can almost see how persuasive he was, telling me that I needed to "man up" and that everything would be fine. He'd reiterated the fact that he ran a multi-million-dollar corporation and he didn't get to the top without knowing a smart decision when he saw one.

"The next day, after I found out what he had planned, I went and enlisted. And then I went straight to my doctor. I was able to have the surgery for my shoulder and recover before I had to leave for boot camp. My grandfather 'bout blew his top. He told me that I was screwing up my future, and that his grandson was meant for greater things. I was either playing in the NFL, or I was going to end up working for him. No other options. Can you believe that, Rayne? What could be greater than serving your country?"

She shakes her head, her eyes still wide and disbelieving. There's stark resentment showing through, and her bottom lip is caught so tightly between her teeth that it's turning white.

"He...God, Jer. He's such a terrible man. I wish I could have been there for you."

We hold each other's gazes, and we're both thinking the same thing. If it weren't for him, we would have been there for each other. Our lives would be really different now. Our son's life would be different. Decker would know he had a father who loved him and would do anything to protect him.

My grandfather's reaction to that adverse time in my life proved to me that I had to get out from under his thumb. That he didn't want what was best for me; he wanted what was best for his image, his legacy. A grandson serving in the military wasn't part of that. A grandson who had a child out of wedlock at eighteen wasn't part of it, either, apparently.

There's an overwhelming urge to confront him. Both of my grandparents, to let them know that what they tried to do all those years ago failed. Even though we've been apart for all these years, somehow my son and Rayne have found their way back to me.

Standing, I start to pace. My breath comes too fast, and all I want to do is punch something. Or get in my car and drive to that beachside estate where my grandparents still reside and tell the old man exactly what I think of him and his controlling nature. I want to show him what I've done with my life. Show him that he couldn't keep Rayne and my son away from me forever. Confront him for trying to take *everything* away from me.

"Son of a bitch!" Shoving my hands through my hair, I want to roar, but one glance at the ceiling reminds me that there's a little boy asleep upstairs. I want that little boy to feel safe when he's here.

Two slender hands slide around me and slide up my abdomen, my chest. I shudder in her arms; her touch siphons off the tension and stress and replaces it with warmth and something much stronger.

Raw desire. Hunger.

I suck in a mouthful of air as her fingers work the hem of my shirt, dragging it upward. Her fingernails scrape against my flesh, and I try, and fail, to bite back a groan.

"Fuck," I mutter, turning to face her while I rip my shirt off over my head.

Have a woman's hands on me ever felt this good?

I've been with women since Rayne. But my heart's never been involved. With the twist and turn of my emotions, the feel of her skin against mine is like a match lighting a fuse. Dynamite. Fiery. Explosive.

The second she's facing me, she leans forward, and my arms encase her. Her hands float up my stomach, my chest, her eyes following the path her hands make.

But my eyes are glued to her.

When her gaze slides to mine, it's burning. Her navy blue eyes are bright and aware, and there's a depth there that comes from the trials and tribulations she overcame when I didn't know her.

She's a different woman now than the girl she was then.

I want to know her. All of her. Every single part of the person she's become.

"I'm here for you now," she whispers as her hands travel to my face, cupping it firmly.

With a groan, I dip my head and take possession of her mouth.

15

RAYNE

When he kisses me, my insides catch fire. Something inside of me snaps, and I throw myself into his arms.

There are so many thoughts fighting for prevalence in my head, a plethora of emotions running rampant in my heart, but I don't want to think right now. All I want to do is feel. And the person I want to feel is Jeremy.

My arms lock tightly around his neck, and I practically climb up his body. Helping me reach my destination, he grips my ass and lifts me so I can wrap my legs around his waist.

He owns my mouth.

His tongue teases, tempts, licking along my bottom lip before slipping inside to entwine with mine. Small laps, like he's tasting me. When he sucks my bottom lip into his mouth, I moan, my fingers playing in his hair. Tugging him closer, pulling him deeper. He walks me toward the couch, but then pauses, tearing his lips away from mine to glance up the stairs.

I can see the wheels in his brain turning. He's thinking

about our son catching us like this. Before he knows that he's *our* son.

Diverting from the couch, Jeremy clutches me tighter to his chest and walks me up the stairs. All the while, he's trailing kisses along my jawbone, down the column of my throat, around the curve of my neck.

Up on the landing, he catches another one of my needy moans with a kiss. He tows me to his bedroom, closes and locks the door behind him, and sets me down on his bed. I tilt my head back to stare at him.

He stands there, eyes searching. "We haven't discussed sleeping arrangements yet. Allow me to assist you in your decision: you're sleeping with me."

A soft giggle escapes me. "Yes, sir."

The corner of his mouth kicks up in a boyish grin, the one I originally fell for. So *my* Jeremy, the one before all the swagger and the army credentials and the ops training…he's still in there.

Standing there in front of me wearing nothing but a pair of low-slung jeans, Jeremy's the picture of male perfection. His broad shoulders and thick biceps have the ability to carry the weight of the world. His rock-hard chest and washboard stomach indicate years of good fitness and a healthy lifestyle. There's a light smattering of golden-brown hair scattered on his chest, and I follow the trail down the center of his abdomen that disappears into his jeans.

When my gaze reaches his again, it's full of fire.

Handsome men crossed my path many times when I lived in Phoenix. But none of them captured my attention; I haven't been with anyone since Jeremy. But now, as I stare at Jeremy Teague, I'm faced with the opposite problem. I might die of the intensity of it all if I *don't* allow him inside me tonight.

Inhaling a deep breath, I pull my tank top over my head and toss it to the floor. Standing, I unbutton my shorts and slide them over my hips and onto the floor. Kicking them aside, I stand in front of him in nothing but my simple cotton bra and panty set and wait.

Jeremy dinks me in, his gaze blazing a slow path down my body. On the return trip, he lingers on my breasts where they nearly spill from the cups of my bra. A flush begins in my chest, traveling to my cheeks. I'm bigger than I was in high school. Pregnancy will do that to a woman. My body has filled out…a lot. I must look like a total stranger to him.

His eyes float back to mine, the shadows of the darkened room casing them to look nearly black. "You're fucking beautiful."

My blush deepens, and my heart riots in my chest. "Your turn."

"Damn…been awhile since I've had a better offer than that." He keeps his eyes trained on me as he flicks the button on his jeans and removes them, kicking them out of the way as two steps eat up the distance between us.

His presence is big—so is his personality. It could be intimidating. Especially knowing that he most likely has a weapon hidden somewhere in this room, and he knows a million different ways to hurt someone. But, as he crowds me, his eyes full of promise, I don't feel an ounce of that intimidation.

All I feel is raw desire pooling in places I haven't felt in a really long time.

Sitting on the bed, I fall back on my elbows and watch as he stalks forward. Leaning over me, he places a knee beside me and cups the back of my head. He kisses me deep. So deep I'm in danger of falling again, if I haven't already.

Reaching behind me with one hand, he unclasps my bra. He slides the straps down my arms, and then pulls back to stare down at me.

"Beautiful," he rasps.

My nipples go tight and hard under his greedy gaze, and he smirks.

"They need attention."

Dipping his head, he takes the peaked tip of one breast into his mouth and sucks, teasing and playing with his tongue until my head lolls back on my shoulders.

That mouth... holy hell. Made for sin.

Pulling back, he takes both my breasts in his hands, palming them softly, teasing the pebbled flesh of my nipples with his thumbs. He pushes them together, testing their weight.

With some amusement, I pipe up. "So, still a boob man?"

His eyes jerk to mine, and his gives me a sexy, rakish grin. "Oh, I'm an equal opportunity lover now, darlin'. I don't play favorites. You'll see."

He follows suit with the same delectable treatment on my other breast, a series of licks and sucks and tiny stinging bites that are enough to drive me insane. By the time he's done with them, I'm writhing on the bed, ready to beg him for *more*.

Dropping kisses along my stomach as he moves south, his

hands continue their play with my breasts, proving they're as skilled as his mouth.

Jesus, Mary, and Joseph, it's like he's certified in making a woman feel amazing.

This isn't the Jeremy I remember. The boy I left behind was a sweet lover. He took care of me every single time and wanted to make sure I was okay. But he wasn't this…*thorough.*

He playfully bites my hip bone before smoothing the sting with his tongue, causing me to arch off the bed. He slides onto the floor in front of me, pushing my legs apart with his hands. His long hair, hanging down around his face, tickles my skin as he leans over me.

I'm quivering all over, just waiting for the first touch from him where I need it most. Everything about Jeremy is overwhelming me right now: his masculine scent, his incredible body and hands, his tantalizing mouth. And when his lips land in the center of my folds, giving me the most searing kiss I've ever felt, I almost come apart right then and there.

"Relax, baby." His voice is low and full of dirty intentions. "Let me take care of you tonight."

The next swipe of his tongue is possessive, demonstrating that in this moment, he owns me. And it's the absolute truth.

Jeremy Teague eats me up and swallows me whole. I'm panting, my fingers digging into the bed beneath me. I'm thrusting my hips forward, fucking his mouth, because it's all I *can* do. I know that it's too much at the same time that I want to beg for more.

Jeremy brings his hand into play, penetrating me in a steady rhythm while is tongue works me over.

"Oh, God." I pick up my head, needing to see him while he drives me wild.

He glances up at me, his eyes dark and full of lust. "If you knew how beautiful you are…how perfect you taste…you're driving me crazy, Rayne."

I'm driving him crazy? Seriously?

As the culmination of everything he's doing to me builds, my inner walls begin to quiver and his finger pumps harder.

"Come for me, Rayne. Let go." His voice is an insistent growl.

My pleasure climaxes, washing over me repeatedly while stars dance before me.

"Jeremy, oh God, yes!" Words tumble from my lips without me realizing exactly what I'm saying.

All I know is if he can do that to me with his mouth and his hand…sex with *this* Jeremy is going to blow my world apart.

Can I handle that? The little thought burrows its way in as I float back down from my orgasm. *If he doesn't decide he wants this life? With Decker and me?*

Scooting back on the bed, I fall against Jeremy's pillows as I watch him stand and crawl toward me on the bed. He hovers above me, bearing his weight on his arms and knees. He scans my face.

"What's going through that gorgeous head of yours?"

Blinking, I stare up at the ceiling while I attempt to sort out my thoughts.

"Rayne." His voice is firm. "Look at me. Talk to me."

I look into his eyes and see nothing there but genuine concern. This isn't just some guy I met. This is Jeremy. And the things I've been assuming about him all these years were wrong. *This* man wanted to be there. For me. With Decker.

"Jer…" My voice breaks. "This"—I gesture between the two of us—"isn't just a roll in the hay for me. Hell, I don't even know how to have a roll in the hay. There hasn't been anyone…not since…" I trail away, unsure of how to finish that sentence.

Understanding dawns in Jeremy's eyes. "Baby…this"—he gestures the same way I did—"isn't a roll in the hay for me, either. You are…God, Rayne. I never expected this. But it's everything. You and Decker. I'm ready to sign on the dotted line. I want this. I want you. But I don't need *this* until you're ready. No pressure, darlin'."

His words sink in, coat my emotional distress, smooth out my doubts and my fears.

Thrusting my arms around his neck, I pull him to me. The only thing I can think about is how fast I want him to sink into me. All of him, surrounded by all of me.

I'm so locked in on Jeremy, so focused on the step we're about to take, that the sound coming from the hallway outside his bedroom door nearly fades into the background.

Jeremy stills. His eyes narrow in the second before he wordlessly slides off the bed.

"What was that?" My whisper is urgent and slightly panicked as my son's face flickers through my mind.

Mild alarm turns to outright fear as, this time, Night's guttural growl comes from the hallway just beyond the closed bedroom door. Jeremy slips on his jeans and turns to me.

Leaping from the bed, I grab my clothes and shove them on

my body, moving more quickly than I've ever moved before.

"Rayne." Jeremy's voice is full of authority. "Stay here."

I gape at him. "Like hell."

"Night can hear noises inside *and* outside, Rayne. Just let me go check things out. It could be nothing. Can you stay here until I get back?"

I shake my head, a resolute *NO* to that madness. "Walk me to Decker's room. I'll stay there until you come back."

Jeremy's expression is a mixture of irritation and under-standing. The conflict would be amusing, if my heart weren't pounding like a marching band on a Friday night. Decker is all I can think about, all I can see in my mind's eye.

"Let's go."

Jeremy eases open the bedroom door. He glances both ways into the dark hallway before he takes my hand and slips out of the bedroom. The room where Decker sleeps is on the other end of the landing, closest to the stairs. We spot Night sitting at the top of the stairs, staring down. He glances at us when we emerge, whining softly.

"God, Jeremy. Do you think someone's in the house?"

In response, Jeremy squeezes my hand.

"Should we call the police?" Cold, oily fear is a bitter taste in my mouth. My limbs are tingling with adrenaline; the high surges through my body and makes the blood pound in time with my pulse in my ears.

Jeremy shakes his head. "Let me see what's going on first, Rayne. It's going to be okay."

He twists open the doorknob to Decker's room. Gesturing that I should stay put, he ducks inside. I can see him walking through the room, making sure all is right. He's moving silently, and I take a second to marvel at his stealth. Basically, if Jeremy Teague doesn't want you to know he's coming, well then…

When he reappears, he nods. It's the all-clear for me to be with our son, and so I pull his face down to mine and plant a hard kiss on his lips before ducking inside. I don't close the door, though. I want to be able to hear everything that's happening downstairs.

I give a quick glance to my son's sleeping form. He's lying on his stomach, his pillow clutched tightly in both hands. His breathing is steady and even. When I peek back outside the bedroom door, it's just in time to see Jeremy and Night disappearing down the stairs.

I've yet to hear any sounds from down there, though. It makes me feel a tiny bit better. *Maybe Night was just growling at the sound of a car outside? Or something as equally harmless?*

It feels like forever, the waiting. I know that whatever happens, this can't be a coincidence. Wagner Horton is used to getting what he wants when he wants it. He may be a spoiled billionaire, but he knows exactly how to close a deal. And right now? I'm a loose end. He knows I can out him, and now I've brought Jeremy into this mess. I need to figure out how to get rid of Wagner without bringing everyone around me down with me.

I know that Jeremy can take care of himself; it becomes more evident every moment I spend with him.

Guilt threatens to swallow me, because I've brought him into my problem when he never deserved it.

There's not a single sound from downstairs. *Jesus. He's like a super-silent ninja.* But as the moments tick by, my anxiety ratchets up another notch. Every sound the house makes pulls an overzealous reaction out of me. When one of the hardwood stairs lets out a creak, I jump like I've just heard a gunshot. When the soft click of Night's nails on the floors downstairs reaches my ears, I draw back like I've seen a ghost.

Finally, I hear the sound of the front door opening. After a moment, it closes again. And then Jeremy's voice whispers to me from the bottom of the stairs.

"It's okay, Rayne. Come down." He flicks the lights downstairs, sending an arc of light creeping up the steps.

With one more glance over my shoulder at my sleeping boy I shoot out of his room and down the stairs. At the bottom, Jeremy catches me and I squeeze him until I know he's safe and that everything really is okay.

"Hey," he croons into my hair. "You're shaking. It's okay, Rayne. Everything's okay."

Pulling back, I scan his face. He gives me a reassuring smile, but there's something else there that sets me on edge again. "What is it, Jeremy? What aren't you telling me?"

Jeremy sighs, and then gestures toward an envelope on the table beside the front door. "That was on the porch outside. Whoever left it is gone."

The struggle within his eyes is real. It goes against everything inside of Jeremy to let me see the envelope, but he knows that keeping me in the dark would be worse.

Grabbing it off the table, I slide out a piece of paper with a handwritten note.

Rayne, you have information that you shouldn't. I'm
not worried about you sharing it with anyone else, because I know what a smart girl you are. Let's talk about
this, so there will be no consequences to those you
love.

My hands tremble, and the envelope falls to the floor. Something falls out of it, sliding across the floor toward me. Bending, I pick it up, and my breath is lost somewhere between my
lungs and my mouth.

It's a photo of Jeremy, Decker, and me on his boat.

16

JEREMY

The following morning, I wake up and immediately reach for Rayne. It's a base instinct that I know will never leave me now. I've had her in my bed for a night, and that's where she belongs.

After she received the note from her asshole ex-boss last night, she was a mess. All she wanted to do was pack up Decker and run. I could see the fight-or-flight instinct driving her, spurring her into action. She said crazy things, like coming back home to Wilmington was a mistake, and how she should have run as soon as she found out I worked at Night Eagle. Like she could have saved me from being involved in all of this.

Crazy shit. Shit that scared the pants off me.

I took her back upstairs and put her in bed with me. Cradled her in my arms. Held her to show her that I wasn't going anywhere and that she and Decker are safe with me. Eventually, she fell asleep, but I stayed awake much longer. Planning all the different ways I could end Wagner's life.

He has no idea who I am or what I can do to him. That much is clear, or he wouldn't have made the mistake of threatening the mother of my child.

Before the incident last night, we'd made progress. I could see in her eyes how she felt, and I know my eyes conveyed the same sentiment to her. She's scared. She hasn't been able to trust anyone but her grandmother since before Decker's birth, and I get that. I get how protective she feels about our son and how much she doesn't want to get hurt by letting me into her life.

But she was ready. It was written all over her face.

Then after she fell asleep I was left wondering where we stand now. All of her talk about running terrified me. She can't do this alone. She shouldn't attempt to, and I'll be damned if I allow it. My mission today is to make sure she understands that. I need to make her realize that she and Decker belong with me from here on out. She needs to pack up whatever she's got at her sister's house and move in with me. Permanently.

It might seem fast to people who don't know us. But I don't give a shit about that. The truth is that I never stopped loving Rayne. And the fact that she carried my child for nine months and then raised him for eight years *by herself* only intensifies that feeling. They're my family, which means they're everything.

The place where my hand lands only encounters cold cotton sheets. My eyes snap open, searching. Rayne is no longer lying beside me. I bolt upright in bed, scanning the bedroom. The bench under the big picture window, the walk-in closet, and entrance to the attached bathroom. No sign of Rayne.

Panicking, I jump out of bed. Venturing into the bathroom, I see that she's not there, so I pull on a pair of sweatpants over my boxer-briefs and exit the room. The absence of my dog is a clue; Night usually sleeps on the floor beside my bed and doesn't move until I do. But he isn't there.

I breeze by Decker's room, doubling back when I realize he's sitting on his bed. Retreating, swallowing my panic about Rayne, I lean against his doorway and shoot him a grin.

"Hey, Deck."

"Hey." He glances around the room and then back at me. "I like it here."

My heart is thrust into my throat. "I like having you here, buddy. You sleep okay?"

He nods, a smile that reaches his eyes lighting up his entire face. "Yeah! Can we have breakfast now? I was waiting for my mom to come and get me."

I beckon him out of the room with a hand, and he joins me in the hallway. Heading for the stairs, I sling an arm around his shoulders.

"Dos your mom usually make you breakfast?"

He wrinkles his nose, causing me to chuckle. "My mom doesn't really cook. So we have a lot of cereal and Eggos."

Laughing outright, I shake my head. "We can do better than that this morning."

He glances up at me. "Awesome."

The downstairs is quiet. There's no sign of Rayne. Or Night, for that matter. But my panic has all but disappeared, because I know she wouldn't leave without Decker. But a nagging worry still tugs at me. *Where is she?*

I've just settled Decker on a stool at the kitchen island, with a mission to help me add ingredients to a batch of pancakes, when we hear the front door open and Night's nails skittering on the hardwood floors.

Backing out of the kitchen with a spatula in my hand, all the breath whooshes out of me. I've been holding it since waking up to find Rayne gone. My gaze finds her now, watching as she bends down to detach Night's leash. My eyes travel down her body. She's wearing the shorts and a v-neck athletic shirt she bought last night when we went out after dinner. Very small, very *tight* shorts. Long toned legs extend for miles. Her body is a work of fucking art, and my cock responds, causing an uncomfortable strain in my own shorts.

Striding toward her, I scoop her into an all-encompassing hug. Discreetly, I press myself against her hip, so she'll know exactly what I'm thinking. Her sharp intake of breath lets me know I've succeeded.

"Someone missed me this morning." Her voice is a low, husky whisper that only makes my situation worse, and small hands slide up my back.

Quickly stepping back, I keep her hand as I gaze down at her. "Decker's in the kitchen."

Her gaze shifts and what was previously hooded is now bright. "Oh? I'm glad he's up. Are you two…doing okay?"

Two small, adorable lines of worry pinch her forehead.

God, she's gorgeous and she's cute. That combination is downright lethal. And then another thought, a shocking one, plunges into my mind like I've been dropped into frigid water.

She trusted me with him. And happiness beyond anything I've felt before lifts me high.

"Come ask him yourself." I can't help the grin that stretches across my lips.

We round the corner into the kitchen, where Decker is still busy stirring dry pancake ingredients. His tongue has poked out of his mouth, and he's giving the task such intense concentration that I chuckle when I see him.

They're a package of cute. Lord help me.

"Whatcha doin', sweetie?" Rayne wraps an arm around him and kisses his temple.

"Oh, hey Mom!" Decker glances up at her, apparently so engrossed in his task he hadn't noticed her arrival. "Hey, Night!"

Night doesn't stop for greetings; he heads straight for his water bowl and starts lapping like his life depends on it.

I take in her appearance one more time, including the bright eyes and rosy cheeks. There's a glistening sheen of sweat coating her cleavage that I have a strong desire to lick away. "Did you go for a run?"

She nods, leaning over the counter to watch Decker. The way she's standing makes her hips jut out, and a vision of owning her body while she's bent over the countertop fill my vision.

She shoots me a sly glance, like she knows exactly what I'm thinking. "Running is how I stay sane. My life doesn't really allow for a gym membership, but I can get out for a quick run most days." She focuses on Decker, worry coloring her tone. "Did you sleep okay, sweetie?"

I return to my task, pouring out the liquid pancake ingredients to add to Decker's bowl, listening to Decker tell his mom that he slept just fine. Our eyes meet, and I can see the relief in hers knowing Decker wasn't disturbed by last night's events.

The safest place for both Decker and Rayne is with me. The work and school week begins tomorrow, and we have some logistics to work out. But I have the entire day today to convince her that this is where they belong. Not just because there's a potentially dangerous predator stalking Rayne, but because they're *mine*.

I let Decker help me finish whipping up breakfast, and when it's ready he gobbles it up like a little man starved. Then he grabs Night's ball and asks to take the dog out into the backyard to play.

I defer to Rayne, who hesitates. "Um, yeah we can go out there for a little bit, sweetie. But not long. We have to go home soon."

She avoids my stare, and I nod to Decker. "Go on out there Deck. We'll be out in a few minutes."

He whoops and grabs the ball. My dog, who seems to have found a brand-new best friend in Decker, joyfully bounces in front of the little boy out the back door. Leaving the door open a crack so we can hear Decker, I turn on Rayne.

She stares up at me, a defiant expression on her face.

I take a step toward her, frustration fizzling around me like an electric charge. "We're going to pick up your stuff. All of it. Then I'm bringing you and Decker back here. It's where you should be."

Rayne folds her arms and locks her jaw, the stubborn set challenging me in a way no woman ever has. No woman but her. "Listen, Jer. I want you to get to know your son. And I...I want..." She trails away, her cheeks flushing and her eyes going bright.

Sensing her vulnerability like a shark smells chum, I step into her space and box her in against the polished stone countertops. She looks up at me, her eyes going dark. Her pink tongue darts out to lick her lips, and my eyes are momentarily stuck there, watching as she moistens first the plump bottom one and then the top one.

"Jeremy." Her hoarse whisper goes straight to my dick, and I jerk my gaze back up to hers.

"Stay." It's a whisper from me, but it's also a request, a demand, a promise.

She sucks in a breath, her chest rising and falling with the movement. Her round tits press against my chest and my entire body tightens in response.

"I'm too much trouble for you right now...and this between us...too much too fast could screw it all up."

Maybe if the situation were different we'd take this thing slow. Maybe I'd take her out on dates, see her at work, test out how our lives would fit together with careful diligence. But life has other ideas, and she needs me to be there for her more than she needs me to be careful. She has to see that.

"Stay." My voice is laced with rough edges, but I can't help it. I bend to kiss the pulse point on her neck and feel her heart racing under my lips. I'm dying to taste her. My tongue slips out to lick her sweet skin, and I nip at her with my teeth.

A deep, low hum leaves her and her head drops back, giving me easier access to her neck. Taking advantage, I use my hips to pin her against the countertop, letting her feel just how much I want her to stay. The evidence is overwhelming, and even though I'm supposed to be torturing her, my cock throbs, begging me to take her right here and now.

"Stay," I growl, biting her neck and using my tongue to soothe the nip.

"This is…" She wraps her arms around my neck and pulls herself closer. "…Coercion. Any answer I give you has been emitted under duress."

Her sexy, breathy voice drives me insane. I'm close to losing it altogether, and it's funny that she has no clue the kind of effect she has on me. Not really.

Pulling back slightly, I lose myself in the sapphire depths of her eyes. "Say yes to me, Rayne."

As she stares back, a sadness that I don't understand crosses into her eyes. A crushing sense of foreboding creeps in, trying to fight its way past the haze of happiness I have when I'm surrounded by all things Rayne. I ignore it.

"Yes. We'll stay."

17

RAYNE

All I can think about is the veiled threat on that clean, white piece of paper and the fact that I won't be able to keep my promise to Jeremy. Staying with him and Decker will only put them in danger. I'm not stupid. I know that Jeremy has the skills and the background to help. But putting him in the line of fire when it comes to Wagner Horton isn't just selfish; it's dangerous, because my son might lose his father before he's even had the chance to know him.

But I don't exactly know how to avoid Jeremy's involvement. When Jeremy keeps me safe, he's also keeping Decker safe. And nothing is more important to me than that. If the opportunity arises down the road for me to take action on my own, I'll do it to save them both. But for now...I have to let Jeremy help.

I leave Jeremy at Olive's house and head over to Macy's with Decker. The second Jay opens the door, he and Decker run off to play a new video game. I close the door behind me, calling Macy's name as I head into her kitchen.

"Rayne, hey! I've been worried about you!" Wiping her hands on a dishtowel, she walks toward me and gathers me into a tight hug. When she pulls back, her liquid brown eyes are brimming with concern. "Everything okay?"

Taking a deep breath to prepare myself to tell her all about Jeremy, instead I burst into tears. Quiet, racking sobs that I can neither control nor cork. They keep flowing and flowing.

With a gentle hand on my back, Macy leads me into her great room, pushing me down on the sofa and grabbing a box of tissues. Then she just sits with me, letting me cry and patting my back until I finally gulp in a big enough breath to curb the tears.

"Oh…my…God," I gasp. "I am so sorry, Macy. I…never… do this." The words are interrupted by the occasional sniffle, and I grab a handful of tissues to wipe my face. "It's been a crazy weekend."

She looks into my eyes. "I'm here for you, Rayne. Why don't you tell me about it?"

And her voice is so warm, friendly, and comforting, that's exactly what I do. I explain that I ran into Jeremy at work, and that he's Decker's father. That he wants to be in Decker's life, and that what he does at work is not even remotely close to in-stalling security systems. That I'm being pursued by someone from my life back in Phoenix that I don't want to encounter again, and that I'm worried for both Jeremy's and Decker's safety.

After the story is finished, albeit modified for Macy's own

safety, we sit in silence while Macy takes it all in. Her expression is unreadable as she sits back on the couch and stares at me, her hands clasped against her chest. Her chest fills just before her gaze shifts to mine.

"So," she asks, her lips curving into a small smile. "You still have feelings for this Jeremy guy."

My mouth falls slack. "That's where you're going to focus first, after everything I just told you?"

She shrugs. "First things first. Are you still in love with him?"

I throw my hands up helplessly before burying my face in my hands and barking out a laugh. "I don't know if I can say that, Macy. The love we had in high school…that was real. He was my favorite person in the whole world. We never wanted to be apart. He picked me up for school each morning and I sat front row at each and every one of his football games. We were…God, Macy. A love like that? I thought it'd last forever.

"Losing him the way I did broke my heart in half. It was like I left the other part behind, with Jeremy. Whether he knew it or not. But as I began to raise Decker, I realized that our high school relationship was so different from what we needed to be as parents. To make that kind of relationship work. I loved him and he loved me. Madly. Deeply. But it had nothing to do with sticking it out, having a kid together, living real *life*. But the pull I have for him now is a different animal. It's like taking that teenage attraction and magnifying it tenfold. And then adding adult emotions and the fact that we have a son together…I can't even describe how I feel. But there's something there."

Macy's head bobs. "Oh, honey. There's more than 'something there.' I saw it in your eyes the day I found you two standing in Olive's driveway together. Maybe you're not ready to admit it yet, but you love that man. And he loves you."

Peeking through my fingers, I give her an anguished smile. "Well, if that's true, how can I put him in the middle of my mess? Especially right as he learns he has a son? This should be a magical time for him and Decker. They should be getting to know each other, and Jeremy shouldn't be having to protect me while he acclimates to life as a dad."

She shakes her head, staring at me like I've suddenly grown an extra nose out of the side of my face. "When a man is in love…there's nothing he'd rather be doing than protecting the woman who belongs to him. I'm guessing that with your ex-army security specialist, that feeling is magnified."

I finger the balled-up tissues still in my hands. She was right about that. Jeremy seemed determined to make this situation better for me…to make sure I'm safe and protected. It's why he's insisting Decker and I move in with him. But how much of that is just him making sure his son is safe?

"I'm going to humor him. I'm packing up Decker and my stuff for now, and we'll stay with Jeremy. At least until this issue has been resolved." I sniffle, glancing at Macy.

Macy's voice is low and her face is serious. "Does Decker know? Who Jeremy is?"

Shaking my head, I offer a small smile. "No, but he seems to adore Jeremy already. Not that either one of them has seen any negative aspects of their personalities yet. But they've bonded."

"Living under the same roof is the best way to get it all out in the open." Macy chuckles. "Jeremy will learn what it's like to be a dad pretty quickly."

A little while later, she walks me to the door and I call for Decker.

"We'll still keep Decker after school, and you and Jeremy can come pick him up after work. And he's welcome here any other time, too. You know that. But do you think there's anything to worry about as far as safety is concerned when I have Decker with me?"

I shake my head. "I really don't think so, Macy. The Night Eagle team is taking charge of this, and they'd never let anything happen. Plus, I'm the real target. You'll be safe with the NES guys looking after everything."

"I'm happy they're involved. I want you to stay safe."

I grab her into an impulsive hug. "I'm so thankful for you, Macy."

She pats my shoulder with her slender hand. "I got your back, girl."

Later that evening, I walk out into Jeremy's backyard to find my son and his father throwing a football back and forth. Night's little tail wiggles in excited anticipation.

A smile tugs on my lips. The thawing sensation building up inside of me can be blamed on the sight of them together, but the way that Jeremy is burrowing deeper into my heart has a lot to do with the way he is with our son. I watch as he praises Decker for catching a difficult pass, and then cover my laugh with my hand when Decker runs and attempts to tackle

Jeremy to the ground after throwing him a perfect pass.

Jeremy plays along, laughing as he allows Decker to take him down, but I notice him protecting the little boy's head as they both hit the ground. And my heart melts just a little bit more.

Jeremy looks up then, as if he senses my gaze on him, and when our eyes meet an invisible thread pulls taut between us. Whatever emotion is flooding out of him reaches inside me and grabs hold, squeezing me until I can barely breathe. It's surreal, but that small moment tethers us together as surely as an actual knotted rope.

I watch them for a little longer, playing together and bonding over what is clearly a mutual love. Football. As much as I tried to avoid it, it's here and Jeremy with it.

And I don't mind nearly as much as I thought I would.

That night, after Decker's in bed and Jeremy and I settle on the couch, I look over at him and take a sip of my wine.

Jeremy waits.

"We should tell him." The statement bursts from my mouth like word vomit. "Shit," I whisper.

Shocked at my own thought, I stare down at the burgundy liquid swirling around in my glass.

I know, in my heart, that Decker is ready to hear this news. I know that Jeremy's ready to tell him. He's been patient, spending time with his son and getting to know him over the past two days. We could wait weeks, but what good would it do? It's only keeping them apart for longer than is necessary. Decker deserves the truth now, and Jeremy deserves the chance to stand in front of him as his father.

Jeremy's hand plucks the wineglass from me, appearing in my vision so fast it startles me. Then he's there, kneeling in front of me with both of my hands clasped in his. When I look into his eyes, they're shining.

"Thank you." His words are simple, but the expression he wears is anything but. It's brimming with open emotion and untapped desire.

And, God help me, I want nothing more than to let him unleash that desire on me.

I hold his gaze, and my throat squeezes as my heart attempts to climb up into my mouth.

"Tomorrow. After we pick him up. We'll tell him then."

He grabs hold of me then, lifting me into his arms. I wrap my legs around his waist and melt against him, my lips pressing hungrily to his. He tugs my bottom lip into his mouth, sucking hard until a moan slides free from my throat.

"Take me upstairs." It's an order, my voice low and husky with everything I want to do to him so close at hand.

If you had asked me a year ago, a month ago, even a week ago about this moment, I would have told you there was no chance in hell it would ever happen. But now that I'm here with Jeremy, and the lies and deceit we've both been victim to are out in the open, all I want to do is pull him closer and closer. I want my son to know his father. I want to experience the passion I glimpse in his eyes, over and over again, know how it feels to be touched, loved, *marked* by this man. And most of all, I want to have my little family together for the first time, without threat of Wagner Horton hanging over us like a poised guillotine blade.

18

JEREMY

My hands want to be everywhere all at once. I don't know if there's ever been a time I've been this frantic about getting as close to a woman as possible. I want to take it slow, enjoy the feel of her against me, but I also want to sink inside her and I want that to happen *now*. In just the short time she's been back in my life, she's changed it forever. I'll never be the man I was again, and I'm glad for it. I'm going to be so much better now. Because of Rayne and Deck.

After carrying her upstairs and closing my bedroom door, I lay her on my bed and stare down at the picture of beauty before me. Her hair is splayed out all around her in waves of dark, her big eyes blinking up at me in the low lamplight.

She stares up at me, her expression vulnerable in a way that shreds me apart inside.

"I want you," she says.

Goddamn. With those three little words, she owns me.

Ripping my shirt off over my head and falling down over her, I cover her body with mine. Our lips find each other, our tongues twisting and tangling in a furious dance. Her fingernails scrape fiery lines up my back, and my answering groan is lost somewhere inside her mouth.

A soft sigh escapes her, and I pull back to glance down. Pulling my brows together, I frown down at her.

"You okay?"

She brings a hand up, brushes my loose hair away from my face. She blinks once, twice, before opening her mouth to speak. When she does, her voice is low and husky. Sexy as fuck. My body is already in overdrive, but her voice does something to my insides, sending me over the edge.

"More than okay. Perfect."

Her words affect me, causing a slow burn of need to start deep in my veins. I reach for the hem of her tank top and pull it over her head. Her bare breasts call out to me, so I dip my head and run my tongue along the plump roundness of one. Letting out a breath between her teeth, she lets her head drop back as her fingers dig deep into my hair. Pulling one peaked nipple into my mouth, I suck hard and am rewarded with Rayne's answering gasp and the tightening of her hands in the strands of my hair.

She arches toward me as I use my teeth, then smooth my tongue over the sting. I switch to her other breast, fueled by the small sounds of pleasure she makes and she way she thrusts herself against me.

My voice is more abrupt than I mean it to be when I lift my head and stare down at her. "Turn around, Rayne."

Her lips quirk into a sexy smile. "You realize I've never been with anyone else? Since you, I mean?"

Pride that I don't deserve to feel fills me, threatening to lift me into the air. Closing my eyes, I exhale. "You know how that makes me feel? Ecstatic. Thrilled. And damn undeserving."

"I've never wanted anyone but you, Jer." The absolute truth in that statement shines out of her eyes like a lantern in the darkness.

I kiss her, and her fingers find the zipper on my jeans as I do.

I slide my jeans off, along with my boxers, and crawl behind her on the bed. Reaching around her, I find the button on her shorts and flick it open before unzipping and pulling them down her thighs. She wriggles free of them, kicking them to the floor and looks over her shoulder at me with a mischievous smirk

"Now what?" she asks.

Kneeling, I pull her body flush against mine. I swallow my groan as the warmth of her skin tempts the rock hard rigidity of mine. Her sweet-and-spicy floral scent overpowers me and I inhale deeply at her neck before trailing my lips from her ear down to her shoulder, planting a kiss on the soft skin. My hips flex, pushing against her ass, and her response is perfection, pushing back against me with a gentle but insistent force.

"God," I groan against her neck. "You feel incredible, Rayne."

Dropping her head back to rest on my shoulder, she sighs. "You *make* me feel incredible."

Nibbling on her shoulder, I run my hands along her hips, up to her stomach, and cup her breasts. Testing their weight in my hands, I allow my index fingers to roam over the hardened tips. Rayne jerks in my arms, her breath coming faster as I continue to explore the sensitive peaks.

"That's it, baby. Feel this…feel *me*."

I let one hand continue to play while the other drops between her legs. Dragging a finger through her folds, I discover how slick she is, how wet and ready for me. Sucking in a breath, I try and steady the intake of air as I draw my finger to her pulsing clit.

Fuck me. I could come from the feel of her alone.

"Rayne." My voice is rougher, harder than it should be, but fuck if I can help it. "I love how ready for me you are."

She moans, bucking against my hips with her ass and a growl leaves me before I can stop it. My finger circles her clit slowly, teasing, before dipping inside her soaked heat.

"Oh, God, Jeremy. Please…" Her words come out in jerky gasps.

"I've got you, darlin'." My finger pumps a slow and steady rhythm in and out of her and a second one joins the first, stretching her just a little bit farther.

Now Rayne's pushing back against me in earnest, her gasps and moans growing louder and more needy with every thrust of my hands. She's riding me hard, her body taking control as she chases after whatever feels good.

And I fucking love it.

I love seeing her like this, carefree and gorgeous. She's always got something important on her mind, whether it's Decker or the fucker who's been stalking her, but right now she's just letting go. With me. It's a heady feeling, one that threatens to take over if I'm not careful.

"Tell me you want my cock inside you, Rayne."

My demand surprises even me. I'm not the possessive type. Even when Rayne and I were together in high school, I knew she was with me and she wasn't a social butterfly so I never had to go caveman. Everyone knew she was mine.

But now everything feels different. Now that I have her again I don't want to lose her. I need her reassurance.

"Jeremy," she pants. "I want your fucking cock inside me. Now."

"Nightstand drawer," I grind out. "Condom. Grab one for me."

Crawling forward, and offering me a stellar view of her perfect ass in the process, she retrieves the condom, rips it open, and hands it back to me. I roll it on, and then position myself behind her once again.

Fisting myself in one hand, I drag the hard tip of me through her wetness before meeting her entrance with one deep thrust that has us both groaning with the sweet rightness of it.

Settling deep inside of her, I pause, closing my eyes and allowing myself to feel this moment. I'm going to savor every fucking second, because I know how damned lucky I am to be here with her like this.

She glances back behind her shoulder, her hair a sexy curtain of inky rain around her face. Her eyes are bright, her cheeks are flushed, and she looks like the most beautiful thing I've ever seen.

"You okay?" she asks with a slight smile. She wiggles her ass for emphasis, and I bite my lip with a wince.

"Just…trying not to embarrass myself by coming in the first minute of being inside you. It's hard, Rayne. Really fucking hard."

An understanding sigh escapes her, and she nods. She sags a little and I wrap an arm around her to secure her tightly to me.

"Yeah…I get that."

Finally under control, I begin to move. Pulling myself nearly out of her before thrusting back inside to the hilt, I flex my fingers against her hips hard enough to make a mark.

"Fuck. Perfection, baby. You're perfection."

She wraps her hands around my wrists like she needs to hold on for the ride, and I take that as my cue to pound into her in a relentless dance of pleasure and delicious, revel-in-the-moment pain. She rocks with me, crying out as our pace repeatedly strokes a spot inside of her that makes her unravel.

"Yes, baby. Let go."

A fine sheen of sweat covers us both as I work to make her pleasure come first, and she works to contain herself underneath the pressure of her impending orgasm.

A few more thrusts of my hips and she comes apart in my arms, trembling and crying out my name with a ferocity that makes me want to pump my fist in the air.

I've been to hell and back more than once, but I've never felt as adrenaline-charged as I do right this second.

When she goes limp in my arms, I gently lay her on the bed, flipping her over so I can see her face. Her eyes are glazed and shining, her lip a glorious red from biting it, and she smiles lazily up at me.

"You're not done yet, darlin,'" I warn, climbing over her and positioning myself to enter her again from a whole new angle.

Her smile grows as she grabs my ass and squeezes, bringing me closer. "I'm counting on it, Teague. I have high expectations for you."

My brow lifts. "Oh, yeah? Why is that?"

Her eyes sparkle. "Well…that body, those tattoos, and the whole black ops soldier thing promises at least two orgasms."

Narrowing my eyes, I swallow the bark of laughter that rumbles up from somewhere in my chest. "Baby, we're going for at least three."

Her fingernails dig into my ass as I plunge back inside her, but the sweet bite of pain is nothing compared to the ache starting to build inside me. There's another ache there, too, in my chest. It's more subtle and indicates that what I'm feeling for Rayne goes so far beyond the feelings a man usually has when he makes love to a woman. She's crawled inside me, buried herself deep, and there's no way I'm going to let her climb back out again.

This little family she's given me has grown to mean everything to me in such a short time. But that's how I know it's real. Rayne and Decker are everything I didn't even know I wanted, and they're mine to protect, cherish, and love.

Love.

Suddenly overcome with emotion, I dip my head and take her mouth with mine, kissing her until my world is dizzy, spinning around me in circles I can't even begin to control. I can feel her clenching around me, the tiny vibrations in her muscles kissing my cock, and her tiny warning cry lets me know that orgasm number two is in the books.

Pulling back, I stare down into her hazy eyes. Without stopping the slow drag and pull of our bodies, I make love to her face-to-face, staring into the bottomless blue eyes, promising her everything I can't say right now. But I know she gets it. The answering emotion in her own gaze tells me that she knows how I feel, and that she feels the exact same way.

The slick slide of our skin against one another is intoxicating; every nerve ending in my body is lit with a flame only Rayne can extinguish. She brushes my hair off my forehead and lifts her legs to wrap around my waist, seating me deeper inside of her. We both groan, her eyes fluttering shut as her hips rise to meet mine over and over again. Feeling her begin to quake just as my own control is fading away, I reach between us and rub her clit with my thumb

"Oh, God, Jeremy," she gasps as she clutches me tighter to her with both her arms and her legs. "I can't…"

"Yes, you can. Just fall, Rayne. I'll catch you." My voice is determined, my thumb insistent, my cock relentless, all in the pursuit of her pleasure.

My own release is racing to the forefront of my thoughts, causing every muscle in my body to tighten and prepare in response, but I push it back and stay focused on Rayne. "Come on, baby. I got you."

Suddenly, her body tenses and her eyes fly open. The sexiest look of pleasure crosses her face as her lips part and her eyes roll back.

"Jeremy!" she screams as her legs tighten around my waist.

"Fuck yes," I groan as I finally let my own release fly.

I pump into her furiously as my seed flows out of me, and

when I'm done, my body shudders as I roll to lie at her side.

She's sprawled on her back and me on my stomach as the world returns to normal and our breathing begins to slow. Opening my eyes, I see that her wide blue ones are staring right back at me.

"That was…amazing." Her voice is full of surprised awe.

Smiling, I reach for her hand and feel all the pieces of my heart click into place. Like they were never broken. But I guess they were.

"Did you think it wouldn't be?"

She shakes her head, still dazed and beautiful. "No…I knew it would be. I just…wow."

Chuckling I bring her fingers to my lips. "This is just the beginning, darlin'. We're about to set the world on fire."

Her smile turns tentative. "What exactly are we doing? I mean…" Her eyes flick down to our naked bodies tangled together before finally settling on my face once again. "I just want to make sure we're on the same page here, Jer."

Turning to face her, I pull her close to the warmth of my body, feeling the heat from hers washing over me. Her midnight eyes search my face for the answers she needs. I can do better than that. I can give them to her straight.

"I thought I had my shit together, you know?" I watch as my thumbs caress tiny circles on the side of her face. "You know—leaving my grandparents' bullshit behind, joining the army, then finding the Night Eagle team. All those things were things I did on my own, independent of my grandfather and his money. I'm a man who can make decisions without a backward glance, and I've made good ones. Finding someone to share all that with....it was always on the back burner. I thought that maybe one day it would happen, but it's never been a priority."

Her hand slides down over my shoulder, my bicep. Looking into her eyes, I see nothing but compassion and understanding. Like maybe there's a part of her who understands what I'm saying because maybe what I'm feeling inside she's feeling, too.

"And then you came back to town."

Her bottom lip disappears between her teeth and a spark of longing lances through me, dragging embers of warning right along with it. I'm so hooked on her already, and I haven't even begun to think of what it could do to me if I lost her. Or Decker.

Slamming my mind shut against that thought, I go on. "Darlin'...you changed everything. The second I saw you I knew I'd never let you go again. And then you gave me the greatest gift I've ever gotten...my son. If you believe one thing out of my mouth, believe this: I'm all in with you. This can't be just a fling. You mean so much more to me than that. You and Decker have just become my number one priority."

Her eyes go wide and her bottom lip quivers just the slightest bit. "You're serious, Jer?"

My gaze is steady on hers. "Don't you want me to be?"

Uncertainty flickers in her expression. My chest clenches when I see it.

What if she doesn't? She didn't come back to Wilmington to look for me. When I first saw her again it was clear that she wished she wasn't seeing me then. So what if this...me...isn't what she wants now?

My pulse is a dull roar in my ears as I wait for her response.

A clusterfuck of emotions chase one another across her face while I watch. Fear, anxiety, sadness…and then euphoric happiness as she slowly begins to nod.

"Yeah, Jeremy…I want this." Her voice is just a whisper, ragged and hung up on the word *yes*.

Pulling her face to mine, I kiss her softly. When I rear back to study her, I let my fingers tangle in her thick locks of black hair. "It's always been you, Rayne. I just didn't let myself believe it until you came back to me."

"Show me," she whispers.

With those words, I can feel myself growing hard again, and dip my head to her neck. My tongue flicks against her skin, tasting the sweetness and sweat from when we did this moments before.

I make love to her. Again.

And later, as I drift off with Rayne in my arms, there's still a lot of resentment inside me. I still feel the need to step up to my grandfather and show him that what he did all those years ago didn't break me, and that my family survives despite his best efforts to stamp it out.

But the main emotion I'm feeling right now has nothing to do with anger and everything to do with the softness the woman lying beside me instills in me.

19

RAYNE

I giggle as I stare out the passenger-side window of Jeremy's Land Cruiser, remembering the way he'd stared into his closet this morning in horror, eyeing the chaos strewn about the built-in shelving and floor.

"I'm going to organize it," I informed him.

Everything I'd acquired since moving here, plus the things I'd borrowed from Olive's house while I stayed there, are congregated in little heaps around the space.

Both of his eyebrows had risen sky high as he whirled on me. "Yeah? I'm pretty sure this would take a professional, Rayne. I'm gonna have to hire someone to come in and sort out all your shit. Jesus."

Embarrassed, because let's be honest: I'm not the neatest person, I avert my eyes as a hot blush crept into my face. Only to feel his finger under my chin, guiding my gaze back to his.

"I'd take three messy closets just like this one," he'd said firmly, "if it meant I got to have you and Decker in the process."

Jeremy glances over, one hand resting atop the steering wheel, the other resting casually on the gearshift. "What's so funny?"

Shaking my head, I glance to the backseat where Decker sits.

"Gonna have a good day today, kiddo?"

His dark hair falls over his forehead as he grins. "Yup. Jay says we have P.E. on Mondays. I love P.E."

I give him a solemn nod. "Yes. I know this."

Jeremy glances at Decker in the rearview mirror as he pulls into the school parking lot. We'll drop him off before heading to work ourselves. His mouth pulls into an affectionate smile that tugs at all the softest parts of me.

"We'll toss a ball around tonight after your mom and I get off of work, all right, Deck?"

Decker's entire face lends itself to his giant grin. "Cool."

When Jeremy looks at me, my face matches Decker's. He tosses me a wink.

After dropping Decker off at school, Jeremy pulls into a gas station to fill up. Grabbing my purse, I meet his eyes over the hood of the SUV.

"Coffee?"

He smirks. "We already had coffee this morning."

My eyes narrow. "You can *never* have too much coffee, Teague."

Chuckling, he shakes his head. Crossing his arms across his broad chest, he settles against the cement post next to the pump and evaluates me with a smug smile. God. How in the world does he do it? His hair, all tied up in his loosely knotted bun is silky and soft, his skin positively golden in the morning sunshine. His green eyes glint and sparkle as he regards me with interest, and the bulge of his biceps on his crossed arms are calling me to wrap myself up in his strength.

"Hey." His voice is playfully sharp. "Eyes up here. I'm not a piece of meat, you know."

Completely unapologetic, I shrug before turning toward the market. "Then don't look so succulent while you're just standing there."

Once inside the bright gas station market, I head straight for the coffee bar and grab two giant cups. Maybe Jeremy doesn't feel the need for a caffeine fix, but I'm sure going to give him one. I fill a third of my cup with vanilla-flavored creamer before pouring it to the brim with the steaming black liquid. For Jeremy, I just fill it up with coffee, knowing he likes it black. A man steps up beside me, grabbing a Styrofoam cup, and I barely spare him a glance as I open two raw sugar packets and shake the light-brown granules into my cup.

"Thought he'd never leave you alone, princess."

The cool, collected voice comes from directly beside me. My entire body stiffens, turning me into a solid statue of unease.

I glance at the man standing beside me, but he isn't looking at me. He's stirring the steaming coffee in his cup, a slow and steady motion of his left hand. His right hand, I notice, is casually resting in his blazer pocket.

His look is nonthreatening. An unremarkable guy with

light brown hair and medium-toned skin. He's dressed casually in jeans and a lightweight blazer. If he hadn't spoken, I wouldn't have noticed him at all.

But I'm noticing him now, and an icy sliver of dread slices down my spine.

"Excuse me?" My voice is an octave higher than usual, but it doesn't shake, and that's a small miracle all on its own.

I'm staring right at the man, but still he doesn't glance my way. His voice chills me way down deep in my bones, wrapping around my heart like a vise. I attempt to make sense of him.

"Your boyfriend. He never leaves your side. But it's good for me that he has now. Put the coffee down. We're going out the back."

The blood that pumps from my veins to my heart slows, sending a cloud of dizziness through my head. This isn't… right. What's he *saying?* Who is…?

And then it clicks, the picture sliding neatly into place in my mind.

Wagner. He sent someone after me.

My teeth clamp together as a river of boiling fury invades my system. "I'm not going anywhere with you."

His stirring hand stills. "Make a scene and I'll shoot you faster than you can scream. This gun in my pocket is the end-all, be-all here. You come quietly with me, or I end your life."

I suck in a sharp breath. "Wagner doesn't want me dead. Or he wouldn't have sent you here to get me."

He shrugs. "Not my problem. I'll bring you back to him one way or another. Either way is fine with me. I'll make sure I get paid."

He's insane. Standing here so casually talking about ending my life like I'm nothing.

Like I'm expendable. Which, to Wagner and this cold, callous man beside me, I suppose I am.

But first... I know that Wagner Horton wants to find out exactly what I know and whether or not I've spread the word.

I glance desperately around me. There are a few other shoppers waiting in line at the cashier's counter, but no one is close to the coffee bar. No one for me to catch their eye or mouth the fact that I need help. And Jeremy is putting gas in the Land Cruiser outside.

Dammit, Rayne! Think!

As I'm standing there, the blazer man, sans coffee, takes my elbow in a strong, threatening grip and begins to steer me toward the back hallway leading to the restrooms. There must be another exit. I don't want to go that way with him, not where we'll be secluded.

But if I scream... will he really kill me right here in the store and then escape?

My stomach begins to somersault over and over again, the flipping motion in my belly causing me to feel nauseated as we near the door. With his hand still on my elbow, he takes the other out of his pocket to push open the door, and that's when I act.

As he pulls me outside, I yank my arm free and use the momentum to propel me toward him rather than away. I shove the heel of my hand up into his nose, feeling a satisfying crunch under my hand as bones break. The sting in my hand is irrelevant; I can't stop moving now. His pained shout is cut off when I grab his shoulders and jam a knee into his groin. The tortured groan is a hefty reward as I silently thank the self-defense teacher I learned these moves from back in Phoenix. I never thought then that I'd have to use them.

He goes down, but not before his fist closes around a chunk of my hair. Screaming in pain, I yank myself away and take off. My heels don't deter me as I sprint for the corner of the building, knowing the back door we just exited will be locked from the outside.

As I skitter around the side of the gas station market, Jeremy's hand freezes on the front door handle when I scream his name.

He catches me as I slam into him, holding me far enough away from his body to scan my face. He takes one look at me before sheer panic registers in his eyes.

"What's wrong?"

My voice is nearly hysterical. "Wagner sent him…he grabbed me, made me go out the back with him!"

Jeremy's eyes widen just a bit before they narrow. "Are you hurt, Rayne? Did the bastard harm you?"

Shaking my head, the panic bubbling through my body threatens to overtake me. I could be stuffed in a trunk right now, on my way to Wagner Horton. Thank God…

"No. No, I'm okay, Jer."

He nods, his lips settling into an angry line. Gripping my hands, he pushes his car keys into them and gives me a gentle shove toward the Land Cruiser. "Lock yourself in the truck. I have to go after him, Rayne."

Sliding my hands down his arm, I grip his wrist. "Jeremy... don't."

My brain says that I know Jeremy can handle himself. But my heart flips with fear. The only reason he's exposed to this danger here and now is because of me. My problems. The fact that I've dragged him into it makes me sick.

Leaning down so that we're eye level, his voice steady, Jeremy wraps one big hand around the back of my neck. "Rayne...truck. Go, now."

Nodding, I head for the SUV. As soon as the door is safely closed behind me, Jeremy turns and springs around the side of the building.

Waiting for him in the silent car, I begin to quake. My teeth chatter, slamming together violently first, and then my limbs start to shake. I suck in deep breaths, trying to control my body, but the shaking doesn't stop. Instead, as the fight I just had for my life begins to flash through my mind in bits and pieces, the quivering and shaking just gets worse.

My hands clench into fists in my lap, all of my muscles constrict as I relive it. I'm not sure which is stronger, the fear or the anger.

By the time Jeremy trudges back around the side of the building I'm a hair's breadth away from convulsions. Yanking his door open, he slams it behind him as he settles into his seat and starts the ignition. Pulling up hands-free calling, he pushes commands from his contacts into the dash screen, and Ronin Shaw's name flashes in blue.

"Shaw."

"Swagger," Jeremy's voice barks out.

"Yeah. What's up, Brains?"

Jeremy quickly fills Ronin in on who Horton is and relays what just happened to me, and Ronin curses under his breath. "You get him?"

Jeremy releases a frustrated growl. "Nah. She fought him off, and I was hoping that'd slow him down. But he must have had a car waiting. He's in the wind."

Ronin's heavy sigh echoes through the car. "I'll let the team know. You coming in?"

Jeremy glances at me, and I manage to nod. I want to go to work. If I don't, I'll crumble. And the last thing I want to do right now is crumble.

"Yeah," he barks. "We'll be there soon."

He disconnects the call and immediately turns to me. He takes one look at me and curses. Then he takes both of my trembling hands in his and brings them to his lips.

"I'm sorry, baby." His voice is tortured. "Damn it!"

"N-not your fault." Why won't my teeth stop chattering?

He lets go of my hands to stroke my face. His eyes examine every facet of my expression before roving over me carefully to check for injuries. "Did he hurt you? Tell me, Rayne. I'm already going to hunt the bastard down, but I need to know if you're hurt. We can head straight to the hospital."

I shake my head. "N-no. I'm okay, Jer."

His green eyes meet mine. His are full of angry pain. "No, you're terrified. I shouldn't have left your side."

I throw my hands up. "This is crazy! You can't stay beside me twenty-four hours a day. This has to end, Jeremy."

Icy fear drags across my skin, raising goose bumps in its

wake. "Decker. God, what if…? I'm going to call the school. They need to be aware that I'm being threatened, and to keep a close eye on Decker at all times."

Grinding his teeth together, he takes the wheel with one hand and intertwines the fingers of his other with mine. "It will stop, Rayne. I'm going to end it."

20

JEREMY

Calling in the authorities at this point would complicate things." My steps halt as I address the Night Eagle team members in the conference room at the office.

The conference room is directly above Jacob's office on the second floor of the building. A long table, more than enough room for all the members of the team, plus any other guests or clients we might be meeting with, stands in the middle of the room. A large screen covers the opposite wall, and when we use it, a blackout screen lowers to cover the windows.

After Rayne and I arrived at the office, she headed straight for the restroom to clean up. I wanted to go with her, more than anything, but she insisted I go and brief the team on what happened and start mission planning. If there's anything I know how to do, it's falling into strategy mode, so I did as she asked and pulled all the guys into the conference room.

Telling them as a group that I have a son was the weirdest and best experience of my life. Their faces mirrored what I'm sure mine looked like when I first found out, minus all the pain. But then they were with me, ready to plan out all the ways we were going to fight for my family, make sure above all else that they stay safe.

Jacob nods, steepling his fingers together while his elbows rest on the table. "I agree. We'll call in the WPD and the SEC when the time is right, but this isn't it. We need to find evidence. And we need to find out where Horton is holed up. If this is as important to him as we think it is, he won't have stayed behind in Phoenix. He's hired people to do his dirty work because that's what men like him do…they gather a staff around them."

"Yeah, the bastard can't do anything on his own. So far he's hired a private detective, who I've collected a file about. He's a thug whose only talent is knowing how to be a slimy asshole. He tried to take Rayne right out from under me. And he almost succeeded." The anger rushing inside of me every time I think of what could have happened can't be contained. I slam my fist down on the table.

"Brains, we've got this. No one will get to her again." Ronin's voice is determined with his promise, but I can't be sure that Rayne is safe until we take Wagner Horton down.

Jacob glances at me. "Can you burn through the software security protocols Horton Tech uses?"

Sucking in a breath through my teeth, I shake my head slowly. "I'm good, but probably not that good. We need to pull in someone to help."

Jacob strokes his chin, contemplating me. "I have someone in mind. I'll call her. She'll be here this afternoon."

"Her?" Ronin's voice carries a note of curiosity.

Jacob beams a bemused glance at Ronin. "You got a problem working with women?"

Ronin leans back in the plush leather chair. "No, sir, of course not. I was just surprised."

Jacob nods. "Until she gets here...Ghost!"

Grisham sits up straighter in his seat, his head snapping to attention. "Sir?"

"Tactics is your thing. Brief 'em on what the team will do once we have the evidence needed to take Horton down with the SEC."

A small smile crosses Grisham's face as he pushes back his chair and stands. I find a seat and prepare to listen, because Grisham fucking loves this part of the job. Planning missions, talking strategy? It's like Christmas for him, every single time.

"We can't get specific until we have a location for him and know exactly what we're dealing with geographically." Grisham moves to the front of the room and plants both hands firmly on the table. "But we can use the people he's hired so far in order to get to him."

Walking over to the laptop that will feed directly to the projection screen, I quickly tap the keys to pull up the file I created on the private investigator who followed Rayne to Olive's home.

"Kevin O'Shea owns a small firm here in Wilmington." I roll through O'Shea's dossier for the team, indicating the location of his office, his past work history, and pulling up a photo for them to focus on.

It's lunchtime by the time we conclude, and I pull Jacob

aside to let him know I need to run out of the office.

He frowns. "I want you working with the hacker I called this afternoon."

Nodding firmly, I look him straight in the eye. "I know. And I'll be here. I want to bring this son of a bitch down more than anyone. But there's something else I need to take care of right now, and I want to get it out of the way. I'll be back with plenty of time to work with your hacker."

He studies me, probably noting the extra lines around my eyes that I'm sure have formed there out of worry. Never has a case hit me like this. It's never been *personal* for me. Making sure that Rayne and Decker are safe is my top priority now, and if there's anyone who understands that, it's Jacob Owen.

"Handling all of this okay? You have to eat, and you have to sleep, son." Jacob's voice is gruff, even when he's concerned. It's just how he's made. He's a scary motherfucker, but I know him well enough now to know that he cares deeply about each and every member of his team. He's got three daughters of his own, and he's recently reconciled with his wife, but each one of us is like a son to him.

"Yeah. I know. Doing my best."

After a pause, Jacob scratches his chin and continues. "I see the way you look at her. You're not just working on a client's case, and you're not just protecting the mother of your kid. It's more than that, and we all know it."

I meet his gaze head-on. Denying nothing. Because, damn right it was more than that. I'd always protect a client with my life if I had to. But this is *Rayne*. I'll protect her with my heart.

He nods and gives me a hard clap on the shoulder. "Go do what you need to do. And get back here by two."

"Understood, boss."

In the outer office, I find Rayne at work on her computer at her desk. She smiles when she sees me, but the same worry I feel in my gut is evident in her eyes. "Hey, you."

"Hey, yourself."

She inclines her head toward the hallway that leads to the lounge. "You wanna go heat up some delicious leftovers?"

She leans forward, theatrically cupping her hand around her mouth and using a stage whisper. "*Leftovers.* It's my first time having *leftovers* for lunch. I usually just eat peanut butter and jelly or takeout. But you see, there's this really hot guy I know who cooks like a damn chef. And he made me dinner last night. So today for lunch? I'm having *leftovers.*"

Chuckling, I match her stance, leaning over the front of her desk. "Wow. He sounds like someone you should keep around."

Her eyes sparkle with mischief, and a thick chunk of her hair falls over her shoulder. My body hums with our closeness, urging me to close the distance and kiss her. But I resist, holding back to continue the banter.

"Oh, he *is.* Because he can cook, and I love to eat."

My eyebrow arches. "That's the only reason?"

Glancing around, she beckons me closer. Rolling my eyes, I lean in farther.

"No," she whispers. "He's also a total *boss* in the bedroom."

I try to keep a straight face; I really do. But her deadpan expression causes the laughter to erupt out of me, and when I lose it, she finally does, too.

When our laughter dies down, my expression grows serious. "Hey. I'm going to be out of the building for a bit. I want you to stay here, all right? No going out on your own. I need to know you're safe."

Her eyes widen in surprise. "Okay. Where are you headed?"

I don't want to tell her. The last thing I want to do is add to the clusterfuck of emotions she must already be feeling. She was attacked this morning. She knows there's a man out there who wants to hurt her. I want to keep her as calm as I can without adding to her stress level.

"Just an errand." Keeping my tone nonchalant, I lean down and kiss her lightly, tasting spearmint on her lips.

Backing away from her desk, I point to her. "Stay put."

Eventually, after it's all said and done, I'll tell her. Just not right now. Not while she's got Horton on her plate. No matter how this afternoon plays out, it's going to hurt me. And I can deal with my own pain. I just can't stand the thought of adding onto hers.

When I stop at the tall, black Iron Gate, my stomach twists. I told myself I'd never come back here the day I left. But now, due to circumstances I never predicated, I'm here again.

It's the last place I want to be.

But I have to do this now. I have the woman I thought I lost and the son I never knew I had in my life. They're filling a hole in the deepest part of me, and I *need* to confront my grandfather, especially before we tell Decker tonight that I'm his dad. I need to know why. How could he have taken this away from me? What did he think he was accomplishing?

It's eating me alive, not knowing.

I roll down my window and touch a finger to the buzzer. The tinny sound makes me wince, and then the speaker crackles as a voice comes through.

"Yes?"

"My name is Jeremy Teague. They're not expecting me, but I'm their grandson."

Silence falls on the other side of the speaker. I wait, staring through the gates onto the winding, asphalt drive. The house can't be seen from here, no way. That wouldn't be nearly ostentatious enough.

Sighing, I lay my head back against the seat and wait some more.

Finally, the crackling on the speaker is back and the distant male voice speaks again.

"Good afternoon, Mr. Teague. You may enter."

The gate swings backward and, ignoring the sinking feeling in my gut, I inch the Land Cruiser forward and travel up the long driveway.

Perfectly manicured flower beds, along with the sharpest, straightest hedges in the history of hedges line the driveway before I round a curve and it opens up to sprawling acres of rolling green lawn. And then the house comes into view.

It's white brick monstrosity with big-ass pillars and a plantation feel to it that screams "I wish we'd won the Civil War!" Just the sight of it causes me to shiver. It's funny because the entire time I was growing up, I thought everything was fine. I knew my grandparents had an absurd amount of money, but I was raised to be thankful that they'd taken me in to raise me after my parents died. They were kind to me, if very set in their ways. Everything about their life and their home was formal, and I didn't realize there was any other way to live until I entered my public high school.

It was the first time I'd attended public school; my grandparents had always enrolled me in private. But when it became clear that college and professional football were a real possibility for me, I begged my grandparents to let me play at the public school level. I wouldn't get nearly the standard of competitiveness in the private school sector that I would in the public school. The people I met there, the guys on the team especially, lived lives that were on the opposite end of the spectrum from my eye. I was introduced to family dinners and mall shopping trips, cheap beach vacations and field parties. Suddenly, it was so very clear how stuffy and snobby my grandparents and all of their friends were. I was embarrassed to bring anyone to my house, and that was fine by my grandparents.

When I started dating Rayne, she was the very first person I brought to meet them, and they weren't welcoming. They never came right out and told me they didn't like her, but she never felt welcome at my house and I didn't blame her. I didn't know what to do about it at that point, though. I'd never gone against my grandparents' wishes before. My grandfather wanted me to play Division I college football as much as I did, so the transfer to public school wasn't as big a battle as it might have been otherwise. But Rayne? She was never going to fit into their scene.

Following the curve of the driveway around the side of the

enormous house, I park in front of the five-car garage and take the walkway to the front door. After ringing the bell, I stand silently on the covered parch, not realizing that I'm holding my breath.

The man who answers the door wears a black blazer and slacks, a crisp white shirt showing underneath. He clears his throat before he speaks, and I recognize the formal voice from the speaker at the gate.

"Welcome home, sir." He bends at the waist in a grand bow that makes my eye twitch. "Your grandfather is waiting for you in the study."

Fucking hell. The study.

It's the place my grandfather receives guests of a business nature. The butler turns and begins to escort me into the foyer. As soon as I'm standing in the grand two-story entrance hall, with a black-and-white-tiled floor, I place a hand on his shoulder.

"Thanks. But I can take it from here. I remember where the study is."

With a disapproving sniff, he turns away from me and stalks toward the kitchen. Sighing, I head in the opposite direction.

Toward the study.

The tall, mahogany door is ajar. During the short walk from the foyer to the grand room covered wall-to-wall in books, my anger and resentment built. With every footstep I think of all the things I lost because of him. Being there for Rayne, my son's birth, every monumental moment of Decker's childhood up until now. By the time I push the door open, the thought of knocking politely is nowhere in sight.

Pushing the door open, I stalk inside and don't stop walking until I'm standing directly in front of the man who raised me.

He stands in front of a large picture window, but as I approach he turns to face me. The years haven't been as cruel to him as they should have been. He stands tall and erect, the same height that I am. At over six feet tall, I'm no slouch and neither is Mason Teague. His hair is stark white, but lies in thick layers on top of his head. His handlebar mustache is distinguished, and bright green eyes, so similar to mine and Decker's, peer at me with shrewd intelligence.

"How could you do it?" The words are grinding out of me before I'm able to stop and think about what I really want to say.

And it's no matter, because the only thing I really want from him is an explanation that makes sense. A good reason for him to have taken away the love of my life and hidden the fact that I was having a child of my own. Because if there isn't a good reason for that, the only logical explanation is that the man who raised me is pure evil.

The sharp expression on my grandfather's face doesn't change as he evaluates me. He takes in my appearance with cool detachment: the long hair pulled back, the plain white polo shirt and jeans, the tats peeking out from my sleeves. I'm nothing like the man he wanted me to become, and his disdain is evident.

But then he shutters his expression and returns his gaze to my face. Innocent nonchalance plays there.

"Well, hello to you, too, my boy. Welcome home."

I bark out a laugh of disbelief. "This hasn't been my home

for a long time. This isn't some heartfelt family reunion. I want answers. And I want them now."

He doesn't flinch at the steel in my voice, but then I wouldn't expect him to. He adopts a leisurely pace as he walks toward the deep leather armchairs on the other side of the room. Even past the age of seventy, he walks upright and without the use of a cane. His body looks physically fit in his golf shirt and slacks.

When he reaches the chairs, he sinks down into one and gestures loosely toward the other. "Have a seat, my boy."

I'm so pissed my voice is almost a snarl. "This isn't a social call. I know what you did, and I want to know why."

With an irritated sigh, he crosses one leg over the other and places an elbow on the thick, rounded arm. Glancing down his nose with a bored expression on his lined face, his lips pull thin. "What exactly are you referring to, Jeremy? I've had a long life, during which I've made many decisions. On behalf of myself and on behalf of my family. But contrary to what you believe, I've never wanted anything but the best for you."

Throwing my head back, I roar with ironic laughter. Walking toward him, I'm moving at a pace slow enough to read the heading on a file lying atop his tidy desk: MERGERS AND ACQUISITIONS: TECHNOLOGY CORPS. With an inner eye roll, I take note.

I thought the old man was retired, but apparently he just can't keep his hands out of the inner workings of his company.

The company that he always assumed one day, after a brilliantly successful college and NFL career, I'd take over.

"You know what? Using your only grandson as a guinea pig

for some insane doctor's science experiment just for the chance he might go pro is one thing. You fucked with my life back then, and thank God I caught wind of it. But attempting to force the girl I loved to abort our *child?*" I take a menacing step closer to his armchair. "That's sick. I would have done right by her, been there for both of them! Dammit, I *wanted* that chance!"

He regards me with his trademark cool stare. His feathers aren't ruffled; his emotions are in check. And it infuriates me. I want him to yell, to scream at me. To tell me that he was pissed that I got a girl pregnant back then and he was trying to get back at me. Any feeling at all would be better than this indifference.

"So, *Granddad?* What do you have to say for yourself?"

He tilts his head to one side. "How did you come by your information?"

With a dark chuckle, I turn around and run shaking hands through my hair. He's unbelievable. Really fucking incredible.

"My information came directly from the source. You see…with all of your meddling and manipulating, you failed, ultimately. You might have driven Rayne away, and thank God you did, because she was strong enough to raise my son on her own. But she and I couldn't be kept apart forever. You get that? We're *supposed* to be together. She's back in my life, and I'm getting to know my son. His name is Decker, and he's amazing. And you'll never get to know him, because of your own selfish ego. How does it feel?"

He sits up straighter. "You're in contact with your son?"

Whirling back around to face him, I realize I'm not going

to solve anything by being here. In fact, coming here at all was a huge mistake. There's no getting through to this man; I shouldn't have even tired. He'll never give me the answers I want. And no explanation he could ever offer will take away the pain of what he did.

My hands fall to my sides with limp indifference. "Yeah. Yeah, I'm in contact with my son. In fact, my son and his mother now live with me. So your plan, all those years ago? It's dust. And I hope you choke on it."

He jerks to his feet, his calm veneer now shattered. His face is an angry red, his lips twisted into a snarl that I've never seen on his face before.

"You idiot!" he shouts. "Everything I did back then, I did for you. But if you have him in your life now...it isn't the time for your stupid pride! You need me. And you have a responsibility to pass on my legacy to my great-grandson!"

I stare at him with sheer disbelief, my mouth falling slack. "You mean the grandson you never even wanted to exist?"

He walks toward me, stopping directly in front of me so that we're almost nose to nose.

"You've always been willful," he hisses. "I knew that. But I didn't know you'd be stupid enough to cut your son out of the destiny he deserves."

"Mason!"

The sound of my grandmother's voice pulls me around to face the door. She strides forward, stopping when she stands beside my grandfather and across from me.

"Jeremy." She reaches up to touch my face, but I jerk away. "You've been away for so long. We've missed you."

My grandmother looks exactly the same as she always has, with a head of white, perfectly styled hair. Her clothes are elegant and refined, and she stands up straight and stately. They're both the picture of good health, with more lines collected on their faces.

"Not enough to apologize for what you both did to me. You knew, right, Grandmother? After all these years, you never wanted to come clean?" My tone is accusatory as I turn my anger on her.

"A baby at that age would have ruined your life." Her tone is matter-of-fact. "We were only doing what was best for you."

I stare at her, and she continues. "But now that our plans all those years ago didn't work out the way we wanted them to, we can see the opportunity we have now. We want you to come back, Jeremy. Back to our family. Come work with your grandfather. Become the businessman we always knew you could be. And now that you have a son, you have someone to pass the legacy down to."

My grandfather nods, smiling like she's saying everything he believes to be true.

Stepping back, I let out a sharp bark of a laugh and scrub a hand over my face. "You were playing God. Both of you. And now that you've found out that Rayne thwarted your plan, you want your grandson in your life? I'll never let that happen. You don't deserve him. Either of you."

Shaking my head, I slowly back up toward the door and look at my grandfather. "You know what? I think my son is gonna be just fine. And any destiny that has to do with you and your goddamn company isn't one I want to pass on to my boy."

Turning, I walk toward the door.

"Don't you walk away from me, boy! We're not done here! Everything your grandmother and I did, we did to secure your future! And I won't regret any of it!"

The words sting my back, but I don't stop. I keep walking, and I don't intend to ever look back.

21

RAYNE

When Jeremy walks back into the office, it's like I'm looking at a completely different man from the one who left before lunch.

An invisible pull yanks me to my feet when I see his haggard face, drained of all emotion and color.

"Jeremy!" My voice is tremulous. "What is it?"

His gait is slow as he heads toward me; his head is heavy as he drops it onto my shoulder and his arms encircle my waist.

Wrapping my arms around his neck, I squeeze him tight. It feels like I've been jabbed in the stomach; I don't know what's wrong with him, but I know he's in pain. And it hurts me like a physical reaction.

He takes a deep breath and his entire body shudders against me.

"Don't do this, Jer," I say softly. His scent tickles my nose and I inhale deeply. "Don't shut down. Tell me what's wrong."

When he lifts his head, he's blinking rapidly and his eyes are red-rimmed and glassy.

"Oh, baby," I murmur. "Talk to me." I place my hands on either side of his face, the gentle pressure coaxing him to talk to me about what made him feel this way.

His green eyes burn into mine, and the pain I see in them is like a sword through my stomach. He opens his mouth to speak just as the buzzer on the office door sounds.

Ignoring it, I stay focused on Jeremy.

"Rayne." His voice is the sound of steel grating against stone. "You need to get that."

With a frustrated groan, I let him go and round my desk to check my computer screen. When the office buzzer sounds, it means someone outside is requesting access inside NES. The camera feed from outside the door shows up on my computer screen so I know whether or not to grant access to the visitor.

"Oh, it's her." My muttered words cause Jeremy to glance over at me.

"Who?"

"Jacob said he was expecting an associate of his to come and consult today. She's holding up her I.D. for the camera." With a click of the mouse, I grant her access to the building and she pushes the door open.

The woman who enters is pretty and petite, definitely a smaller package than I am. She strides toward my desk, not sparing Jeremy a glance as she homes in on me. As she approaches, I notice that what I thought was merely pretty before is actually gorgeous.

Her thick, chocolate black hair is streaked with red, although she wears it in a messy bun on top of her head. She's plainly dressed in jeans, a tank, and a short-sleeved hoodie. The white terry cloth of the lightweight jacket makes the dark, golden-bronze color of her skin stand out. Her sneakered feet shift as she eyes me.

"I have a meeting here." Her tone is blunt, and I blink at her.

"Uh, yeah, okay." Trying to keep my tone bright, I glance at Jeremy before looking back at the woman before me. "Mr. Owen told me he was expecting you. Let me just buzz him and I'm sure he'll be right out."

Jeremy clears his throat. "Actually, your meeting is with me."

His interjection causes both the new woman and me to cast our glances in his direction.

My stomach tightens. The thought of Jeremy, my Jeremy, working closely on a project with this beautiful woman makes me feel a little queasy.

"It is?" I try to keep my tone even. "Jacob didn't tell me that."

Jeremy gives me a reassuring smile. "Go ahead and buzz him, Rayne." Turning to the newcomer, he holds out his hand. "I'm Jeremy Teague. I'm a member of the team here at Night Eagle, and we're going to be working together today on some tech surveillance for a case we've taken on."

She hyperfocuses on him but doesn't extend her hand. "It's nice to meet you. I'm Sayward Diaz."

"Sayward!" Jacob emerges from his office, a small smile on his face.

I'm astounded to even see the small smile, because it might

just be the first one I've seen out of Jacob in my time here. He stops just short of hugging Sayward, and she offers him a big grin.

"Hi, Jacob."

"Thanks for coming. We really need your help on this one." He glances at Jeremy pointedly.

"Yeah," agrees Jeremy. "I'm good with computers, really good. But I can't break through on this one, and your expertise is gonna save my ass."

Sayward gives him a firm nod. "Saving asses is my specialty."

I attempt to thwart the rolling of my eyes, and I *think* I succeed.

"Perfect." Jacob nods at Jeremy. "Take her to your office, and don't come out until you have a breakthrough."

"Got it." Jeremy gestures to Sayward to follow him, but before he disappears down the hallway he leans over and kisses my cheek. The soft, warm press of his lips on my skin sends tingles down the length of my body, and it lifts my spirits just a tiny bit from where they've fallen.

"We'll talk later." His whisper is deep and husky in my ear, and then he's gone.

Staring after him, I'm left wondering what caused his emotional breakdown a few moments ago, and what the hell I'm going to do with a gorgeous computer genius like Sayward hanging out in his office for hours at a time. With a sigh, I sink down into my chair.

Jacob clears his throat. Startled because I forgot he was still standing there, I glance up at him. He shoots me a wink before heading into his office.

Settling back into my chair with a slack jaw, I decide that today's the day I'm going to buy a winning lottery ticket. Because now that Jacob Owen has winked at me, I've pretty much seen everything.

At 5:00 p.m., I call Macy to check on Decker and ask if he can stay for dinner.

"I'm so sad I couldn't pick him up from his first day." I sigh into the phone.

Macy is quick to reassure me. "I'm sure he'll tell you all about it when you see him. You're protecting him, and that's the most important thing."

Jeremy and Sayward are still closed away, working on whatever computer issue has to do with Wagner Horton. Even thinking his name nearly causes convulsions. I've never wanted anything to be over as much as I want Wagner to go to prison, for everything he's done to me, but there's still a cold little voice in the back of my mind that tells me Night Eagle isn't going to be able to end this for me.

Pushing that thought to the very darkest corner of my mind, I smile as Ronin perches on the corner of my desk.

"Headed out?"

He shakes his head, his pretty, clear green eyes studying me. "Nah. We're a team, Rayne. So we're all working overtime on this, because your safety is at the top of all of our priority lists."

A warm sensation fills me up. Even when I lived at home with my parents, they were so critical and conservative I felt suffocated more often than not. And when I was in Phoenix and my grandmother was still alive, I knew I was loved, but the stress level from taking care of both myself and Decker was often more than I could bear.

I've never felt like I had a family I could count on. But now this group of guys who barely know me are giving it their all just to keep me safe.

"Thank you, Ronin. Jeremy's lucky to have a friend like you."

He smiles. "You know…I've known the guy a long time. We've been through a lot together. Conquering life-threatening missions together makes for tight bonds, you know? And there's always been something…missing for Brains. Like he'd left something behind. And I always knew he wasn't close to his grandparents and he had no wife or girl or kids so…I could never figure it out."

His eyes pierce mine, and with each one of his words my heart has squeezed just a little tighter inside my chest.

"But then you came to town, and everything started to make sense. That thing he was missing? It was you. And Decker."

Warmth floods into me. "He told you."

Ronin grins in response.

Color rises in my cheeks, warming me from the inside out. "He didn't even know about Decker."

Ronin strokes his clean-cut chin. His look is so different from Jeremy's, but when you saw them together you knew instantly they had a brotherly friendship. "Didn't matter. Something inside him knew that there was something else out there he needed. I'm glad you're here, Rayne. You're one of our own now, and we'll protect you both with all we have."

The back of my eyelids sting, and a giant lump clogs my throat. My voice is nothing but a raspy whisper. "Thanks, Ronin. That means…everything to me."

"Hey." Jeremy's voice reaches us from the entry to the front office lobby where Ronin's still sitting on my desk. "You hitting on my girl?"

Ronin, winking at me, drawls out his response. "*Well*…You leave her alone for too long, and…" He trails off suggestively, and Jeremy points a finger at him.

"Put that swagger away. Go use it on someone else."

Ronin heaves a dramatic sigh and rises, walking toward where Jeremy's standing.

"Where's Sayward?" I ask.

He inclines his head toward Jacob's office. "We just got done briefing Jacob on what we've accomplished today. She's still in there."

Ronin stares at Jacob's door. "Anybody know how she and Boss Man know each other?"

Jeremy and I both shake our heads.

"Not a clue." Jeremy holds out a hand to me, pulling me up from my chair and wrapping a strong arm tightly around my waist as he plants a kiss in the top of my hair. "They seem to go way back, though."

Ronin lifts a brow. "She cool?"

Swiping a hand over his exhausted face, Jeremy shrugs. "Hard to tell, you know? She's a computer chick. Really into her tech, not so much into socialization. So we'll see. Seems like Boss Man's gonna want her around more. He shared with her stuff on the level we don't usually include consultants in."

Disentangling myself from Jeremy's arm, I shut down my computer and gather my bag while he and Ronin finish their discussion.

"You two go home, get some rest. First thing tomorrow, we're back at it. Grisham should be able to form a more specific plan by then."

Jeremy's expression is full of frustration. "We're close, but this isn't moving fast enough for me, Swag. I want this asshole out of our hair."

Ronin gives him a solid nod before patting his shoulder. "Yeah. I get that. We all do. But you know these things take time, and we need to do it right. The cargo is too precious, right?"

Glancing down at me, Jeremy's' expression softens in a way that sends a flash of heat through my stomach. "Yeah. It is."

Glancing between us with a small smile, Ronin rubs his hands together. "When do I get to meet the little guy?"

"Oh! Um…" I glance at Jeremy, unsure.

Jeremy's face transforms with a full smile. He's so handsome, so full of perfect male beauty that my heart stutters. "Tonight we tell him I'm his dad. I want you guys to meet him soon. Really soon. He's an amazing kid. His mom has done an incredible job."

Jeremy pulls me toward him with an arm slung over my shoulder and I can feel a hot blush creeping into my cheeks once more. He and Ronin bump fists, and then Ronin heads out the front door.

Looking down at me, Jeremy's face is alight with excitement and the tiniest hint of anxiety. "Ready to do this?"

Smiling up at him, trying to be sure he knows exactly how ready I am, I wrap an arm around his waist and squeeze.

"I'm so ready for our son to know you're his dad. Let's go tell him."

22

JEREMY

I watch, leaning against the doorway between the kitchen and the great room as Rayne tosses her purse haphazardly on the countertop. Her keys skitter along the gray stone, sliding until they tumble onto the floor just as the contents of her purse spill out onto the counter.

I bit my lip against a grin.

"Dammit!" she grumbles as she bends down to retrieve her keys.

Tossing them on the counter, she turns to Decker whose expression is very reminiscent of mine. Oblivious to either of our humor, she places her hands on her hips.

"Okay, kiddo. Upstairs to get ready for bed. Then I want you to come on back down here. Jeremy and I have something to talk to you about."

"Okay, Mom." Decker turns for the door, my lovesick dog bounding into action in front of him in his rush to beat my son to the stairs. But as Decker passes me, he gives me a wide, devious grin as he turns back around.

"Oh, and Mom?"

"What, babe?"

"Put your keys in your purse, in the pocket where they belong, or you'll have no clue where they are in the morning." He almost chokes on the last word, he's trying so hard not to laugh.

My answering snort is met with an icy stair from Rayne just before she turns it on Deck. "You two ganging up on me? Not a good plan for either one of you. "

"Also," adds Decker helpfully as he turns to go, "you need to put a dollar in the swear jar."

Night takes off, his nails clicking wildly on the floor as Decker races him for the stairs.

"There's no swear jar at Jeremy's house!" she shouts behind him.

Chuckling, I watch as she whirls away from me. Kicking off her heels so they're lying on their sides next to the island, she heads for the refrigerator. She tugs it open, and her skirt rides up high on the backs of her thighs as she leans down to grab a bottled water out of the lower drawer.

Immediately, I push off the wall and stalk toward her, led forward by instinct and the surge of lust-tinged desire.

Coming up behind her, my hands smooth up the backs of her legs, sliding around to palm her thighs as I yank her toward me. Her surprised gasp makes my now rock-hard erection strain against my pants. I'm a mixed jumble of emotions after today, my head cloudy with the memory of the meeting with my grandfather and the high from the successful hack into the mainframe at Horton Tech. But right now, all I can see is Rayne.

"You know," I whisper as I nibble the shell of her ear and am rewarded by a low moan from her lips. "There's a different kind of swear jar at this house. And I don't want to hear you calling it 'Jeremy's house' again. It now carries the title of 'our house.'"

Bracing her hands against the refrigerator shelf, she rocks her hips back against me. All the blood rushes straight to my dick, and my fingers tighten their hold, digging into her thighs.

"Aren't you getting ahead of yourself a little bit there, Mr. Confident?" Her throaty voice is like my Kryptonite, pulling me toward an out-of-control spiral of need that I can't deny.

"Damn, darlin'. What is it about you? I can't get enough…can't control how much I want you. Our son is going to be back downstairs any minute, I'm about to tell him I'm his father, and I should be prepping for what I'm going to say. But all I want to do right now is rip off this skirt and fuck you."

When she presses her lush ass against me again, this time I'm ready for her, using my grip on her thighs to meet her with a powerful thrust. One of my hands slides over her mouth to cover her moan.

"Shhh. Not now.…but later? I need you. I need you so bad, baby." I slide my lips from her ear down to place open kisses along the side of her throat.

Night's clicking nails on hardwood are as good as a cowbell, and I drop another kiss to her skin before stepping back and adopting a casual stance at the island.

Decker, moving at full speed, flies into the kitchen just ahead of Night and he whoops in triumph. Night lets out a short bark to match, and Decker laughs.

"You can't whoop, Night! I'm the winner, only I can whoop!" He scolds the dog while scratching him behind the ear.

Night butts the boy with his big head and barks again.

"Fine." Decker sighs. "You can have the win this time. Brat."

He climbs onto a stool and tosses me a grin before reaching into the jar at the center of the island for a chocolate chip cookie.

"Hey!" Rayne's tone is half-jovial, half-commanding. "At least grab a plate."

"I'm on it." I saunter toward the cabinet, grab a plate from the shelf, and lower it onto the countertop in front of Decker. Then I grab two more cookies to add to his pile. "How was your first day of school, Deck?"

Decker shrugs, his mouth too full of chocolate and sugar to answer. Rayne nails me with an eye roll. "This is what it's like, living with an eight-year-old. Never more than a one-word answer to the question 'how was school today?'" She pulls up the stool beside Decker and pulls me in with a sexy smirk. "Watch and learn, mister. Hey, Deck?"

Decker swallows his cookie and turns to face her. "Yeah, Mom?"

"Did you write anything down at school today? Say, maybe some sentences about some topic or other, or maybe some numbers that were added together to create new, bigger numbers?" She places her chin in one hand, focusing on him with a winning smile.

Decker contemplates, before his face lights up. "Oh, yeah! The teacher put a picture on the screen of this awesome giant panda fighting with an orangutan. They were in some kind of tropical jungle or something. And I wrote a paragraph about it that the teacher asked me to read for the class. And then in math we worked together in a group to solve a story problem about making change at the mall. Pretty cool, right?"

She beams at him, tousling his hair.

I'm floored, watching the interaction with pure amazement. I pull out the stool across from them and sink onto it, my eyes never leaving Rayne's face. "That was…how'd you know exactly what to ask to make him talk?"

She shrugs, leaning back and folding her arms across her chest. "It's called Magical Mommy Juice. See, I drink it in the morning? And then it helps me interact with my son in a productive way all day."

"Huh. Magical Mommy Juice? Do you think they make something called Delivering Dad—" I cut my words off abruptly as my eyes widen, realizing what I almost did.

Shit. I almost jumped the gun there.

Rayne isn't fazed; she gives me a reassuring smile as she wraps one arm around Decker. "So remember how I told you that Jeremy and I have something to talk to you about?"

His green eyes slide to mine with curiosity before nodding. "Yeah."

"Um." She searches his face, looking for the words that will make this monumental discussion easier for him to grasp. "Jeremy isn't just a friend, Decker. He's so much more than that to me…and to you."

Picking up his second cookie, he takes a bite and munches, waiting. "Okay. So what is he, then?"

There's a tiny hint of worry in Decker's face as he glances around the kitchen. He looks down at Night, lying faithfully on the floor beside him before finding my gaze again. "Do we have to leave?"

My heart stalls; just the thought that he might think I don't want him here, with me, brings the words that I want to say to the surface.

Catching his eye, I glance at Rayne for the OK. She nods, and I take a deep breath before plunging right in.

"No, Deck. You never have to leave. I mean…I don't want you and your mom to go because you're both really, really important to me."

Decker tilts his head to the side, a quizzical expression crossing his face. Then he nods, as if in understanding. "Oh, because you want my mom to be your girlfriend?"

God, how am I messing this up this badly?

I know that Decker won't be able to wrap his head around it, but Rayne is so much more to me than a girlfriend. And she always will be.

"Not exactly. Well, kind of. I mean, I care about your mom *and* you, Decker."

His little face screws up in confusion. "Me?"

Rayne's arm tightens around him as her eyes fill with tears.

Seeing them starts an ache in my chest that won't go away until I reassure him that I care about him because he's mine. I more than care about him. I love him with every fiber of my being, and not because he's earned it, or has done something to make me happy, but because I'm his father and my love began unconditionally the second I knew he existed.

I reach out and take his hand, dwarfing it in my large one. "I care about you, Deck, because I'm your father."

Silence creeps in from the edges of the room, covering us in its heavy blanket until Rayne can no longer stand it. Decker is staring at his plate, his cookies forgotten, and I'm staring at Decker, waiting for his response. Any response.

"Decker, sweetie?" Her voice is soft, nudging. "Did you hear what Jeremy said? He's your dad."

Decker glances at her. "I thought you said you didn't know where my father was?"

She nods. "I didn't, sweetie. I mean…Jeremy and I went to high school together. That's when we met and that's when we created you. But after that, we lost touch and I didn't know where he was. It was coincidence that I ran into him here…or fate."

Decker glances at me. "Why didn't you call me? Or tell me happy birthday? Or send me Christmas presents?"

His voice isn't accusing; it's just demanding. He genuinely wants to know why I never reached out to him. And my heart hurts, just knowing that he thinks I ever would have purposely neglected him.

Rayne steps in again. "Honey, that's not Jeremy's fault. He never even knew he was a daddy."

Another round of silence covers us while Decker thinks this over. "You just found out that you're my dad?"

I nod, never taking my gaze from his face. I'm watching him, studying him, wanting nothing more than for this to be okay with him.

"Yes. There're a lot of reasons, Deck…grown-up reasons, I mean, that I didn't know about you before. There's no fault here, not mine or your mom's and especially not yours. But now that I know, all I want is to be here. I want you and your mom with me. Can you understand that?"

His eyes, finally full of understanding and now a little bit of uncertainty, stare me down. His dark hair falls into his eyes and his bottom lip disappears between his teeth. "You…want me? I mean, you want me to stay here? And Mom, too?"

Unable to stay seated any longer, I round the island and stop in front of him. Pulling another stool around so we're face-to-face, I put a hand around his neck as I stare into his eyes. I'm begging him to see the sincerity there. "Yeah. I want you. More than anything in the whole entire world. I'm so happy about this, Deck. Happier than you could ever know. And I hope that eventually you'll be happy about it, too."

Finally, finally, his face breaks into one of his true-blue grins. The sight almost causes me to break down, but I swallow the enormous ball of emotion in my throat and return his smile.

"I'm happy about it."

I glance up at the ceiling, thanking God.

"But…what am I supposed to call you?" Decker's uncertainty shows in his little confused expression.

Still looking into his eyes, I make sure he knows I'm not going to be disappointed by anything he does right now. "You can call me whatever you want. It doesn't have to be 'Dad' right now. Not until you're ready."

He nods, giving me one of his grins, and my chest constricts.

Everything is out in the open. Glancing at Rayne, her eyes are glistening with tears and she nods at me with a smile on her face. The enormity of this moment is taking up so much space in my heart there's no room for anything else but the two of them. My family.

My everything.

23

WAGNER

As I glance around me, my skin crawls. The hotel room I've been holed up in since my arrival in Wilmington is so far beneath my usual accommodations. I now know for a fact I can never be anything but filthy rich. Which means that silencing the little assistant bitch who forced my hand is even more important than I originally thought.

The private investigator I hired, who came highly recommended from my new business partner, actually had the nerve to suggest I lower myself to even dirtier standards. He suggested that I stay in a roach-infested motel, which I laughed uncontrollably about until he informed me of the serious nature of his advisement. At which time I told him to get the hell out of my face and proceeded to book a room at the Amenity Inn and Suites.

And apparently, in places like this the word Suites is a blatant and inexcusable fabrication.

Leaning back in the uncomfortable, stiff-backed desk chair,

I stare toward the darkened town alight outside the fourth-story window. My thoughts are calm, despite the fact that my emotions are heightened and frenetic, something that never bodes well for those around me. The cell phone beside me on the desk vibrates and I snatch it up.

"This better be good news."

"It's not."

With a barely stifled snarl of infuriation my back teeth snap together as my face contorts.

"I hired you to do a job. That job needs to be successfully completed or you'll receive nothing from me other than a promise that your life will become hell on earth from this point on." My voice, layered with subdued fury, is staccato and sharp.

"I understand, sir. We'll be trying a different tack. We sent one man after the girl, thinking it would be sufficient. She was able to get away, and because of that we'll adjust our tactics and the next time we'll be successful."

Standing, the phone clenched tightly in my hand, I suck in deep breaths in order to calm myself. "And exactly when do you think that will be?"

My vision is hazed with red. In my head, I picture someone trying to grab the gorgeous, raven-haired ex-assistant and my cock grows instantly hard. She's a feisty one, she would have fought. Hard.

I want to be the one she's fighting. I'll enjoy it, relish it, even. I want her kicking and screaming and beating my chest as I make her body mine in every despicable way I can think of. And I won't stop until she's pleading for more.

Because I'm going to make her like it. And then she'll learn that my way is the only way she'll get to keep breathing. I don't want to kill a body like that. Not if I don't have to.

I want to *appreciate* a body like that.

Adjusting myself, I focus again on the conversation, catching him midexplanation.

"I don't care how you do it. Get her and bring her to me. Soon. Do you understand?"

I can almost hear the man on the other end of the line nodding. "Yes, sir."

I end the call and drop the phone down on the desk. And then I lower myself into the chair and open my laptop. My fingers fly across the keyboard until I find the file I'm looking for, clicking OPEN.

It contains the details of my new business deal, contingent on the rolling out of the new tech that will change the way everyone in the world communicates. My lips pull into a hopeful smile.

This deal will go through. I will become the most successful and innovative technological powerhouse on the planet. Horton Tech will become even more successful than I ever could have believed, thanks to my new partner.

And I'll have the incomparable, newly tamed Rayne Alexander in my bed.

And all will be right with the world.

24

RAYNE

Seeing the look on my son's face tonight when he looked into Jeremy's eyes and realized for the first time that he was looking at his father nearly broke me. The longing he's been feeling for the man who helped create him, the ever-present hole in his life that existed no matter how hard I've tried to fill it…it's all been repaired. Now Jeremy and Decker can begin the road to finding the bond that they should have had from the very beginning.

The one that was stolen from us, thanks to Jeremy's grandparents' calculations and their manipulation of two teenagers.

Mason and Alyssa Teague have been on my mind very little over the past nine years. I chalked their cruelty up to being rich, entitled assholes. I assumed they had gotten to Jeremy and corrupted him, too. After I escaped Wilmington and never looked back, I just never wanted to give them the satisfaction of dwelling over what they'd tried to do to me. How they, along with my uber-conservative parents, had tried to take my choice away.

"Why do you think they did it?" My hands shake the tiniest bit as I lift my wineglass to my lips and sip the crimson liquid.

My legs, sprawled across Jeremy's lap as we sit on the love seat in the cozy sitting area of his bedroom, coil with tension as I bring up the topic the Teagues.

"Do you think it's because they really hate me that much? They couldn't stand the thought of you having a life with me? Of me being the mother of your child? What'd I ever *do* to them?"

Jeremy's strong fingers, massaging the stress from my calves, still. "No, baby. It had less to do with hate and everything to do with control. My grandmother is one thing, a snob on her best day, but my grandfather couldn't stand the thought of not being in total control of my future. You were a wild card, especially when you got pregnant. He saw an opportunity to work the situation to his advantage, and he pounced on it."

Staring down at the wineglass, absently swirling the drink around and around, I sigh. "Well, I guess I put the kibosh on that real quick when I up and left without a word. And he must have known that I was somewhere out there raising his grandson. You know? And he never said anything to you. And he never tried to contact me, ask about Decker…nothing."

Jeremy had resumed the massage, but then his fingers go still again, and this time he squeezes as the muscles in his hands tense up.

"What, Jer?"

He glances at me, his gaze pensive and a little bit cautious.

"It's just…that part doesn't sound like him. Now that I think about it, I can't imagine that he'd just let you go like that and never attempt to find you. It's not his style. He'd want to know where you were, and he wouldn't have stopped until he did."

All the blood in my body slows as I contemplate that chilling thought. "You think he knew where I was? And he never said anything?"

Jeremy smoothes his hands up my legs, trying to reassure me. I take comfort in his touch, letting his hands warm me where I'm suddenly cold. "Baby…I went to see him today."

I sit up, my spine straightening so fast that Jeremy's hands fall away from me. "What? Your grandfather?"

He reaches for the wineglass, setting it down on the small oak table. Gathering my hands in his, his thumbs rub calming circles over my skin. "Yeah. And it wasn't a good visit, not by a long shot. It's the first time I've seen him since I left for the army years ago."

Pushing away from him I stand and pace away, reaching the other end of the room where the bathroom door lays closed before spinning back around to face him. "Are you fucking serious right now, Jeremy? And you didn't think I'd want to know?"

He stands, too, spreading his arms out wide in an open gesture. "I had to do it, Rayne. And I knew it'd upset you. I had to get it off my chest. How pissed I am about what they did to us. I wanted to get answers. I said my peace, and then I got the hell out of there."

My breath is coming fast, and the anger inside me curls my hands into fists as I stalk back toward him. "I don't want anything to do with them! I don't want them near Decker. Not ever!"

Jeremy's voice is calm, but there's an edge to it that lets me know he's just as upset as I am. "I know that, Rayne. I don't want them to have anything to do with our family either. But they essentially stole my family from me. I couldn't let that go without telling them exactly how I felt, and finding out the reason why."

Closing my eyes and pinching the bridge of my nose with one hand while the other floats to my hip, I attempt a calming breath. It helps to slow down my racing thoughts, so I take another. "Okay...yeah, I guess I get that. Just...the thought of them trying to insert themselves in our lives again after everything...it scares me, Jer. And I don't handle being scared very well."

His hands rise to the sides of my face, his palms so big they span my cheekbones to the top of my neck. "Rayne...you have to trust me. You have to know that now that I have you and Decker in my life, you're both my first priority. Your safety, Decker's well-being...they come first with me. I'll never let anything happen to you again. Look at me." He tilts my head slightly, forcing my eyes up to his. "Tell me you trust me. I need to hear that. I need to know it, and I need it to be true."

I stare into his unwavering gaze. His eyes tell me a story; they let me know that every word he says to me is something he'd swear on. They say that he might not have known what anchored him before, looking for his purpose in the armed forces, in the team, in his house, and on his boat...but now he's found it in us. In me and in our son. They tell me that he would absolutely lay down his life if he had to in order to protect me.

And I trust it. All of it.

But with that trust comes a certain amount of fear that I can't deny. Now that Jeremy and Decker have found one another, they deserve a chance. They don't deserve to be torn apart because of a mess I've made.

I trust him completely. But I don't trust the universe to keep us together when it's all said and done.

Gripping his wrists with my hands, I return his stare with a fierce one of my own. Then, keeping my eyes locked on his, I let him go and slowly remove my clothes. My shirt is the first thing to go, yanking it up and over my head before tossing it over my shoulder. My skirt is next, sliding down my thighs and finding itself in a heap right beside my shirt. Jeremy's throat works, his Adam's apple bobbing as I reach up for the clasp of my bra, loosening it and tossing the garment on the floor. When my thumbs hook into the side of my panties and drag them down over my hips, his eyes flare with heated intensity and his hands curl into fists at his sides.

"Rayne...what are you doing?"

Instead of answering him, I grab him by the belt and yank him toward me. I pull his shirt up over his chiseled abs and rock hard chest, tugging until he finally grabs ahold of the collar and jerks it over his head. Taking a second to feast on the expanse of his golden skin, accented by a smattering of curls over his chest and the winding lines of his ink, I finally lift my eyes to his once more. And that's where they stay as I drop down to my knees.

Jeremy's pupils dilate, his tongue darts out to lick his lips but he doesn't say anything, just watches me with fiery heat building and surging in his gaze. My eyes drop to watch my hands work as I undo his belt and flick open the button on his pants, dragging the zipper down and shoving them down his legs. He helps me, stepping out of them and then his hands settle on my head.

"Rayne." His voice is hoarse. "If you feel like you have something to prove—"

"I do have something to prove." I interrupt him, grasping hold of his firm, erect cock and giving it a stroke.

His breath hitches, and as I glance up at him his head has dropped back and every single muscle in his body has gone taut.

"I've never gotten down on my knees for any man, Jeremy. I've never taken another man into my mouth. Not even you. If you had told me a year ago, hell…even a few months ago that I'd be doing this, I would have called you a damn liar. This…this is trust. I know you'll respect me. I know you'll protect me. And I know that no matter what happens, I can trust you with our son."

Leaning in, I lick him. From the base of his cock to the swollen tip, my tongue blazes a path of the sweetest skin I've ever tasted, with just a hint of salt. He groans, his hips jerking with the feel of it, and I take him fully in my mouth with pleasure.

"Fucking…hell…yes." He grunts out each word, punctuating it with a gentle thrust of his hips. Even now, he's being careful not to hurt me.

This is a brand-new experience for me…something we never did back when we were teenagers. And although I never engaged in a serious relationship with anyone in Phoenix, it's something I never even would have considered doing with a casual date.

I never expected it to feel so…empowering. Jeremy's fingers flex in my hair and he's quivering—*quivering!*—under my touch. It's heady and wonderful and intoxicating.

His feet are planted wide, his thick and corded thighs bulky, and I grip the backs of them. Releasing him with a popping sound, I swirl my tongue around the lush head. Then, plunging him back inside my mouth, I suck and taste until I find a steady rhythm, working my hand on the base of him to make up for what I can't reach with my mouth.

Over and over again, I take him deep, loving the taste and the feel of him in my mouth. Who knew I could love this? Who knew I would relish the feel of him thrusting against my pumping sucks, his fingers tugging on the long strands of my hair, his guttural groan as I bring him so close to the blink of erotic pleasure?

I never did.

"Damn, baby. I'm gonna come…you might want to pull back for this." The strain in his voice as he tries to hold back is evident, and I take it as a challenge.

Removing my other hand from his thigh and lowering it between his legs, I caress his supple sac in my fingers, rolling them before squeezing with intention.

His choked-off cry of release, flowing hot and steady into my mouth, doubles as my shout of triumph.

As I swallow, I pull back from him with a smirk. Glancing up at him with nothing but sincerity, I grasp his outstretched hands and hop to my feet.

"I trust you, Jeremy. With everything I have."

His answering groan is lost somewhere as he pulls me into his arms and crashes his mouth to mine.

Hoisting me into his arms, I wrap my legs around his waist. His cock stiffens again in response and he groans, tossing me onto the bed and climbing over me. His mouth devours mine like a man who's been starving for weeks.

Kissing Jeremy is familiar because I've known him before. But kissing this older, more mature, more experienced Jeremy makes my heart beat fast and twists me up into a tangled knot of desire. My hips thrust of their own accord, searching for the relief that my body craves. Tingles of exhilarated pleasure radiate from my core to my limbs, and I squeeze him tighter with my legs.

Breaking free, he glances down at me before he dips his head to my neck. "Easy, baby. I've got you."

His voice is nothing but a rasp as he finds the sensitive spot above my collarbone, the one he used to spend so much time licking and sucking when we were younger. My nails dig into his shoulders as I buck against him.

Jeremy kisses a hot path down my body. His tongue meets parts of me that haven't felt the touch of a man in so long: my breasts, my stomach, each of my hip bones. When his warm breath blows against the wetness of my tightly coiled heat, I cry out. I don't know whether to beg him to stop or pull him closer.

But my body does…my hands tangle in his hair as I urge him toward me. "Please."

His eyes, darkened with his own frantic desire, meet mine. "Absolutely."

With one deft finger, he parts my folds, his skin sliding along my wetness. I push my hips forward, begging, pleading. He obliges. His tongue meets my clit, and my fingers dig into the soft bedclothes beneath me.

Oh, God. It's a very real possibility that I might explode. My hips jerk and buck with each lick, and when he inserts his finger inside me and curls it upward my mouth falls open on a deep moan.

Has anyone ever died from a freaking orgasm? Because I can feel mine building, and I think it's going to make me implode.

"Jeremy…please!"

He pushes my knees apart even wider, burying his face against me. When he hums against my heat, the vibrations from his mouth combined by the furious lashes with his tongue push me over the edge and I fall. My entire body trembles as the pleasure washes over me, and I reach for him.

"God, Jer…I need you inside me. Please."

With a low humming sound in the back of his throat, he swipes my neck with his tongue before reaching over to the nightstand and pulling out a shiny packet. Tearing it open, he sheaths himself.

Impatient, I grasp him in my hands, causing his eyes to close tightly.

Leaving him there and waiting for the explosion of deliciousness I know is about to come, I close my eyes.

And wait.

I can feel Jeremy at my entrance, but he doesn't push inside and my eyes snap open as he teases me. He rubs the head of his cock over my clit and I moan and push myself against him.

Drawing back, his eyes are dark and mischievous. "Impatient?"

With a sound that's half irritated and half amused, therefore rendering it ineffective, my hips rise again.

But he continues to tease me, his measured strokes against the tiny bud of pleasure pulling me into a vortex of sensation. Then, with his other hand, he reaches and pinches my nipple between two fingers. I gasp, my hands flying above my head in helpless defeat as my orgasm rolls through me. The one that was brought on by a cock *that wasn't even inside me.*

Then, when I'm still spiraling, he enters me, plunging deep and his lips are at my ear.

"That might be the sexist thing I've ever seen." His whisper is intense, and I shiver in response. "What you just did for me was amazing, and the only thing I want to do right now is return the favor."

With that, he draws back, so slowly it creates an ache somewhere deep inside. My walls are clenching with the need to keep him close and make him move faster.

When he slides back inside, his teeth clench, and as he stares down at me the expression in his eyes is sinful. "God, darlin'...you feel amazing. I can't...fuck, it's so good."

Unable to help himself any longer, he begins to slam into me like a man possessed, and I'm meeting him thrust for thrust, my body responding to his in a way that I never thought was possible.

I've never thought of myself as a sexual person, because who has the time? I was a mom. That's it. But now…now I'm like a tigress in the bedroom with Jeremy. I can't get enough, and I want him to give me everything he's holding back. Harder, stronger, and more intense.

"Yes…oh, God yes!"

In response to my pleasure-filled scream, Jeremy places a hand over my mouth and continues to pound me until my body stiffens around him with my impending climax.

"That's it, Rayne…fall. I've got you. Always." He's breathless, his skin slick with sweat as my hands grip his shoulders hard enough to leave a mark.

But I do. I fall. Because that was always going to happen with Jeremy.

It was inevitable.

Above me, he trembles. His mouth is tight, his forehead creased with the strain. But he doesn't drop eye contact while he releases into me. Instead, he brushes my matted hair out of my face and gently touches his lips to mine.

His sweetness nearly breaks me.

When it comes to Jeremy Teague, why did I ever think I'd outgrown him? Why'd I ever think the love we shared so long ago, the love that created Decker, would have faded away?

25

JEREMY

When Rayne follows Jacob into the conference room the following afternoon, I catch her eye and shoot her a reassuring smile. She glances around the table at the members of the team, minus Ronin and Grisham, with a nervous smile before sitting down in the big leather chair beside mine. Reaching for her hand under the table, I give it a small squeeze to let her know that I'm going to make sure everything will be all right.

Every member of NES will.

"We're ready to take action on your case, Rayne." Jacob indicates the screen, which displays the findings in my and Sayward's report.

Rayne's body goes tense and rigid in her chair. I stoke her leg, trying to surge warmth and reassurance from my body into hers. "What are you going to do?"

Jacob aims a pointed glance at me, and I point to the screen. "As I told you yesterday, Sayward and I were able to find a way into the Horton Tech server. And this morning, we found what we needed. We tried not to leave a trail, but time isn't on our side here. We don't want Horton to catch on that we have what we need before we pick him up. We want him neutralized before we call in the authorities, for your safety first and foremost."

Her big blue eyes are blinking rapidly as she processes what I'm saying. "You did it? You found the proof?"

Nodding, I smile. "Yeah. You were absolutely right in what you saw. He's a slimeball thief, and there's proof there in the system. We downloaded what we needed this morning, and we can hand it over to the SEC when we're ready. I also want to pass on the threats he used against you to the police so he can also be charged with stalking and attempted kidnapping. The asshole is going down, darlin'."

Relief breaks across her face and her smile curves softly on her lips. "That's…oh, my God." She glances around the table. "All of you are so amazing. Thank you."

Jacob offers a tight smile. "Don't thank us yet, Rayne. The bastard's still out there. Ronin and Grisham are out right now, tailing the P.I. guy to see if he'll lead them to Horton's hideout. When we get him, we'll let you know."

She glances at me, and the worry is back on her face.

"I'm staying by your side, Rayne. Until this is over."

And for a lot longer after that.

"And Decker? He's unprotected at school." The anxiety bleeds through in her voice.

"We'll have someone situated outside the school within the next few minutes. Our son will be safe, Rayne." That's something I'll always make sure of.

Relaxing, she nods. "Sounds good to me." She glances around the table once again. "Is there anything I can be doing to help?"

Dare shakes his head. "Nah. This is what we do. Your man there is the brains behind the tech. He loves gadgets and all the things that make a mission fun. Makes sure we're outfitted with the most up-to-date materials. Ghost is practically a tactical genius. I can fix and drive just about anything…better than most stuntmen can."

He swivels his chair to face me at my snicker. "What's that, Teague? Something to say?"

Clearing my throat, I flick a hand at him. "No, of course not, Wheels. Carry on with your descriptions."

With a confident, crooked grin, Dare smoothes his dark hair back from his forehead and continues. He gestures toward Jacob. "Boss Man here is the best there is. He's seen it all, and he's taken down monsters worse than Horton. Dude picked the wrong woman to mess with when he came after you, Rayne."

Rayne has been listening to all of this with an amused expression, rapt with curiosity. She places her elbows on the table, leaning forward. "And what's Ronin's…I mean, Swagger's specialty?"

I roll my eyes skyward while Dare mimics her position, leaning in. He keeps his face completely deadpan. "Swagger? He's an interrogation expert. He excels at all the ways to torture a man without killing him."

Rayne's quick intake of air has me pushing back from the table. "Are we excused, Boss Man?"

Jacob nods, and I pull Rayne up from the table. I keep her hand wrapped up in mine as we walk back to the lobby.

Standing in front of Rayne's desk, I wrap my arms around her. She settles into me, her sigh muffled against my chest.

"This is all really going to be okay?" Her voice is full of uncertainty that rips through my insides like wildfire.

"It is." I pull back, holding her out from me a little bit so I can get lost in the dark blue ocean of her eyes. "I told you that you and Decker were safe with me, and I meant it."

Her tongue runs across her plump lips as she nods, and there's a dark, sweet stirring in my chest. I let my hands slide down her shoulders, caressing her arms. Her smooth skin is exposed thanks to her sleeveless top, and I catch her hands in mine.

"Hey," I murmur. "Call Macy. Let's go out for a little bit after work today. Not too late, just something to help take your mind off of this while the guys are rounding things up."

Her face lights up. "Really? You want to take me on a date, Jer?"

Chuckling softly, I rub my head. "The fact that you sound so delighted and surprised about that means I've been doing something wrong. So yes. Drinks after work to start making up for the lack of dates so far."

Her smile turns coy. "Well, things have been complicated. And hectic. And I mean, maybe taking your baby mama out on a date..."

Spluttering, I pull her against me. "Please do me a favor and don't ever call yourself my baby mama again."

She smirks. "I want fancy drinks. Like ones in glasses that'll break if we drop them and that have snazzy names I've never heard of."

"Snazzy?"

She gives a firm nod. "And then you have a deal. I won't call myself your baby mama anymore."

"God…it's like negotiating with a terrorist. Deal."

The restaurant, a classy establishment located just steps from the beach, is close enough to NES for us to walk. In the warm orange glow of the dusky sun, I hold Rayne's hand, and I can't remember the last time I felt my stomach shifting with nerves.

It feels just the way it did the first time I ever took her out, back in high school. And that's probably the last time I was so ripe with nervous energy. Everything is so different now—we're adults, we have a kid together, and I've been all the way around the world and back again more than once. But yet, staring down at her with the backdrop of the ocean behind us, my vision is filled with everything I ever wanted and never thought I'd get.

Holding the restaurant door open for her, I place my hand on the small of her back and guide her inside. Strolling up to the bar, I pull out her stool and signal the bartender that we'd like to order a drink.

"What do you want?" I ask her as she peruses the wall of liquor bottles before us.

The glass-topped bar is sleek, just like the rest of the place, and glancing around I take in our surroundings with meticulous precision. Date or not, I haven't forgotten that Rayne was almost snatched out from under me once already. I need to make sure every aspect of her life is safe until the bastard Horton is brought in. My fingers twitch, itching to grab my phone and check in with Ghost and Swagger, who are still staking out the sleazy private investigator.

When I glance back at Rayne, she's holding a cocktail menu in her slender hands.

"Hey. What sounds fancier? A sloe gin fizz, or a Delancey?"

Deciding that all the patrons in the bar area seem unsuspicious enough, I focus on her. "Definitely the Delancey. I mean, from the name of it, you can't even tell what kind of alcohol is in it. That's the true trademark of a fancy drink."

She nods, solemnity on her face. "Absolutely. And what will you have?"

The bartender appears in front of us, tucking a towel into his black slacks. "What can I get you two?"

Inclining my head toward Rayne, I smile. "A Delancey for my lady. And a Yuengling for me."

Rayne gasps. "Um, excuse me? We're going fancy, Mr. Teague." She zeroes in on the bartender, her hair swinging over one shoulder. "He'll have a Bowery Fix."

I bite my lip around a groan. "Darlin', I don't even know what's in that."

She shoots me a devilish smile. "Exactly. Live a little, Baby Daddy."

The bartender's eyes bug a little, but he smiles and turns away to fix our drinks.

I clear my throat. "I thought we had a deal?"

Rayne nods. "We sure did. I agreed that if you took me to a fancy place for drinks I would not call myself your baby mama anymore. But I said nothing about calling you my baby daddy."

Gripping the back of her neck, I pull her toward me until I can taste her. Moving my lips against hers, I nip and suck until the bartender returns and sets our drinks down in front of us, disappearing discreetly. Glancing down at them and then returning my attention to Rayne, I take her mouth once more.

When we finally pull away, she's breathless and my heart is thumping wildly against the cage of my chest.

"Were you trying to shut me up?" she asks, her eyes bright, her lips plump from my kiss.

My whole body now wide awake thanks to the taste of her, I shake my head. "Maybe. Either way, it worked for me. How about you?"

She grabs her drink and sips without breaking eye contact with me. "Works for me."

She watches me while I take my first sip. "How is it?"

Screwing up my face, I blow out a breath. "It tastes like it looks. Very yellow."

Rayne gives me a doubtful look. "How can a drink taste yellow?"

Taking another sip, I shiver. "This one does."

Turning toward me, she crosses her legs. The movement catches my attention, because the skirt she's wearing has ridden up to midthigh. I turn toward her and place my legs on the outside of hers.

"Jeremy..." Her tone grows serious.

"Uh-oh."

Slapping me gently on the thigh, she smiles and my hand engulfs hers. "Thank you."

"You don't have to thank me, Rayne."

She sighs. "Why? Because you feel obligated to take care of me?"

Whoa. Is that what she thinks?

Holding her chin in my hand, I hold her stare. "There is no obligation when it comes to you. There is no obligation when it comes to my son. All there is, is love."

Her eyes go wide. "What are you saying, Jeremy?"

I pick up my fruity drink and drain it in a gulp.

Taking a deep breath, I let the words fall from my lips. Not only because she needs to hear them right now, but because I need to say them. There's a pressing need to make sure she knows what's inside of me, and how vital she is at this point. Losing Rayne is not an option.

"I love you, Rayne. I never stopped. I never will."

When I glance at her again, her eyes are glistening. Her voice is nothing but a whisper. The bar around us, the buzzing of the bartender, the chatter of the patrons, it all drains away. Fades to black. "I thought I'd never hear you say those words again. At one point, I had convinced myself that I didn't need them."

She sniffles, and I lean forward so that our foreheads are touching. "And what do you think now?" My voice is rough with emotion.

"I think that I've never needed anything so much in my life. I love you, too, Jer."

I'm saturated with feeling. The feeling of her skin touching mine. The feeling of my heart filling up with all things Rayne. The feeling of my tongue growing thicker in my mouth and my head buzzing with rain clouds.

Wait...what?

Pulling away from Rayne, I overshoot the movement and almost fall backward off the stool.

Rayne frowns. "Jeremy? What's wrong?"

Shaking my head to clear it and finding out that I can't, I glance around me. Everything in the bar has gone hazy.

Somewhere in my mind, my instincts try to lock down, attempting to help my brain wrap around the situation.

My words are thick. "Something's wrong, Rayne."

Alarm creeps into her expression, her eyes stark with fear. "Are you sick? What can I do?"

Glancing around me once more, there's a man only two seats away from me. When I look at him, he smiles and touches the brim of his baseball cap.

"Rayne." I try to infuse the urgency I feel into my voice, but I come off sounding tired. "I've been drugged. Call Ronin. Don't leave the bar. Call *now.*"

It's the last thing I remember.

26

RAYNE

I'm watching in absolute shock and terror as Jeremy lurches forward, his hand jerking out to knock over my glass. I've only taken a sip, and when I glance at Jeremy's glass to see that he's downed the entire thing, it all clicks into place. Jeremy is conscious, but barely, as his head collapses onto the bar top.

"Your man having trouble holding his liquor?" The bartender's critical accusation comes from lips twisted in irritation as he mops up the spill.

"More like he has trouble keeping it together when our drinks have been drugged," I snap, glancing around the bar.

When my eyes land on two men who are watching me intently with scowls on their faces, my stomach flips over twice. Pulling out my phone, I hold their gazes and raise my voice.

"Ronin? It's Rayne. Yeah, I'm at The 501 with Jeremy, and someone drugged his drink. I will stay put, Ronin, I promise. Five minutes? Okay."

I slam the phone back down on the counter and glare at the unknown men. "Five minutes to move your ass before reinforcements get here. I'm not going anywhere with you, ass-holes."

One's eyes narrow as he assesses Jeremy and then glances at my empty glass. Hopping down from his stool, he pulls out his phone and starts to speak urgently into it as he pushes through the crowded bar to get to the front door. The other follows behind, clearly knowing they can't cause a scene in a crowded bar.

"Get us some water." Snapping out of his surprised trance, the bartender grabs a bottle of water and slides it across the bar top.

"Hold on Jer." I rub the cool bottle over the back of his neck. His skin is damp with sweat and his breathing is ragged. "Help is on the way."

"Rayne…" His voice is a garbled murmur. "Stay."

"I'm right here, baby. Not leaving. I'm okay."

I rub his face and attempt, and fail, to get him to drink water as I wait, and it doesn't take long before Ronin Shaw is walking through the door.

"Okay, Rayne?" he asks as he helps Jeremy to his feet.

Right behind him, Grisham takes my arm and glances around. "Perp still here?"

Shaking my head guiltily, I frown. "Two of them. They're gone. I snapped and told them to leave. I'm sorry I confronted them. I should have waited. "

We exit the restaurant, Ronin and Grisham both heaving Jeremy's large body with them. Jeremy's taking dragging footsteps, doing his best to help his buddies out, but he's in rough shape, and fury burns through me.

"What did they think they were going to do?" The question shoots out of my mouth as I walk beside Ronin.

Ronin grunts as he places Jeremy into the backseat of an SUV. "They likely wanted to drug you both. Take Jeremy out of the picture so they could grab you. My guess is that Horton is sending men after you to bring you to him alive. He wants something."

Shuddering, I picture Wagner's intense blue eyes and twisted, furious mouth. "He wants me."

Ronin glances at me as he gently nudges me into the front seat of the vehicle that Grisham is now starting. "Not gonna happen, sweetheart."

Twisting around to look at Jeremy in the backseat, I sigh. "Is he going to be okay?"

Ronin, climbing in beside Jeremy, nods. "Oh, yeah. He'll have a hell of a headache in the morning, but he'll be fine."

Biting my lip, I pull out my phone. "I'm going to call my friend Macy. She has Decker; I need to make sure he's okay."

Ronin grunts. "Dare will continue to keep watch on him. He'll call if there's trouble."

Letting out a sigh of relief, I make the call and ask Macy if Decker can stay the night with her and inform her that a member of Night Eagle is keeping watch over her house. I don't want Decker seeing Jeremy like this. We plan for me to pick him up after school tomorrow.

Glancing into the backseat again, I note that Jeremy's head is against the window and his eyes are closed. Settling into the front seat with a frustrated sigh, I speak to Ronin and Grisham. "What now?"

Grisham glances over at me. "Now we take you guys home. Swagger will stay with you tonight, watch over you while Brains is out."

Wringing my hands, and watching the scene change from beach town to downtown, my heart sinks. "He's going to be so upset in the morning. I don't know how to thank you guys for everything you're doing for me. I've brought so much trouble into your lives."

Ronin leans forward, his hand landing with gentle force on my shoulder. "Hey. You're family now, Rayne. Doesn't matter how long we've known you. We protect our own. And you're ours. It'd be the same with Dare's wife, Berkeley, or Grisham's fiancée, Greta."

Nodding, offer up a weak smile. "Thanks."

When we arrive at Jeremy's house, Grisham pulls all the way around to the garage in back and both guys help Jeremy, who is now almost completely unconscious, out of the car. Hurrying ahead to open the door for him, they drag him inside the house to a chorus of distressed barks from Night.

Rubbing the big dog's head, I talk softly to him. "It's okay, boy. Jer's just had a rough night. He'll be good as new in the morning."

Ronin and Grisham herd Jeremy up the stairs while I scoop out Night's food and place it in his dish. After I've filled his bowl with fresh water, Grisham and Ronin are heading back down the stairs. When they enter the kitchen again, I lean against the countertop.

"Ghost is going back out on surveillance. Private Eye hasn't led us to Horton yet. Something tells me that he's going to, though, so we're not giving up. If he doesn't make contact again with him, either by phone or in person, we'll find another way to get to the bastard. I promise you that. This will end, Rayne."

Unsure, my thoughts turn dark.

What if this doesn't end? What if he just keeps coming after me and the next time Jeremy ends up hurt, or…worse? I'd never be able to live with myself. And what if one of the guys lost their life over me? I'd never be able to look their wives in the eye. Ronin's right, this does have to end. But what if I'm the only one who can end it?

My phone buzzes on the countertop, and I pick it up to read the screen. A text from a blocked number. My stomach clenches as I read the scrolling words.

I'm growing tired of this game, Rayne. This will end. One way or another. Come to me, and no one gets hurt. Don't, and I'll take you forcibly, and take down everyone around you in the process.

My knees buckle and my heart buzzes too fast in my ears. The color must have drained from my face because Ronin grabs hold of my arm to steady me while Grisham grabs my phone from my trembling hands.

His mouth sets in a line, and he shows the text to Ronin.

"Don't even think about it, Rayne," Grisham warns. "He's trying to scare you, get into your head."

"It's working."

Ronin rubs my shoulder, trying to reassure me and place me onto a barstool at the same time. "You're safe with us. He can't get to you, Rayne. Trust us, all right?"

Shutting my eyes tight, I cover my face with my hands and take a deep, shuddering breath. "I do."

And it's true. I do trust these men to protect me. Each and every one of them wears his own special brand of a badass hero cape. Their competency is on another level. I've never seen anything like them.

I don't miss the concerned glance exchanged between Ronin and Grisham. Standing up, I give each man a hug on impulse. They have lives; I know they don't usually work twenty-four/seven. But apparently, my case never ends.

"Thank you both. I need to check on Jer."

Ronin nods. "Settle in for the night, Rayne. I'll lock up as soon as Ghost leaves and arm the security system. I'll probably watch Brains's camera feeds for a while, just to make sure everything is quiet. I'll be on the couch all night if you need me."

Grateful, I give him a nod and head out of the kitchen with Night on my heels.

Opening the door to the bedroom, I take note of Jeremy's prone form on the bed. Night trots over and drops his big, blocky head down on the mattress with a quiet whine, staring at his master with an anxious gaze.

"It's okay, buddy," I whisper, pulling my clothes off and grabbing one of Jeremy's T-shirts to slip into. "He'll be good as new in the morning."

Sliding under the covers, I attach myself to Jeremy's side and rub a hand over his hard chest. He stirs, but barely, turning into me and wrapping an arm protectively around my mid-section. Even drugged and passed out, his body is trained to protect me.

With a sigh, I close my eyes and drift to sleep.

27

JEREMY

I cracked my eyes open and immediately shut them again, the light filtering in through the two bedroom windows slicing through my head like a sword. With a silent curse, I roll over to face the opposite side of the room and gingerly pry my eyes open again. They are grainy, and the pain in my head is a motherfucker, but the sight in front of me is worth all the pain in the world.

Rayne is still sleeping, one arm thrust above her and the other draped across her middle. Her face is so peaceful in the early morning light that I go still while I stare. Trying to recall the previous night with her, I frown as the fuzzy details evade me.

Dinner…right? No, drinks. She was stressed about everything happening with that sick fuck Horton, so I took her to that swanky place near NES…

Frowning, my face screws up with the effort to remember. Did I drink too much? Not likely, not when I had Rayne with me and a known psychopath stalking her every move.

A picture from the previous night slams into me: men sitting near us at the bar, smug smiles; one stares at Rayne and tips his hat at me.

"Son of a bitch!" Sitting straight up in bed, I rub my head when it protests the quick movement.

"Jer?" Rayne's sexy, groggy morning voice draws my attention back down to where she lies.

Lying back down beside her, I study her face, using my fingers to trace the delicate lines. When my thumb scrapes gently across her full bottom lip, her eyes flutter open completely.

"Hey." Her face lights up with a sweet smile, and all I want to do is pull her into my arms and kiss her.

"You okay, darlin'?" My voice is urgent. "Last night…I went down, right? Motherfucker drugged my drink?"

Her lips roll between her teeth and her eyes show concern. "You remember? How are you feeling this morning?"

I prop my head up on my elbow and study her face, scan her body where it's visible, and cup her cheek. "You're safe. Thank God. What happened, Rayne? And where's Decker?"

Sitting up, I pull her with me as agitation and a serious sense of pissed-offness invades my system. Pulling her close, I feel her touch is the only thing that can bring any sort of calm to my chaotic brain. All I can think about is the fact that I was out of commission the previous night, leaving her to fend for herself against the maniac hunting her.

Goddammit. I can't do this for one more day. We have to bring Wagner Horton down.

"Well…" Rayne curls her body against mine, worrying her

bottom lip as she peeks up at me. "Decker's safe. He's at Macy's with Dare keeping watch. And you were really amazing, considering. You realized what had happened immediately, told me your drink had been drugged. You knocked mine over before I could take another sip, and you told me to call Ronin, which I did."

"Swagger? He here?" Glancing at the closed bedroom door, all I see is Night curled up on his dog bed close by.

Rayne nods. "Yep. Downstairs on the couch all night."

I take a deep breath in through my nose, hold it, and release it slowly through my mouth. "Good. When I think about what could have happened, Rayne...I could kill someone. With my bare hands."

Shaking her head, she rests it on my shoulder and squeezes my arm with one of her hands. "Don't. I'm safe. Decker's safe. Everything is okay."

As the anger surges through me to a point I can no longer control, I shove the covers away and shoot out of bed. Walking to the window, I pull both hands behind my head and stare out onto the quiet tree-lined street. "This needs to end."

Turning back to Rayne, I stutter to a stop. Because she looks so damn gorgeous, sitting up against the headboard with messed-up hair and wearing my T-shirt. She's exactly the picture I want to see in my bed every single morning from here on out. But I can't truly enjoy it, not when I know someone's trying to rip her away from me.

"Baby...I want you to pull out a bag for you and one for Decker. Start packing. I'm going to go down to talk to Swagger."

Moving toward the door, I stop when I hear the alarm in her voice. "Packing?"

I glance over at her. "I'm getting you and Decker out of Wilmington. My family has to come first. I want you guys out of here while the team wraps this up."

Her eyebrows scrunch together in an adorable frown I want to kiss off her face. "I don't want to leave without you, Jeremy."

Striding back to the bed, I lean down and take her mouth. She tastes so sweet, even first thing in the morning. When the pounding in my head reminds me that I still have a nasty hangover courtesy of Wagner Horton, I pull away with a whole lot of fucking regret.

"I'm sorry," I whisper, leaning my forehead against hers. "But I didn't mean I was sending you and Deck away. Neither of you are going anywhere without me."

Pulling back, the corners of her mouth tip up in a smile. "Really?"

Nodding, I focus on her deep blue eyes. "Yeah, darlin'. Not letting you out of my sight. The team can go in and get Horton at this point, as soon as they pinpoint his location. Then they'll call in the authorities, he'll be arrested, and we're back here in a matter of days."

She releases a happy sigh. "I like this plan."

Giving her a quick kiss before turning for the door once more, I throw back over my shoulder, "Me, too."

Night rushes off his bed, stretches his front paws out in front of him and arches his back, and then bounds in front of me to beat me down the stairs. I find Swagger in the kitchen, sipping from a mug of coffee.

"You need a shave." Indicating the few days' worth of dark scruff on his face, I head straight for the coffeemaker.

Without glancing up from his mug, he fires back. "Scruff is sexy. No one told you?"

Rubbing a hand over my usually clean-shaven face, I smirk because I've had too much on my mind to shave for the past few days. "Yeah, I got the memo."

Grabbing a mug from the cabinet and pouring a cup of the steaming black liquid, I carry it to the counter across from Swagger. He glances up and I hold my fist out.

"I owe you."

"Bullshit. We're a team, always have been. She's important to you, she's important to me."

"She's the mother of my kid." Saying it out loud still freaks me out, but in a good way. "Thanks for keeping her safe."

Swagger leans back on his stool, folding his arms across his chest. "When do I get to meet the kid? I'm pretty sure it's gonna blow my mind, seeing you as a dad."

The thought of Decker brings an immediate smile to my face. "If it weren't for all the crazy shit going on, everyone would have met the little dude already. I'll plan a cookout for when we get back. Everyone's invited."

Swagger frowns. "Back from where?"

Holding up a finger, I retrieve my cell phone from the charging dock where someone placed it last night and bring it back to the island. Pulling up Boss Man's number, I hit SEND and place the phone on the counter.

"Heard about what happened." Boss Man's voice barks out of the speaker. "Everything all right this morning?"

"Yeah, thanks. But it's too hot in Wilmington right now. I'm thinking I need to take Rayne and Decker away for a few days while the team neutralizes Horton."

Ronin lifts a brow, and I lift one shoulder in a shrug.

I've never walked away from a mission before. But in this case, my family *is* my mission. And getting them out of harm's way is my first priority. I know I can count on the rest of the NES team to finish what I started. And I'm the only one I feel comfortable enough protecting my family."

"I can compute with that plan, Brains." Jacob Owen's voice is thoughtful. "But I don't want to send you alone. Take Wheels with you. Have any idea where you're going?"

"Haven't gotten that far, Boss."

"Mountains. I have a cabin in the high country that's off the beaten path. You three can hole up there until we bring Horton in. Shouldn't be long."

Relief swarms around me, mixing with gratitude. I would have found a place to take Decker and Rayne, someplace off the grid where we wouldn't be easily found, but Jacob had just made things that much easier.

After discussing logistics a few minutes further, I end the call. Taking a long swig of my coffee, I lean back and just breathe for a minute. Having a strategy in action for getting my family out of the fray brings me a sense relief. And an overwhelming feeling of determination to implement the plan as soon as possible.

"Rayne's upstairs packing." Chugging the rest of my coffee, I push it aside and glance at Swagger. Every muscle in my body is tense. No matter how many plans I make I'm not going to be able to relax until the threat to them is eliminated. And as important as it is for me to be the one keeping them safe, it's gonna drive me fucking insane that I'm not the one going after Horton.

"Hey." Swagger's voice breaks into my thoughts. "Don't sweat it. You know I'm gonna do this for you, bro."

"Yeah." I glance at him without smiling. "I know."

Swagger shoves back from the counter. "I'm headed home to shower and then I'm headed into the office. Today, Brains. We bring him down today and hopefully you can bring your family back home tomorrow."

Tomorrow.

This will be over tomorrow, and then I can start a life with Rayne and my son.

Tomorrow.

28

RAYNE

So where are we going?" Decker's voice is brimming with excitement, and I turn around in my seat to glance back at him.

The huge, elated smile on his face is all the reward I need. Maybe this trip isn't just a spur-of-the-moment vacation with my son and the man I'm newly reunited with, but couldn't we pretend? Can't I just imagine that I'm not running away from Wilmington because my ex-boss is on the warpath and I'm his number one target? Can't I imagine that the sole purpose of this trip is for my son and I to bond with his father, as a family, for the very first time?

I can and I will, dammit. The fact that Dare is following behind us in his truck is of no consequence. None at all.

Glancing at Jeremy, my cheeks threatening to split my face, I raise my brows. "Should we tell him?"

He twists his lips to one side, feigning contemplation. "Mmmm. Not sure. Don't know if my son is rugged enough to handle a trip to the mountains."

"I'm rugged!" Decker's tone was completely indignant. One hand reaches down absently to stroke Night's head, which is settled comfortably in Decker's lap as he's curled up on the seat beside him. "What does *rugged* mean?"

Laughing, I reach back to grasp his chin in my fingers. "Rugged is a rough and tumble kinda guy, sweetheart."

Jeremy chimes in, "Yeah. And we fish, and hike, and we like to shoot stuff. And we do stuff on boats. Oh, and we grunt."

Decker's giggling, but at the last he pauses. "Grunt?"

Lifting his head, Jeremy's best grunt echoes through the Land Cruiser. Turning from Decker to Jeremy, I blink twice in amazement. Then I burst into laughter. Not just giggles, either. The kind of laughter that has me leaning forward, gripping my cramping stomach.

"Hey." Jeremy scowls.

When I can't stop the peals of laughter, and Decker joins in from the backseat, he raises his voice. *"Hey."*

Gasping for breath, I reach over and grab the rock-hard muscle of Jeremy's thigh. My laughing fades as his muscle twitches under my touch and my thoughts turn in a completely different direction. "Um, was that your very best grunt, Mr. Teague?"

With a tiny twitch of his lips, he nods. Glancing in the rearview, he beseeches Decker. "It was a damn good one, right, Deck?"

Decker's response is prompt. "Swear jar!"

Jeremy chuckles, rubbing his jaw with one hand while the other maneuvers us onto the famed Skyline Drive, heading into the Blue Ridge Mountains. "Gonna be hard to remember that."

"That's okay with me." Decker's voice is full of amusement. "You know I get the money when the swear jar is full, right?"

Jeremy turns mock shocked eyes into the rearview mirror. "What? I smell a scam!"

Leaning my head back against the seat, the only thing I can do at this moment is smile.

The smile is still hanging there an hour later, when the car is quiet except for Decker's heavy, even breathing.

"Hey." Jeremy's deep voice reaches me across the center console, reaching inside me to entice a shiver. "What's going through your head over there?"

He picks up my palm, his large fingers sliding between mine and threading them together. Bringing my hand to his lips, they brush softly against my skin.

"I'm pretending." I steal a quick glance at his handsome profile: the strong jaw dusted with golden hair, his straight nose, and his gorgeously plump lips. He's chiseled male perfection, all grown up from the boy I first fell in love with. The fact that he's sitting here beside me with our son in the backseat is nothing short of a miracle.

"Pretending?" His tone is half-amused, half-bewildered. "Pretending what?"

I bring our hands to my mouth and plant an openmouthed kiss on his hand. "That this is real."

His returning glance is sharp, his brow furrowed with worry lines. "Darlin', this *is* real."

I shake my head, suddenly urgent for him to understand. "It's not real in my head yet, Jer. Not really. I mean…we're taking a break from reality right now. We're pretending like we're on a vacation for Decker, when we know what's really going on. And you and I…it's all been so amazing between us, and with Decker. Despite what' s going on with Wagner, it feels like it's too good to be true."

"Rayne—"

"No, I'm serious." I continue, suddenly amped up like I've been chugging Mountain Dew all day, when in reality my brain is working on overdrive as a result of all of my heightened emotions. "It's like, I know that you're here with me and Decker because you're this amazing guy, kind of like a superhero, really, with all the muscles and the alpha complex and the computer skills and not to mention the fighting and superior use of weapons—and I know that no matter what happens you're going to do your best to protect us. But when it all ends and we're just back home in Wilmington, and it'll be time for Decker and me to find our own place and it's back to work as usual and Olive is going to come back and if your grandparents decide they want to be in your life again—"

"Rayne."

Jeremy's voice is low and growly and stern, and it stops me midsentence, and my head immediately drops to study my hands. They're twisting around and around in my lap. I'm not even sure when I let Jeremy's hand go, sometime during that insane tirade of word vomit.

"Look at me, darlin'."

Turning my head and tilting it up, I watch his profile. He glances at me before setting his sights on the road again. "First of all…I'm not just here to protect you. I mean, yes—this is what I do for work and I'm damn good at it. We all are. But

I'm here with you right now because I want to be. I've had you in my bed because that's exactly where I want you to be."

From the backseat, Night lifts his head and gives a soft chuff.

Jeremy glances in the rearview mirror. "That's right. Tell her, Night."

Night barks again, then stands up, stretches, and turns himself around three times before settling with his head against the door. His eyes close once again.

"Baby." Jeremy's eyes plead with me to understand him. He takes my hand again and squeezes. "Did you say something about *finding your own place?*"

I nod.

"Because, I'm gonna pretend you didn't. You trying to find your own place would mean I'll have to beg you to stay, and I'm not much for begging. I want you and Decker to stay right where you are. Even when your sister gets back from Europe. Even if my grandparents come sniffing around, at which point I'll tell 'em to go straight to hell. You and me and Decker are together now. I don't want that to change."

His voice goes lower, softer. "Do you?"

I'm about to open my mouth to answer when Jeremy's cell phone rings. Pressing the Bluetooth button on the dash screen, he answers the call. "Yeah."

"Brains." Dare's voice barks from the speakers. "Take me off Bluetooth."

Immediately, Jeremy releases my hand and relinquishes the Bluetooth, picking up his phone and putting it to his ear. Searching his face, I see his eyes flick to the rearview mirror and back again. Then he does the same with each side mirror.

"Yeah. Nah, it's clear. What?" Jeremy listens to his phone, and I can see the way his posture has changed. His body is rigid in the seat, and his eyes are continually darting, roving, scanning the road in front of us and the expanse behind.

My heartbeat skyrockets. Glancing back at Decker, I'm relieved to see he's still asleep. But my hands grip my thighs, my eyes glued to Jeremy's face.

"Shit. Get Swagger to run the plates. Okay, Sayward, then." Jeremy listens to whatever Dare is explaining on the other end of the call.

Suddenly, his open palm slams into the steering wheel, and I jump in response. Checking the backseat again to see that Decker is still asleep, I breathe a little easier. But Night is sitting up in his seat, his eyes glued to Jeremy's headrest. He whines when he catches me staring.

"Goddammit." Jeremy's jaw is clenched, the muscle there ticking as he tries to stay calm.

"What's wrong?"

"Wheels," Jeremy speaks out of the side of his mouth. "Says there's been a sedan on his tail for the past twenty miles."

My eyes widening in alarm, I suck in a breath. "What does that mean?"

Jeremy shakes his head, contemplating. Both hands are gripping the wheel. It's obvious to me that he's trying to remain calm, and if this were any other situation for him at work, he probably would be. It's the fact that Decker and I are in the car with him that's making him tenser, more nervous that he usually would be.

"Okay…what do we do?"

"We change our route. Get off the highway, test out some back roads. If the sedan follows, we'll know they're not just a motorist on their way into the mountains."

I take a deep breath and count to ten, letting the air escape slowly with each second. "Jeremy? What happens if it's not just a passing motorist?"

His lips thin out, going white. "Normally, we'd use evasive procedures. We all know them, but Wheels is the best driver out there. I'd just follow suit."

Fear grips me by the throat, squeezing until barely any air gets through to my lungs. "But this isn't a normal situation, is it?"

Instead of answering, Jeremy focuses even harder on the road and drives on. I see the exit as it approaches, and Jeremy swerves onto it at the last minute, rather than turning on his blinker and slowing. I send up a silent prayer that it's the end of summer rather than the dead of winter. No icy mountain roads to worry about.

But I'm still scared shitless.

The thick mountaintops rising up to greet us in the distance, the sun is slowly sinking behind them. The sky is a violent blaze of orange and pink in the last waning light of day, and ordinarily this would be the most relaxing, picturesque drive possible. But now I can't even focus on a bit of the scenery. Not until I know what's going to happen next.

We've turned onto two different two-lane highways, twisting, winding country roads that serve as mountain passes when another call comes through on Jeremy's phone. This time, he keeps the Bluetooth on.

"Verdict?" Jeremy's voice radiates tension.

"Suspicious as hell. Still behind me. Thought he was gone for a minute there, he dropped his distance. But yeah, he's still back there."

"Fucking hell," mutters Jeremy.

"It's your call, man. Your family is in the car with you. Want me to take point?"

"Yeah." Jeremy grounds out, and I know that it kills him to give up the frontal position to Dare.

"Evasive?"

Jeremy frowns, glancing in the rearview at a still-sleeping Decker and then over at me. The turmoil in his expression is real, and my heart squeezes tight enough to ache just watching him.

"No. Can't take that kind of risk with Rayne and Decker."

Dare answers like he already knew what Jeremy's answer would be. "Copy that. Only one alternative, bro."

Jeremy's angry growl reverberates through the car, stirring Decker in the backseat and drawing out another low whine from Night.

"Yeah. Find a confrontation point."

29

JEREMY

Fuck. Fuck!

This is the absolute last thing I want to do with Rayne and Decker in the car.

It's funny, because I've never been afraid of a confrontation. They happen all the time when you're manning a battlefront, sweeping a hostile environment, or tracking down an enemy. Confrontation is what I've been trained for, although it's not always the wisest action. When I had to do it, my body always kicked into high gear and I acted off of training and instinct.

Right now, though, my instinct is telling me that I need to get my family the hell out of here. Right now, I'm truly afraid to face whoever's in that car, because it means that my Rayne and Decker have to face them, too. I could let Dare shift into evasive maneuvers, knowing that he's the best out there when it comes to driving and getting us out of harm's way. But the risk is too great. Having to weigh my options between bad and worse with my family on hand is the most difficult thing I've ever had to do.

A thin sheen of sweat coats my skin and my heart hammers with a pulsing rhythm against my ribs. Too fast. Too much adrenaline pours into my system, readying me for a battle I'm prepared to lay down my life for.

And the idea of that sacrifice means so much *more* now. More than it ever has before.

"Confrontation?" Rayne's voice rises to a level just below panic and just above anxious. "We can't do that, Jeremy."

"Mom…Jeremy? What's going on? Are we almost there?"

Decker's sleepy voice from the backseat rips my thoughts off of Rayne and toward him. "Nah, buddy. Not yet. We're just about to stop for a few minutes, that's all. You know what I want you to do? I want you to stay in the car. No matter what you hear. Got that, Deck?"

When I glance in the rearview to check for Decker's reaction, his face is all screwed up in confusion. "Yeah. Got it. Can Night stay, too?"

With a tight smile, I nod. "Pretty sure I couldn't tear Night away."

Rayne's voice, full of the strength and determination I've learned is her MO, rests a light hand on my thigh. My muscle twitches under her touch.

"Jeremy." She keeps her voice soft. "Promise me this is going to be okay."

Up ahead, Dare increases his speed, and I follow suit, glancing back in the rearview mirror at the sedan that's been following a couple hundred yards behind us. There's a bend in the road up ahead, and I know that's exactly where Dare is headed. Our speed ratchets until the suspect sedan is only a tiny dot in the distance and the curve in the road approaches fast.

"I promise you, darlin'. This will be okay. You stay in the car, too." My voice is just above a whisper, for Rayne's ears only. The last thing I want to do right now is scare Deck.

It's a damn stupid move to make that kind of promise. But after everything that Rayne's been through, in part because of me, I refuse to do anything else.

But why can't I keep the wave of dread surging through me at bay?

We were careful. No one should have followed us out of town. We took roundabout routes and kept our eyes glued to our backs the entire time. So if this is Horton or his men, how'd they find us on the open road deep into the Appalachians? The thought gives me pause. From the moment the whole story about her ex-boss poured out of Rayne, we've been behind the eight ball. We haven't caught up to the guy, we haven't been able to apprehend any of his accomplices. We've been jumping through hoops to locate him, and based on the fact that I haven't heard a word from the team back home, we're still searching.

I'm missing something vital when it comes to this case, and that fact is what slams me with icy fear right now.

"Bullshit. I'm not staying in the car, Jeremy. This case is about me, right? I want to be out there with you."

A rumble of anger rockets through my chest, at the same time a sliver of fear slices through my gut. "No fucking way, Rayne. You stay."

I can almost hear the stubborn streak settling into place as she lifts her chin. "I go."

Up ahead, Dare pulls off to the shoulder, far enough off of the main road not to be hit. His taillights are the brightest things in the darkening landscape. There's nothing around us for miles. This is it.

Pulling up behind him, I reach across Rayne and open the glove compartment. I have more weapons in the trunk, including an M-16 assault rifle with a scope and a brand-new, wickedly curved hunting knife, courtesy of NES weapons locker. Grabbing hold of my 9 mm and pulling it out of the glove box, I level my gaze at Rayne.

"You have one job right now, Rayne. And that's to stay with Decker."

"What if something happens?"

God, I have to give this woman credit. Her voice, which was rising with anxiety before, is now mostly controlled. I can hear the slight tremor, but her tone is even and she's trying like hell to keep her composure. I know it's for the sake of our son, who's petting Night in the backseat.

"Rayne." I grind the word out through my teeth. "I've gotta go. Stay in the car."

I can't wait for her to acknowledge my order. Dare's already out of his truck, armed, and moving with rapid steps toward the back of my SUV.

Slamming my door, I join him at the back and we both holster our guns. Our hands are free as we assume unthreatening positions, two guys just checking on an issue with our car on the shoulder of the road.

"Plan?" Knowing that my whole life is inside the Land Cruiser, I try hard to focus on my teammate.

"Wait. See if he stops. If he does, we're ready. He's either gonna barrel out of that car shooting, or he's gonna have something to say. Let's hope it's the latter."

At the sound of an engine roaring around the bend, we loosen our stances, turning our bodies so that we can conceal our weapons by our sides at the ready beside the car.

"Better yet, let's hope that whoever is in that sedan just blows on by." My grumble is lost somewhere in the wind.

Headlights breach the dusk, and the sedan rolls around the bend. The brakes send a soft screech into the night, and I can't remember the last time a sound scared me.

But this one does.

"Here we go," murmurs Dare.

We both rise to our full heights and face the sedan now rolling to a stop some fifty feet from where we stand behind the Land Cruiser. The headlights remain on, and I stare just off to the side of them so I won't be blinded. Four car doors open, and four men remove themselves from the car and stand to face us.

They're all dressed casually, except for one who apparently believes that dress shoes, slacks, and a tailored shirt are the best wear for a mountain excursion. As the group begins to approach, Dare and I pull our weapons.

"Stop." My voice is deadly as my training kicks into high gear. "Not another step, or I will shoot to kill. Who are you?"

"Oh, I think the formalities are unnecessary at this point, don't you, Mr. Teague? Or should I say Sergeant

Teague, elite member of the Night Eagle Security Team?"

My blood begins to simmer in my veins as I lower my gun just enough to get a good look at the speaker. He moves to stand in the center of the pack of four, obviously claiming the leadership spot.

And from the polished appearance that matches every picture I've discovered online, I can see that this is Wagner Horton, in the flesh.

"Decide to come yourself this time, huh, Horton? Tired of seeing the dickheads you send coming back empty-handed? Ready to settle this like a man?" My voice is low, dangerous, taunting. I want to see how far I can push this asshole before he breaks. Before I break him.

Beside me, Dare shifts, and I know it's because he's covering all four men with his weapon. None of them have drawn, but each of their hands linger near their waists, and it doesn't take a genius to guess why.

"Taking a vacation, were you?" Wagner continues, seemingly unimpressed by my question. He gestures around him at the gorgeous landscape. "Mountains this time of year...very pretty. The air is just about to turn chilly, the leaves are readying themselves for a change..."

Horton's tone indicates that he has all the time in the world. I don't.

"What do you want? Ready to come on into our headquarters, tell us why you've been stalking Rayne?"

Horton tsks, and the sound of it sends a jolt of rage through my body. "Oh, yes. Let's talk about Rayne, shall we? My former employee. She ran away without giving me her two weeks' notice, did you know that, Mr. Teague? Very unprofessional of her. Also very unprofessional? The way she dressed around the office. She liked to tempt and tease me, you see. The woman has a hell of a set of legs on her, that's true. And that ass, in a tight skirt…well, I can see why you're taking her on a spur-of-the-moment getaway."

He's trying to bait me. It's obvious and it's pathetic, and I'm trained way better than that. He can't get to Rayne. Not unless he goes through me.

"Again, I'm asking you. For the last time." I take three steps closer, and the men on either side of Horton bristle, stepping forward.

But Horton only smiles, his teeth gleaming in the semidark glow of the early evening. "Not a patient man, I see? That, I can understand. Neither am I. So let's get down to it. Your Rayne has seen something that didn't concern her. And if you release her to me now, I promise not to hurt her. I just want to know what she knows, so I can do a little damage control. Explain it to her properly."

Lying son of a bitch.

"Liar!"

Rayne's voice approaches from the side of the car, and I let out a whole slew of curses in my head.

"Stay. Back. Rayne." Each word is ground out, and I don't turn my head to look at her because I refuse to take my eyes off of Horton. But I can hear her footsteps crunching against gravel, retreating once more and I breathe a silent sigh of relief.

From inside the Land Cruiser, Night begins to bark.

The fact that I don't know where this standoff is going to

go, the virtual unpredictability of it, threatens to drive me insane. Dare and I are outnumbered, that much is obvious. But I know that it doesn't matter. These men are hired muscle.

Not trained, lethal soldiers.

But underestimating Horton would be a mistake. The fact that he's here himself says something. He's done waiting, he's ready to capitalize on his end game, whatever that might be. And thus far, he's had the upper hand. The strong desire racing along inside of me to end this can't get in the way of my own common sense.

Without verbally communicating with one another, Dare and I begin to edge out. Our movements are so marginal, it shouldn't be apparent to the four men standing before us that we're slowly going to close in on them from either side.

Keep talking, Horton.

"The way I hear it, you're a thief. Isn't that right, Horton?" My voice is calm, steady, smooth. Collected. Thank God for desert ops training. Dealing with snakes in the desert is exactly the same as dealing with snakes on your own soil. No sudden moves, and always come at them from behind.

Dare and I can't inch any farther unless we force them to break their tight formation.

Lowering my weapon, I slowly place it in its holster. "See? We can be friendly here, can't we? We can sort all this out. Why don't you tell me what Rayne saw."

Let me hear you lie through your teeth some more, you son of a bitch.

The growl of an engine drifts toward us from the distance, and Dare tenses beside me. We could put our guns down for the sake of the passing motorist to prevent calling attention to ourselves, but I'd be willing to bet that the second our weapons are no longer drawn, Horton's men will strike. So through an unspoken agreement, we keep our revolvers trained at the enemy. But as all four men glance at the bend in the road, Dare and I each take a step farther away from each other and toward them.

At this point, I hope the motorist calls 9-1-1. Having the cops show up right now would be a relief, not a hindrance. Even though at this point I wish I was still in Wilmington, where I have PD connections from when Swagger and I were on the force.

A black SUV tears around the bend, blowing past us, moving too fast for me to get a good look. But then the screech of breaks warns us that the vehicle is stopping, the loud crunch of tires on loose rock alerting us to the fact that the SUV is turning around.

What the hell? This person have a death wish?

Keeping my eyes trained on Horton, something inside me crumbles when his calm smile grows into a sneer. And I know right then that we're in trouble. I hear the sound of more than one car door opening, but no resulting slam of the doors closing.

"Wheels." I grind out, the sick feeling in my stomach ramping up to ice-cold, panicked terror. But it's too late.

Rayne's startled cry forces me to turn toward her.

Dare acts on instinct: he pivots toward the closest man to him and uses the butt of his revolver to smash it into the guy's temple. Going down like an anchor at sea, the guy crumbles as another man pulls his gun from his waist holster. Dare's hand snaps out, grabbing the guy's wrist and twisting. The gun clatters to the pavement but Dare keeps twisting, snapping the man's wrist before planting a good into his knee and bowing the man's leg out. A scream of pain rips from the injured man as he slumps to the ground.

But I can't go after the last man or Horton, because Rayne is behind held against a newcomer's chest. I recognize the sickly pale face of Kevin O'Shea, private investigator. His white-blond hair is slicked back away from his face and his lips curve upward in a leer as he bends down close to a struggling Rayne's ear.

"Now, I'd hold still if I were you, sweetheart. Gonna get your man or your boy hurt acting like that."

She stills, all the color draining from her face.

"Let her go." I don't recognize my voice. It's sandpaper brushing over rough stones, and I clear my throat as I level my gun at the man clutching my world to his chest.

"Stop." Horton's voice slides over us all, but I don't turn to face him.

Dare stops, alerted by the sound of my pain, and when I glance at him he's standing at the head of one of the men he put on the ground. He's barely winded, and he now has his gun leveled at Horton while the last remaining casually dressed guard has his pointing at Dare's head.

From the Land Cruiser, Night's barks have reached an epic level of canine apprehension.

"I've never been a fan of weapons myself," Horton continues. "Too Neanderthal. Too messy." With a lazy wave of his hand, he gestures toward the other side of the Land Cruiser, where two more men, these two in a matching uniform of gray suits, stand waiting. Their suits clash absolutely with the nasty-looking rifles in their hands.

Horton aims his command at Rayne. "Instruct your son to remove himself from the car without releasing the attack dog."

"No." Rage blooms inside me, partially because Horton has the fucking balls to order Rayne around, and partly because of the utter helplessness of the situation. We're outnumbered, Rayne is in the hands of the enemy, and now they're bringing my son into the fold.

Dare stands motionless, his eyes darting, moving, missing nothing.

At least he took down two. But there are five more remaining, including Horton. And I don't like those odds, not when the lives of Rayne and my son are on the line.

I can't take any action that will risk their lives right here and now.

"Fuck you, Wagner." Rayne spits the words like knives, straight into Horton's smug face. I can't help the tendril of pride that curls through me at the show of her strength.

That's my girl.

"Very well. The alternative is that my men will start shooting into that car and we'll drag him out afterward. Is that the route you'd rather take?"

Rayne's gasp mingles with the nighttime sounds that have begun to descend on the landscape. Crickets, frogs, and an occasional stirring of leaves in the wind echo happily all around us.

With a growl ripping from my chest, I lunge at Horton, who takes a hasty step backward. His guard steps in front of him, pulling a Glock from the waistband of his jeans. He points it at me, and I freeze, but I don't lower my weapon.

I just don't know where to point it anymore.

If Rayne and Decker weren't a factor, Dare and I could have taken our chances fighting our way out of this.

But now? I might as well be weaponless and untrained.

"I will murder every single one of you. Painfully. If you hurt a fucking hair on my son's or my woman's head. I hope that's really fucking clear." Gathering myself, I toss the words out for the group, pulling myself to my full height and aiming my weapon around our little cluster.

"Noted," Horton drily. "Do it, Rayne."

Rayne's hands are balled into fists at her sides, her chest heaving with her own fury. Leaning down, she knocks on the window to the Land Cruiser and gestures that Decker should get out of the car.

"Fucking hell," mutters Dare.

Everyone's eyes are on Decker as my son steps from the vehicle, shutting the door on Night's frenzied barks. The dog throws himself against the door, trying like hell to force it open again.

Decker surveys the scene with wide, disbelieving eyes.

"It's okay, sweetheart." Rayne's voice trembles. "I'm right here."

Decker glances at her, and then at me and the weapon gripped in my hands. "Dad?"

Pain as pure as freshly fallen snow explodes inside me. It

mingles with the most unsullied type of love I've ever felt. The emotion is so strong, so goddamned *true* that I almost stagger backward under the weight of it.

It's the first time he's ever called me "Dad," and I'm about to lie to him.

"Everything's gonna be fine, Deck." Attempting to keep the absolute fear I feel right now out of my voice physically hurts.

Decker doesn't say anything else, not even a cry as one of the men in a suit grabs him and hustles him to the black SUV.

"Wait! What the fuck are you doing, Horton?" I turn to the calmest man on the scene. "You don't need my *son*. You don't need Rayne! She doesn't have any proof. I know everything she does, and I'm a computer hacker. Military trained. I'll teach you how to clean your system so there's not a trace of anything you don't want. Just leave them out of it."

"This is your only chance to take that deal." Dare's voice is pure steel laced with dangerous, dark promise. He wants to murder the man just as much as I do.

Horton tilts his head to the side. I can hear Decker struggling with the man placing him in the SUV, but then the sound is cut off as he slams the door on his cries. When I glance at Rayne, she's staring at me with tears streaming down her face. Willing me to do something.

But I just used the only card I have. I want—no, I *need*—Horton to take me instead of my family.

Horton's eyes land on Rayne, and the expression I see in them scares the shit out of me. It turns my stomach, sending fingers of dread snaking through the heart of me.

"That's an interesting offer, Mr. Teague. But Rayne here and

I have a history. I'd much rather have her by my side as I prepare to take over the tech world. She knows what I like."

I lunge again, and this time it's Dare who reaches out a vise-like arm to hold me back.

"Not letting you get a bullet put in you today. Stand down." His harsh whisper does nothing to lessen the anger fueling me into action.

"We'll be going now. Put her in the car with me," he instructs O'Shea.

Despite the fact that Rayne's struggling for all she's worth, O'Shea wrestles her toward the sedan.

"I'll kill you, O'Shea. I'll fucking kill you, I swear to God." My words are a promise, and O'Shea pauses with the slightest hint of fear in his eyes. But he follows orders, herding a kicking and biting Rayne to the car.

"We'll go after them." Dare's voice is low, for my ears only.

But I barely hear him, because all I can do is watch as the last man, gun trained on us, backs away. Moving his gun off of us long enough to shoot out all four tires on the Land Cruiser, his face breaks into a sinister grin. *Fuck.*

"You shoot, everyone goes down." Dare's words thrown at him are a warning.

The man blows us a kiss as he jumps into the backseat of the SUV with my son.

"Wait! Just fucking wait a minute!" I throw open the trunk of the Land Cruiser and grab Decker's backpack.

Sprinting to the man now waiting and watching me from the door of the SUV, I thrust the bag at him. "Take his bag. At least let him have his stuff."

With a sneer, the man grabs the bag, closes the door on my face as I take one last look at Decker's stricken face, and the big engine roars to life.

I watch as the two vehicles disappear back around the bend, probably standing there a beat too long, before Dare's voice breaks into my desolate thoughts.

"We need to regroup. Check in with the team. Boss Man will say we need to turn this over to the FBI. It's a kidnapping now."

My head snaps around. "I'm not reporting shit. That's my fucking *family*. I'm going after them my damn self, and if you aren't on board then this is where we split."

Dare studies me, his dark eyes brooding and wary. "Man…"

Holding up my hand, I head for the driver's seat of the Land Cruiser. As soon as I open the door, Night's ferocious barks turn to an anxious whine.

"What if it were Berkeley? I worked her case when she went missing. No one could tell you shit. You were gonna be in on it, no matter what, right?"

Turning back to Dare, I stare him down. "I won't ask you to help me, you know that. Going rogue like this could hurt us both. It'll definitely earn us a suspension from NES. Can't ask you to do that."

With a heavy sigh, Dare steps toward me and offers me his knuckles. "No way I'm letting you do this alone. Your family might as well be mine. I'm in. And as soon as we let Swagger and Ghost in on the situation, they'll say the same thing."

I suck in a ragged breath. It's what I'd hoped he'd say. "So the entire team is going off the books?"

Dare gives a curt nod. "Damn straight."

Adrenaline races through my veins, amping me up, sending my brain and my muscles into overdrive. "Then I guess it's a good thing I have this."

I hold up my phone as I pull up a special GPS app I installed only a few days ago. There's a red dot on the screen with concentric circles pulsing out from it. There's also a green triangle. The red dot is moving, while the green triangle stays static.

"What the hell is that?" Dare leans over my phone, trying to see it closer.

"That's the tracker I set up. The bug is attached to the inside of Decker's backpack, concealed inside a pocket."

Dare stares at me, awe and admiration in his eyes. "You're one smart son of a bitch."

Shrugging, I place the phone back in the car. "Instinct told me I should make sure I have tabs on him and Rayne both. Get Swagger and Ghost on the phone. They need to be in the car and headed this way…yesterday."

Dare turns and jogs back to his car.

The GPS tracker gives me hope that I'm going to find them again. But it doesn't change the jarring truth of what just happened. The truth that—if I allow myself to settle into it, really absorb it—will pull me under and drown me where I stand.

I lost them.

30

RAYNE

I don't know where we are, but I'm with Decker and at the moment that's all I care about.

We drove only for another hour or so before pulling off the road and onto an unmarked dirt pass through a thick wood. The headlights only illuminated a few feet before us, enough to shine on the back of the SUV that I knew held my son. My eyes stayed glued to that vehicle, even when Wagner would try to engage me in conversation.

I remained mute.

Pulling up in front of an elaborate log mountain cabin, completely hidden from view and off the path in a clearing, surrounded on all sides by nothing but forested mountain land, I rush to slide out of the sedan.

I ignore Wagner's chuckle behind me as I race for the SUV and pull the back door open. Decker tumbles out and into my arms.

"Mom?" His voice is raw, probably from screaming, and my heart breaks in two equal pieces.

Grasping the sides of his face, I study him from head to toe. "Did they hurt you, sweetheart? Tell me the truth."

He shakes his head, his green eyes wide with fear. "What's going on, Mom? Who are these guys?"

Wagner steps up next to me on the brush-strewn path. "Decker, right? I'm Wagner, your mother's old boss. I've heard so much about you, but it's very nice to meet you."

Everything that I've been thinking and feeling for the last hour and a half boils up inside me, a volcanic eruption of rage, emotional turmoil, and paralyzing fear. Turning to Wagner, my hand raises almost on its own and the slap rings out through the night.

"Don't you speak to him," I snap, putting my arm around Decker and leading him away from Wagner.

My hand stings, but I ignore it as I'm hustled up the stone steps, my grasp on Decker never weakening, and led inside the elaborately styled cabin. Knotty pine walls, a gorgeous, cavernous vaulted ceiling with wood shiplap and wooden beams painted white, and all the luxurious furniture and decor you'd see in a rustic home magazine.

Turning to Wagner, I'm satisfied to see a red stain on his cheek where my hand left its mark. "Why do you have this house?"

Wagner shrugs, his blue eyes piercing me where I stand. "It belongs to a business associate. Came in handy, didn't it?"

Glancing around once more, pulling Decker tighter to me, I see that the two men in suits and Kevin O'Shea came inside with us. The others must be assigned to outside guard duty.

Grabbing my arm in a hold that's too rough to be gentle but only harsh enough to border on painful, he steers me toward the spiraling staircase.

When I'm wrenched away from Decker, I cry out and he stands as tall as he can.

"Hey!" He raises his little voice in a shout I've never heard from him before. "Let go of my mom!"

He sounds absolutely enraged, and it's not a side of him I've witnessed often. Decker is usually a pretty even-keeled kid, relaxed and fun loving and happy. I hate that there's a possibility this experience can change that forever.

With a smirk, Wagner gestures toward O'Shea. "Watch the kid."

Tugging my arm painfully out of his grasp. I dig in my heels. "I'm not leaving my son alone!"

I'm still having trouble even wrapping my mind around the fact that we're here. Just under two hours ago, I was sitting in a car with the man I love, the father of my child, escaping all of the problems that had followed me to Wilmington from Phoenix. Then, those same problems caught up to us, ripped us apart, and carried not only me away with them, but my son as well.

And the last thing I ever wanted was for Decker to be dragged into any of it. Now he's downstairs alone, scared, and clueless about why we've been taken or whether or not we'll be hurt.

I didn't miss the fact that he called Jeremy "Dad" for the first time. That should have been an epic moment for the three of us, something that we could stop and revel in. I can only imagine how Jeremy's feeling. The look on his face when Decker said it, and when he realized that he was probably going to lose us, nearly broke me.

And I put every ounce of trust I had in Jeremy. I should have known that no one would be able to protect me from Wagner forever. The man has never failed at getting what he wanted. He didn't get to be a billionaire by sitting around waiting for things to happen.

But I was naïve to think that Wagner only wanted me. I never truly believed that he would hurt Decker. But now Decker and I are here on our own. There's no way Jeremy will be able to get to us. Even though we aren't too far away from where we were snatched, it would be like searching for a needle in a haystack. For all he knows, we could be driving through Tennessee by now, on our way to God knows where.

The thought of never seeing him again makes my knees buckle, and I trip up a step. Wagner hoists me up and pulls me the rest of the way up the stairs and into a bedroom where he shuts and locks the door.

"Have a seat, Rayne." His voice is cool and polite, but I can hear the command in it even with the layer of saccharine on top.

"I'll stand."

His lips twist in amusement, and he presses hard on my shoulders. I plop onto the bed and then scramble backward, pulling my knees up to my chest.

"What do you *want*?"

Instead of answering right away, Wagner tilts his head to the side, studying me. I want to close my eyes and pretend invisibility under his stare, but I know that showing weakness in front of Wagner is a mistake. He smells it, the same way a shark seeks bloody chum in the water.

When I don't flinch or cower under his probing gaze, he turns away and heads for the big picture window. Looking out onto the black night, he says nothing for so many minutes I'm about to open my mouth and ask the question again.

Without turning, he speaks. "I want you to understand me, Rayne."

Reeling back, my mouth opens and then closes again. It's not what I expected him to say. He wants me silenced. He wants to be sure I don't have proof of the corporate espionage he used to steal information from Prednar. And from the looks I've interpreted, he wants my body.

But for me to understand him? I never would have put that on a list of things Wagner Horton wants.

"What do you want me to understand?" I whisper.

Finally turning, his hands clasped behind his back, I expect him to walk toward the bed. Even though he takes in my tight gray leggings, short, heeled boots, and clinging tunic, his eyes going dark, he takes a seat on the edge of an armchair instead.

"I want you to understand that the only crime I've committed is conforming to the way the business world works. I'm a creative genius, Rayne. I have people who breathe down my neck, demanding the next best thing in order for the company to continue to grow and flourish. But that's not the way my brain works. I can't come up with the 'next best thing' on demand."

Cautiously, I nod. "I can imagine that would be hard. Lots of pressure."

With an eager nod, he looks up into my eyes. "Unrelenting pressure, Rayne. All the time. When the opportunity arose to borrow an idea from another company, I bit. It felt wrong, but do you know something? Ideas are rarely ever original. They're just recycled, over and over again. Revamped, yes. And that's all I've done with Red40. It may have originated at another company, but I've tuned the software to my own needs, and it's really quite different now."

Is he seriously trying to convince me that stealing is okay when you're a genius billionaire?

All I do is nod, because he's talking. And when he's talking, he's not touching me and he's not hurting me. I have an urgent need to get back to my son, though.

"Wagner…I need to go back downstairs. I can't stand leaving Decker alone."

A glow of something stronger and harder than irritation glows in Wagner's eyes, but it's gone so fast I can't even be sure I saw it. Then his face is a mask, hiding his emotions as skillfully as a chameleon blending into its surroundings.

"Give me a few more minutes, Rayne. I have a proposition for you."

Shaking my head, I scoot forward on the bed until my feet touch the floor. "Let's just lay it all out on the table, Wagner. You know what I saw, and I know that you want to keep me from singing to the authorities. You let my son and me go, and I'll keep my mouth shut. Does that work for you?"

He leans forward on his elbows, watching me like I'm a

show he just can't turn off. His lips curl into a smile that hides more than it shares. "Just like that? I should just let you and your son walk away?"

Trying to keep my face impassive, I nod.

The silence in the room stretches, growing thick and heavy until it might as well be a suffocating blanket covering us. I jump when Wagner bursts into laughter.

He laughs so hard and so long that his face turns red, and I can feel myself growing more furious and more humiliated with every passing second.

He's just playing with me. This is a game to him.

"Nothing is more important to me than my son, Wagner." There's a warning note in my voice.

Wiping his forehead, his face turns serious. "Oh no? Let's talk about that, shall we? If nothing is more important to you than your son, why have you been shacking up with Jeremy Teague?"

Wheeling back like I've been slapped, I snap. "We're not shacking up. I love Jeremy. And he's Decker's father. You know he won't stop until he finds us, right? And he's trained to do it."

Wagner leans back in the armchair, crossing one leg over the other, his expensive leather boot dangling over his knee. "Yes, I think I've heard some information to that effect. It's rather interesting, really. Did you know that your son is an heir of sorts?"

Narrowing my eyes, my teeth snap together as a wave of fear ripples through me. "What are you talking about?"

He waves his hand. "Never mind. I have a counter deal for you. Are you ready to hear it?"

Mutely, I nod.

As if he's been waiting decades for my response, he launches himself off the chair and before I can take a breath, I'm on my back, staring up at his hovering face.

Attempting to struggle is futile, Wagner has me pinned underneath him, my hands pinned above my held, held in place by his.

"What are you *doing*?" I hiss through my teeth.

"Are you angry, Rayne? I always thought I'd really love to see that. Have you like this—pissed-off and spitting venom like the little harlot you are, right underneath me. I plan to have you like this again and again. Ready to hear my deal?"

His mouth is so close to mine, hot breath floats from his mouth to my face and I want to squeeze my eyes shut, but I'm too afraid to take my eyes off of him. I can feel his hard-on pressing into my thigh, and bile rises in my throat. I cough as I choke it down.

"I'm going to let your son go."

Waiting for more, my heart beats a frantic rhythm in my chest. "Why…why would you do that?"

His smile is cruel, sure. "Because I have you. I don't need him. He can sail off in the sunset with his daddy, for all I care. But you and I are leaving on a private plane, out of the country, tonight. I have a private deal going down, a merger with a very lucrative corporation. Once that deal is done, I won't need to run the day-to-day nonsense at Horton Tech anymore. I'll be free to just collect my paychecks. And if I have you with me, you'll keep your sexy little mouth quiet. So much better than killing you."

I'm having a hard time remembering how to breathe. "That's…you're insane. Why would you want me to stay with you when I despise you?"

He leans down and takes my mouth with his, a rough and harsh and stomach-turning kiss that leaves me gasping when he finally pulls away. Running a hand over my thigh, he grips is tightly and wraps it around his waist, pressing into me.

Oh, God. This isn't real. Please let me wake up and this will all have been a horrible nightmare.

"Because hate and love straddle a fine line, Rayne Alexander. And I've never wanted a woman as much as I want you. The fight in you?" He dips his head, running a tongue along my heck until he reaches my collarbone. "It's something I'm going to enjoy tearing out of you."

The fight to keep from gagging has black dots dancing on the outside of my vision.

"No response? No biting reply, no snide remark? Would you rather I beat it out of your son instead?"

I snap to attention, cold and oily fear coiling in my gut. All the fight leaves me then. Since the first moment I laid eyes on him, I always knew I'd do absolutely anything for Decker.

My answer for Wagner is easy.

"Let Decker go. You make sure he gets back to Jeremy. And we leave tonight."

31

JEREMY

Early September in the Appalachians brings crisp night air. The scarred and scuffed wooden tabletop at the coffee shop adjoining the service station where the Land Rover is getting four new replacement tires is filled with the writings of previous customers. A slew of Sharpie in a rainbow of colors reads like a love song, but I'm not studying the poetry.

I keep glancing at the glass door leading to the service station, checking the status on my SUV, my fingers drumming anxiously on the table.

"If they aren't here by the time the car is done, we're leaving without them." My tone warns Dare that I'm dead fucking serious. It's been two hours since I watched a psychopath drive off with the woman I love and our son. There's only so much waiting a man can do before he snaps.

And I'm at the tipping point.

The tracker stopped moving an hour and a half after they left, and I've had eyes on it, waiting for it to start up again. But it hasn't. They're still in these very same mountains, and I need to get on the road so I can get to them.

The *thump, thump, thump* of my fingertips hitting the table and the beeping of the tracker on my phone, combined with the continuous whir of the espresso machine behind the counter are the only sounds in the room.

"No, Brains. We wait. You can't do this alone, that's why you have a team. Swagger and Ghost are on their way...should be here any minute now."

When we called them, they were staking out a hotel where they'd had confirmation Horton had been staying. As soon as we informed them of what had happened on the mountain road, they abandoned that post and we decided as a group not to put Jacob on the line by telling him what we were doing. We collectively made the decision to go rogue and take the consequences later.

But we knew damn well that if Boss Man were in any of our positions, he wouldn't hesitate.

I hope he's not too pissed off at me later, but at this point I really don't give a fuck.

Thoughts of what Horton could be doing to Rayne and Decker while I'm sitting on my ass waiting for my car to be fixed threaten to drive me over the edge. Dare insisted that taking his truck and going in alone without a plan was a bad idea, something that would surely be more dangerous to my family than waiting and planning.

When the little bell over the shop tingles and I glance up to see Grisham and Ronin walking through the door, I shoot out of my seat.

Ronin locks eyes with me and the sympathy in them almost breaks me.

He walks over and places a hand on my shoulder. "We'll get them back."

With a curt nod, I rake both hands through my disheveled hair. "No other option."

Grisham takes the seat beside Dare and places his tablet on the table. "Show me your app with the tracking device information."

I slide my phone over to him but there's no way I can sit down again. Instead, I pace the small space, listening as Grisham starts to strategize.

"Brains." Grisham addresses me with such a serious note in his voice that I pause in my pacing and glance at him. "I hate to ask this, but…can you handle this? There's a reason why teams like us aren't supposed to execute rescue missions for our own families."

Three sets of eyes focus on me. My jaw tenses, every muscle in my body going rigid with irritation. I feel like an open fucking wound; the extreme rawness of my emotions scrapes with each painful reference to my own capability.

"Ghost. I want you to listen to me." Each word is succinct for perfect clarity. "There's no way in hell anybody can keep me from going after them. I'm on this mission. Period. Let's get a plan in place so we can stop sitting around. Now."

He studies me for a minute, his pensive gaze probing, before he finally lifts a tattooed arm in a "come here" gesture. Gathering around him, we all stare down at the devices.

"The location is densely wooded. It's kind of the perfect

hiding spot, way up in the Blue Ridge Mountains. The town borders Tennessee and North Carolina, and it's known for its nearly impassible road conditions in winter. We're damn lucky that there's no ice and snow to contend with right now, because if there were we wouldn't be able to drive in at all."

With a groan, my head falls back . "I know that area. Used to go there a lot as a kid."

Grisham glances up, surprised. "Good. The fact that you know the terrain will help. We'll drive in, test out the lay of the land. It's probably good we're gonna have the Land Cruiser. We'll probably need to take Dare's truck, too, since this is a rescue mission."

From the floor beside the table, Night looks up and gives a short, low bark.

Grisham grins. "Yeah, we'll use Night, too. If they're not inside a residence, he can follow a scent."

Nodding, I crouch down and pat Night on his blocky head. "Yeah. He's good at that."

"We don't know until we get there whether they're being held in a house or a cabin, or some kind of facility. I don't like the idea of going in blind, of not having time to conduct surveillance first. So none of us can afford to be emotional. Cool heads here, you understand?"

Grisham's looking at me, but I know he's addressing everyone. When one of our own is taken, it affects the entire team. I'm not the only one who's feeling this in my gut. The other guys are like my brothers. They know what's at stake, and all of our emotions are running high.

We all nod. "Roger that."

The glass door to the service station opens, and the tall, lanky mechanic in gray coveralls lumbers over. "All set."

I head straight to the cashier and pull out my credit card. By the time I'm finished paying for the tires and service, Dare, Ronin, and Grisham are headed out the door. Night sits, waiting for me.

Resting a hand on his head, I crouch down and look him in the eye. His are blue, deep, and full of trust and understanding.

"Ready, Night? Let's go bring our family home."

32

WAGNER

Pure, unadulterated exhilaration.

That's what I feel when I'm lying on top of Rayne Alexander.

The feel of her tight little body all fueled up and ready to go beneath mine offers me a tiny window to the pleasure she's going to bring me.

Her thigh is firm and supple beneath my hand. Squeezing it sends a jolt of need straight to my dick, and the erection that was previously interested, is now raging and painful. Her face, contorted in anger and fear, calls to me. She's like a perfect doll, gorgeous and flawless and ready to be molded to my very own design.

Just like a software program, I can create her to my exact specifications.

Her chest heaves beneath me, pushing her plush breasts against my chest in a way that nearly makes me lose my mind. If I were a lesser man, a weaker man, I'd take her right now.

But I can't let the fire her body and her fear creates inside me lure me away from the true goal. My company is on the verge of greatness. I've signed on the dotted line. But there's another piece of the bargain that I have yet to deliver on. And after I do, I can take my new little project far away from here and get started making my life perfect, with the perfect woman by my side.

She tastes like silk and sugar, with a hint of darkness. That darkness is what I'm going to cultivate, stretch, intensify. By the time I'm through with Rayne, she'll be a writhing mass of wanton need, there to serve me.

I use a finger to trace the heart-shaped outline of her lips. "I can feel the way your body responds to me. The same way you just agreed to my terms, your body will merge with my plan."

Her delicious shudder stokes my fire.

Turning her head to one side, she plays coy. "I want to check on my son."

Ah. Getting rid of the brat is the first step. His presence here couldn't be helped, but he's too much of a distraction. I want nothing to do with him. I'm more than happy to shift him into the hands that have requested him. *More* than happy.

With a pained sigh, I push off the bed and straighten my sweater. My raging hard-on is going to be impossible to calm, especially if I continue to stare at her while she scoots off the bed and fixes her clothes. Licking my lips, I turn away from the sight of her and grasp myself, squeezing until the pain overwhelms the needy ache.

When I'm finally limp, I clear my throat and turn back toward Rayne. Offering her what I hope is a friendly smile, I proffer my hand. "Shall we?"

Ignoring my hand, she heads for the bedroom door. A smile twists my lips.

Oh, yes. I'll enjoy beating that sass right out of her.

She runs to the boy when she sees him, sitting on the couch with a dramatically wounded expression on his face. Rolling my eyes, I stride to my phone and remove it from the charger. Pulling up the contact information I'm searching for, I wait for an answer.

"Yes?" The voice on the other end of the line has become so familiar over the past few months.

Turning away from Rayne, I lower my voice. "Our deal is about to be complete."

"Is that right? I've been waiting. I'll send a driver to retrieve him. Better yet, I'll come. I'm nearby. Make sure he's outside in an hour."

With a smile, I turn back to face the room and lift my voice higher. "Yes, I will pay you very handsomely if you will return the boy, completely unharmed, to his father."

There's a chuckle on the other end of the line just before it goes dead.

"Yes, exactly. We'll walk him outside in one hour and you will take it from there."

Rayne's face is a mask of worry, and I give her a reassuring smile. "Young Decker here will be leaving us shortly."

Rayne's face contorts with pain. "How can you expect me to let him go without making sure he gets to Jeremy?"

Oh, the dramatics! If it's a child she wants, I'll make sure we create another one. One that can be raised under my own thumb and molded accordingly. One that's the perfect combination of Rayne and myself.

Striding over to her, I grasp her chin in my hands. Her eyes go wide but she doesn't pull away. Beside her, the boy shifts away from me. "Trust me. I have your best interests at heart."

Her eyes full of mistrust, she doesn't answer. It's no matter. Everything is working out exactly the way I want it to.

Rayne clutches her son to her. "How do I know he'll really make it to Jeremy? I need to talk to Jeremy…tell him to expect Decker and to let me go."

My first instinct is to refuse. To deny her access to her former love every again. I don't know the background of their union, how they got together all those years ago and made a child. I don't know the full extent of what they've been doing together since she ran from me, but I know that I don't like the thought of them together. Rayne belongs to me, not to him.

But a deep breath and a calm and peaceful mind help me to see that allowing her to sever ties with this man, allowing her the closure that one last conversation might bring, will only serve me better in the long run. If I allow her to make a clean break from him now, maybe he'll be smart enough to stop sniffing around. Maybe having his son will be enough for him and he will let Rayne go once and for all.

I imagine her pussy is a hard one to forget, but if he wants to live, he'll do it.

My mouth waters at the thought, and I shake myself to stay focused.

The thought of driving into this woman's body until I'm

limp with exhaustion threatens to overpower me. It's a high similar to making billions of dollars. I must remain in control.

I snap my fingers at O'Shea. "Bring me a burner."

Straightening up from where he's been leaning against the wall beside the fireplace, he frowns. "Fine. This job has gone on longer than I planned for. I need to get back to Wilmington and to my business, which means I need to get paid and be done here."

Silence blankets the room. My guards shift with unease, and Rayne stares between the idiot private detective and me.

Crossing the room with purposeful steps, I draw near him until my face is merely an inch away from his. Reaching down, I grab hold of his peanut-size balls through his slacks and squeeze. His eyes bulge and his mouth goes slack. Gathering them tighter, I give a slight twist and he gasps. His breath comes fast and hard, and the fear and pain in his eyes is almost enough to rile me up again.

Almost.

My voice is filled with frosty calm. "You want to get paid? Do what I tell you. This will be over for all of us soon enough. But until then, you work for *me*." Squeezing him just a little bit tighter pulls a yelp from his throat. Then I release him and pat his face with an open palm. "Understood?"

When I glance at Rayne this time, her face is green. That's good. Showing her that I'm not to be fucked with can only help her.

"Now. How about that phone?"

With a trembling hand, he reaches into his jacket pocket and pulls out a small black cell phone. With a smirk, I take it and hold it out to Rayne. When I don't move from my spot, she's forced to let go of her son and walk over to me to retrieve it.

When she attempts to pull it from my fingers, I grip her wrist and pull her against me. Leaning down to her ear, I run my tongue along the outer shell, tasting her.

"What do you say?" I whisper.

I hear her teeth snap together, but I don't release her until I hear her reply.

"Thank you."

Releasing her, I watch her carefully as she walks back to her son's place on the couch and sits. Powering up the phone, she waits. When the screen lights up, she stabs a finger against the keys, inputting Teague's phone number.

With a smile, I wander over to the large window overlooking the front clearing and wait.

This is a good-bye I want to relish.

33

JEREMY

As the road grade steepens and the forest growth grows denser, my anxiety ratchets up until my stomach is nothing but a tight fist of nerves. Not for myself, but for Decker and Rayne. How is Decker holding up? He's only eight and he's never been faced with this type of adversity. What about Rayne? Knowing that her son is in danger must be breaking her. Is she holding it together? And has Horton put his hands on her?

Shaking my head to clear it, I focus on the device in my hands. Ronin is driving the Land Cruiser so I'm able to pay attention to the tracker app on my phone. We've also pulled Sayward in, and from time to time her voice breaks in over the vehicle's Bluetooth.

"You guys are getting close." Sayward's tone is measured and calm. "You're only a couple of miles away from where the tracker is located. What's the terrain like? Do you see any houses around?"

Sayward and I were able to connect my phone to her laptop,

and my tracking application was showing up on her screen. I'm thankful as hell for Grisham's forethought to bring her in on this before they left Wilmington. They came outfitted with earpieces and wireless devices so that we can all keep in constant contact with one another, and with Sayward, throughout the mission. The covered bed of Dare's truck looks like a mini-weapons locker with additional reinforcements, and we're walking into this rescue far more prepared than we could have been.

Ronin studies the surroundings as he turns onto a dirt path that we almost missed. "It's pretty crazy up here. Definitely no properties in sight. Whoever owns this land owns a big ass chunk of it. There're NO TRESPASSING signs all over the place."

Scanning the woods around us, I note the signs, and from that, coupled with the rough terrain of the road, it's obvious that whoever owns this property wants it to stay tucked away from prying eyes.

I'm hit with a sense of déjà vu the farther we progress down the path. *I know this property.*

I'm about to voice the thought when my phone rings. My body going tense, I check the screen, only to see that the number is blocked.

Sayward is cut off when I answer. "Hello?"

"Jeremy!"

When I hear Rayne's voice calling out to me from my car's speakers my heart riots in my chest. "Rayne? Are you hurt, darlin'?"

Trying to keep my voice level and calm, not relaying the pure panic I feel over the line is a feat, but I think I accomplish it.

"Jeremy, he's letting Decker go. Someone's going to pick him up and bring him to you."

Her words come out in a tumbled rush, and she sounds so very un-Raynelike my stomach flips. "What? Why would he do that?"

The engine revs as Ronin pushes through a particularly steep incline. When we crest the ridge, he pulls to a stop. His headlights illuminate the path in front of us, and I know we've driven as far as we can. Now it's time for us to get out, gear up, and follow the remainder of the path on foot.

"Jeremy, listen. I made a deal."

My heart plummets. Blinking rapidly, I focus on her voice and will myself not to bolt from the vehicle to get to her. "What kind of deal, Rayne?"

Her voice cracks and it's my hard limit. I want to feel Horton's throat in my hands. I want to feel the life leaking out of him. But more than any of that, I need to get my hands on Rayne, check her for injuries, and cradle her to my chest.

I need her to be safe.

"He lets Decker go. He has someone coming to take him to you. But you have to stop looking for me, Jer. You have to let me go."

Her voice breaks again on the last word. Shaking my head, the despair I feel is in danger of taking over my entire body. "Rayne…can he hear me?"

"No-no."

Speaking so quickly my words tumble over one another, my voice pleads with her to hold on. "I'm coming for you and

Decker both, Rayne. We don't need Horton's deal. Do you hear me? Stall him. If he said he's letting Decker come to me, it's a damn lie. Because I'm close, baby. *I'm coming for you both.*"

A sob bursts from her just before her voice rises in a strangled cry and the phone is ripped away from her.

"You heard her. Whatever fantasy you have of a happily-ever-after with your son and his mother are now obsolete. Let. Her. Go. Be thankful for your son and all he stands to inherit."

My open palm slams down on the dashboard. "Fuck you, asshole. If you hurt her, or touch my son, I will dismember you. One limb at a time. Got me?"

His chuckle fills the air in the car before the line goes dead.

34

RAYNE

I'm close, baby. I'm coming for you both.

Jeremy's words whirl around and around in my mind, even after Wagner snatches the phone and turns it off. The glimmer of hope that Jeremy just dangled in front of me is enough.

"Your Mr. Teague is a caveman." Wagner spits the words like he can't get them out of his mouth fast enough. "You should be happy that I'm rescuing you from a life with him."

Glancing up at him with venom in my eyes, I stand up and walk away from Decker. As I thought he would, Wagner follows.

"Is that what you see yourself as? Some sort of hero? What kind of man has to kidnap the woman he has affection for? If you even have affection for me."

His lips curve upward, but there's nothing warm about the smile. It chills me through and through. "Having affection for you is a bonus *for you*." He leans forward until his lips brush my ear, and I shudder involuntarily. "Originally, my new business partner was going to kill you. I saved you from that. But then you ran, so *my* first thought was to kill you. I don't trust you to keep my secrets. But I kept thinking about what a waste that would be." He pauses, glancing all the way down my body before whispering again. "This way, you live. And I get to enjoy you. I plan to share the fortune I'm making with this new merger with you. So, yes. I fancy myself as your rescuer."

Stepping away from him without a word, I return to Decker on the couch. He sidles closer to me, whispering, "I miss Dad."

Pulling him against me and kissing the top of his dark brown head, I whisper back. "Me, too, buddy. You know he's coming for us though, right?"

Looking up at me with the same hope I know is mirrored in my eyes, he gives me the first smile I've seen on him in hours. "Yeah. I know."

O'Shea storms toward the window. He's been increasingly antsy since entering the cabin. I've been watching his irritation with this entire situation ramp up. Maybe before this, he was a private investigator on the correct side of the law. If that's the case, I feel sorry that he hooked up with Wagner Horton.

After the way Wagner hurt him a few moments ago, I think he's sorry, too.

"Now what?" O'Shea's voice is hollow, resigned. "We just have to sit here and wait?"

"We wait until we can release the boy back to his father. And then you get paid and out of my sight, and Rayne and I here head to the private airfield where I have a jet waiting. Easy enough." Horton walks to a chair facing the fireplace and sits, looking like the most comfortable man in the world.

* * *

When the sound of an engine pulling up in front of the house alerts us all to a visitor, my heart stutters, and on reflex I pull Decker to my side. Wagner's phone chirps, and when he glances at the screen his face transforms into a genuine smile. A genuine smile from Wagner means nothing good for my son or me.

"Well then." His voice is cheerful as he stands from his chair and walks toward the couch where Decker and I sit. "Guess it's time to get the boy back to his daddy."

I stand, moving myself in front of Decker. "I want to make a new deal."

Wagner throws his head back and laughs. "Ah. You're a funny girl, Rayne. I'm going to enjoy having you by my side. Now get the boy up."

His last words are laced with a warning, but I can't move. I can't hand my son over to be taken away from me. Not when I know that Jeremy is on his way for us. "Can we just go upstairs and talk about this for a minute, Wagner?"

Trying to install a note of pleading, of gentleness that I don't feel into my voice is more than a challenge. I stare up at him, the picture of innocence and openness, but Wagner doesn't hesitate. Reaching around me, he grabs Decker and yanks him up from the couch.

"You'll thank me for this later, Rayne."

Decker begins to struggle as I cry out, "Wait!" I reach for Wagner's arm and pull as hard as I can.

The two suited guards who are standing beside the doorway to the open kitchen move, but Wagner holds up a hand to them. Whipping his arm from my hold, he rears and back-hands me, brutally hard, across the face.

I've never been hit. The impact of the blow that I wasn't prepared for knocks me off my feet, my face on fire. But I don't stay down. I'm rolling and back up on my feet in seconds, but I sway as a wall of dizziness slams into me.

Though my vision is blurred, I start forward again, a scream lodging in my throat when I see Horton pass Decker off to O'Shea.

And O'Shea drags him out the door.

"Decker!" This time, the scream rips through the air of the cabin.

I surge forward, just as strong arms grab me from behind. I struggle like a wild animal: biting, kicking, striking out. Nausea rises in my gut and I'm in serious danger of hurling all over the gray suit holding me in place. Through my haze of rage and panic and pain, I note that Wagner has calmly closed the door and is now striding toward me with something in his hand.

"Rayne. I was hoping I wouldn't have to do this, but you're making this much too difficult. When you wake up, we'll be on a plane over the Atlantic."

I glance down and see the syringe in his hand, and my scream rents the air.

At the same time the sound of an explosion blows toward us from the kitchen.

"What the hell?" The guard behind me loosens his hold and I fly forward right into Wagner's arms.

The sharp prick in my neck registers, but then the darkness creeps in from all sides.

35

JEREMY

As we pull to a stop, Ronin speaks up. "Out. Let's gear up."

Climbing out of the car, I take the Kevlar that Grisham offers me and pull off my black T-shirt. Dare's truck is bumped up right behind us, and both cars are pulled off the path.

Be thankful for your son and all he stands to inherit.

The line thrown from Horton's lying mouth tugs at something in my gut. What the hell was that supposed to mean? Inherit? Giving me back my son was never going to be an option for Horton. And he taking Rayne away from me is never going to happen. When he spouts crazy shit out of his mouth like that it scares me even more that my family is currently in his hands.

When I pull my shirt back down over my bulletproof vest, I fit the headpiece that connects me to the team in my ear. Sayward's voice crackles through it.

"You guys set?"

Ronin answers her, pulling a rifle out of the truck bed. He tosses one to each of us, and we each check the ammunition. Flipping open the cargo pockets on my army-green pants, I stuff extra cartridges inside.

"Sayward," says Dare. "When we breach the perimeter of the property, I want you to call in local law. I want these assholes funneling straight into handcuffs when we drive them out of there."

"Copy." Sayward's answer makes me grin. The girl is a sponge; she's been soaking up military lingo since she first began working with us. She might not have the social graces the rest of us do, but she's a fast learner and proving to be a valuable member of the team.

As we trudge forward, the nighttime sounds of the wood shrieking all around us, our feet nearly silent on the brush and our gazes focused on the path ahead, Grisham murmurs softly, but we hear him perfectly through our earpieces.

"Plan. Two at the entry: Brains and Swagger, Brains at point. One at the back, that's me. I'll create an explosive diversion; try to draw as many interior guards toward me at the back as possible. Wheels posted at the sniper position. We don't have schematics, this we're blind rats in this maze. So we better make sure we're the strongest damn rats in the area."

"Copy," we all mutter.

We take a sharp twist and the path opens up into a clearing. And sitting in the center of it, about a hundred yards away from the trees where we're hidden, is an ornate mountain cabin. We all stop and take in the sight, but I can't hear anything over the sound of my heart pounding in my ears. My knees feel suddenly weak and wobbly, and I place a hand against a nearby tree to steady me as my mind turns somersaults around what I'm seeing.

We don't need schematics. I know this cabin inside and out. It's been over ten years since I've been here, but I'll never forget my grandparents' mountain vacation home.

The magazine-worthy log architecture appears quaint and cozy nestled in the clearing, alight with lights burning in the windows and large lantern porch lights glowing yellow in the nighttime darkness. In front of the house, the two vehicles that took Rayne and Decker away from me earlier this evening are parked.

"Fuck me," I breathe.

My three teammates send puzzled glances in my direction.

"I know this house. It belongs to my grandparents."

"Damn." Ronin's muttered curse is all he gets out before our heads all snap toward the sound of a vehicle approaching from another direction.

A black Suburban with dark tinted windows pulls into the clearing just east of our hidden location. It crawls to a stop, but no one makes a move to get out of the car.

"Think that's whoever Horton sent to pick up Decker?" asks Ronin.

My teeth grinding together, I stare at the SUV. I know exactly who's here to pick up my son and I want to break into a run, pull the SUV doors off the hinges, and pull him out of the car by the lapels of his three-piece suit.

"Horton has six guys with him that we know of. Two of

them are at the front door right there. Horton has no reason to believe we're coming. He thinks he's free and clear, so chances are there's no on posted at the back. You saw them on the road. We can take them down, but we go in hot. No hesitations. If you have to fire, don't shoot to kill. Everyone who comes out of this alive serves time, remember that. The goal is to incapacitate, and pull Rayne and Decker out safely."

The front door of the cabin opens, and I take the first breath I've breathed in hours when Decker appears, held steady by Kevin O'Shea. My blood erupts in my veins like lava when I see my kid, and every instinct I have screams at me to get him.

"I'm out," murmurs Grisham as he begins to move swiftly away from us. "I'll skirt the perimeter until I reach the back. Wheels…hit the west side and find a perch. You two… watch the kid, but don't give away our approach unless you have to."

Gritting my teeth, I shake my head. "I'm not letting Decker leave here in that Suburban."

We can't see Grisham anymore, but his voice comes in loud and clear through my earpiece. "Wouldn't expect you to."

I watch, my heart thumping a jarring rhythm against my ribs, as O'Shea tries to lead Decker to the SUV. Decker is struggling like no other, and I'm filled with pride and fear. I don't want them to hurt him for fighting.

"Wheels," I hiss. "What's your position?"

"On my stomach and at the ready," he replies.

"Can you take down the two at the door?"

In answer, there's a whizzing sound as Dare's silencer-equipped rifle fires. One man by the door goes down, holding his knee. In less than a second, the other falls much like the first.

Kevin O'Shea, confused as fuck, turns to look at them, and Decker takes his opportunity. Swinging his backpack around to hit O'Shea as hard as he can, he wrenches free and breaks into a run.

Straight for the tree line where I'm standing.

As I step out to catch him, the driver of the Suburban breaks into a run to try and catch him. But with another quiet bullet from Dare, he goes down with a scream, holding his shoulder.

Decker slams into me, and my arms go around him. In the darkness, he struggles. All he knows is that he was free and now he's not. Leaning down to his ear, I whisper urgently.

"It's me! It's me, Deck. I got you."

He stops struggling immediately, his small body going limp in my arms. Crouching down in front of him, I watch as his eyes go wide.

"Dad!" His arms go around my neck, and it's the best fucking hug I've ever had.

I smooth his hair as I hug him, and then I pull away and scan his face. "Are you hurt?"

He shakes his head, glancing back toward the cabin. "Mom...she's still in there!"

Nodding, I gesture toward Ronin. "I know that, Deck. Look...this is my friend Ronin. He used to be a soldier, like me. Stay with him while I go in there and get your mom, okay?"

Decker opens his mouth and I know he's about to argue, so I give him a serious look as I grip his shoulders. "Listen, Deck. This is a rescue mission, okay? And I need you to follow orders so I can get in there and get your mom. Do you think you can do that for me?"

He nods, and Ronin steps in.

"Don't like sending you in alone," he warns.

"Don't have a choice." With one last look at Decker, I step from the tree line and sprint toward the house. Just as I'm passing the Suburban, a loud explosion sounds from the back of the house.

"I got two down." Grisham's voice in my ear.

That means there's only one guard and Horton left.

I'm at about the bottom of the steps when the sound of a car door stops me.

The Suburban. Not empty.

"Hello, Jeremy. I didn't expect to see you here. Where's my grandson?"

When I turn around, it's to face my grandfather.

And he's pointing a Glock directly at my chest.

"Granddad."

The fact that my own grandparent is leveling a gun at me should be disturbing. It should be surprising. It should be devastating.

But it isn't, because I know Mason Teague. He was always ruthless, you don't get to the top in business unless you have that trait. But over the past ten years, since I cut all ties with that world, he's gone to the dark side. I saw it that day at his house in Wilmington, and I'm definitely seeing it now.

"Granddad? Shit." Dare's curse crackles through my earpiece. "I have a shot, man. You want me to take it?"

I shake my head, knowing that Dare will see it and know it's for him.

I take a step closer to my grandfather when a scream from inside the house rips through my insides like wildfire.

My body tenses. That was Rayne. Fuck, fuck, *fuck*.

"Granddad…you gonna shoot me? Because if you're not, I need to get in there." I jerk a thumb over my shoulder.

His hands are steady. *"My great-grandson."*

A growl rumbles in my chest. "Will never know you. He's gone. You think I'm just gonna hand him over? I'd let you shoot me first."

Grisham's voice, inside the house, sounds through my earpiece. "Hey, hey, hey. Easy now, Horton. You don't want to do this."

I trust Grisham with my life on a daily basis, but he's not the one who should be inside that cabin if my woman is in trouble. It should be me. A cold sweat breaks out on my skin as a thousand scenarios of what Grisham's seeing right now flash through my head. None of them are good.

"This mess is because of you?" I spit the words. "That Mergers and Acquisitions folder I saw on your desk? Tech companies aren't in your wheelhouse, are they?"

His face remains stone cold, and dead serious. "They are if bringing them under the Teague Industries umbrella gets me what I want. And I want another chance to raise a Teague heir who has the balls to take over my legacy when I'm gone."

Grisham: "You hurt her, Horton? Why is she unconscious? You know this won't end well, right? Why don't you hand her over to me? Then you can run if you want."

She's unconscious? Horton is a fucking dead man. Rage boils within me, and now I direct it right at Mason Teague for keeping me away from Rayne, back then and right now.

"How long have you been planning this? Have you known about Decker all along?" My anger is seething just below the surface, and if I don't contain it I'm likely to explode.

His right eye twitches, a habit he's always had when dealing with stressful situations. "Do you think I would have let that stupid little twit run off all those years ago without making it my mission to find her? She'd changed her name, but when I finally found her, Decker was about six years old. I watched, and waited for my opportunity. When she began working for Horton Tech, I researched the company. I knew it was my chance to get close to her and bring my great-grandson home."

My jaw tightens painfully as my back teeth grind together. "And so, what? You pay out of your ass and Horton somehow kidnaps my son for you and takes my woman? And you really thought I was going to let that happen?" My words might as well have been tinged with venom.

He takes a step forward and I can almost hear Dare's trigger finger tense. "When I figured out that he was alive, do you really think I would let my great-grandson grow up without me in his life? Or that I would let Rayne get away with defying me? Once I knew she had your child there was no way I was letting a Teague be raised by anyone else. I did this for you, you ungrateful idiot! I brought him back here for you, so you would have a chance to raise him…the right way. It was time to get rid of that little bitch once and for all. It was time for you to get your head out of your ass and for the Teague men to run my business. It was time for both of you to come home!"

I raise my voice. "There's a red dot on your back."

He freezes.

Inside, Grisham continues to talk to Horton. "You can drop her and walk right out that front door. I'm pretty sure the cops will be here any minute, so you don't have much time."

Atta boy, Ghost.

I don't know if I've ever been so grateful to a member of my team before now.

But I'm done with my grandfather.

"That's right. Did you think I came alone? My whole team is here, and there's no way we're letting either you or Horton walk away. So you have a choice. You can either pull your trigger and end up dead yourself, or you can lower your weapon and let us take you in to the local authorities."

The rage in his eyes is due to the loss of control. If there's one thing that matters to Mason Teague, it's control. And he just lost the upper hand in a situation he thought he had all figured out.

His hand shakes as he raises his weapon, and I know what's going to happen before I hear the whistle of the shot that Dare fires. I only have time to see the Glock fly out of my grandfather's hands and to hear his cry of pain as he registers the fact that his hand has been grazed by a bullet before I'm turning and sprinting up the stone steps of the cabin.

"I'm grabbing him." Dare's voice sounds like he's running, and I know that my grandfather won't be able to run.

I burst through the front door just as Horton reaches it. His arms are full of an unconscious Rayne, whom he throws at me and shoulders by.

Catching Rayne, I sink down to the knotty pine floor with her in my arms. Grisham kneels beside me.

Pushing Rayne's thick hair from her face, my stomach turns and I can't seem to swallow past the enormous lump growing in my throat. "I'm so sorry, darlin.'"

As sirens reach us in the distance, the only thing I can think about is getting medical attention for Rayne. I look her over, being as gentle as I can. "What'd he do to you?"

Grisham looks her over, too. "I think he hit her."

When I look at Rayne's face, I go rigid with fury, because Horton's fucking *handprint* is etched in an angry red mark on the side of her face. But it doesn't explain why she's unconscious. Her chest rises and falls, so I know that she's breathing and her heart is beating. But the paleness of her skin other than the mark on her face scares the shit out of me. She's so limp in my arms and she feels so damn far away.

Conscious of possible broken bones, I pull her to my chest. Kissing her hair, I whisper in her ear. "Come back to me, Rayne. Come back to me and Deck."

The steady beeping of the monitors has been my saving grace. If the room had been quiet for the past four hours, I would have ripped the place apart. I would have gone completely fucking crazy. I've been sitting in a chair I've pulled next to the bed, watching Rayne's still face as she sleeps.

After she was admitted and the doctors examined her, they didn't find any bodily injuries that would have caused her to lose consciousness. And even after being grilled by local law enforcement, Horton wasn't talking. The doctors completed a tox screen that revealed that Rayne had heavy tranquilizers in her system.

The son of a bitch had tranked her.

So now I've been waiting. And while I wait, I've had a lot of time to think.

I could have lost Rayne and Decker. The situation worked out, but the fact that Wagner Horton and my grandfather nearly succeeded in taking everything I love away from me isn't lost on me. I almost lost everything, and it makes me realize how damn lucky I really am.

Rayne walked back into my life by accident, but I'm going to make sure she's here to stay. I'm going to make sure that she and Decker know how much I love them, and there's one way that I can make that very clear.

I'm staring toward the window when her slender fingers clench around my hand. Glancing down at her, I see her eyelids flutter before her long, dark lashes open and I'm staring into her gorgeous blue eyes.

"Jeremy?" Her voice, always sultry and raspy, sounds even more so than usual. I pull her hand to my lips and just try to keep myself from losing it right then and there.

"Hey, beautiful."

She glances around the room, and her eyes go wide. "Where's Decker? Oh, my God…they took him!"

"Shhh, it's okay. It's okay, Rayne. He's here. He's safe." I move to the bed so I can be even closer to her while she's freaking out. I can't imagine what it must feel like, waking up to think you've lost your son.

Her eyes close, but it doesn't stop the tears from leaking out. When she begins to tremble all over with the force of her quiet sobs, I flip a giant middle finger to hospital rules and lie down beside her, pulling her to my chest.

"It's okay, baby. Let it out…I'm right here and I'm not going anywhere." My words are meant to soothe her, but they're truer than any I've ever spoken.

She just cries. My shirt soaks up every single tear, but I couldn't care less. I'd change shirts and let her soak up another one if I could.

When she finally takes a deep, shuddering breath that shakes her entire body, she lifts her head from my chest, and I wince at the sight of the bruise forming on the side of her face.

With gentle fingers, I caress it. "He hit you. You don't know how bad I want to hurt him for that."

"It happened when he let Decker go with O'Shea. All I could see was Decker leaving me, and I know what you said about stalling, and I didn't want to fail and lose our baby boy, and…" Fresh tears spring to her eyes and this time I turn so that I can cradle her face in my hands.

"You did so good, darlin'. You really did. Decker ran when he got outside and I caught him. He was with Ronin the whole time. And now my grandfather and Horton, along with his crew, are in police custody. I think the team is making the calls that need to be made for them to be turned over to the feds."

Her forehead wrinkles in confusion. "Your grandfather?"

Trying to hold my anger in check, I explain to her how my grandfather caved under police interrogation and said he initially approached Horton in order to get to Rayne.

"He wanted to invest in Wagner's company so he could get close in order to get you out of the picture. He wanted to kill you so that I would automatically have custody of Decker." Just saying the words makes bile rise in my throat. I can't even stand the thought of something happening to her, and it was *this* close to all going to hell.

"Then, when Decker was here, my grandfather was going to try to manipulate me into coming back into the family business so I could give Decker the 'right kind' of future. As if a future with Mason Teague would be superior to growing up without a mother.

"But my grandfather found out that Horton wanted you for himself. Since my grandfather didn't care what happened to you he allowed Horton to do all the work, which worked out perfectly. My grandfather wouldn't even have to get his hands dirty and he could still get his way. Horton was going to fly off with you, someone would say you disappeared and abandoned Decker. Then Decker would be under my custody. Horton could have you as long as you never reappeared in public. But then you saw the Prednar coding and ran. You screwed up their plan Rayne. And thank god you did. Thank God you came home, because as bad as this was,

I can't imagine what would have happened if their plan had worked."

"Wait a minute. The whole time, he was acquiring Horton Tech because he wanted to get his claws in our *son*? *He wanted to kill me*?" The rage in her voice is familiar, and I nod with total understanding.

"Yes. And now he'll be charged with attempted kidnapping, among other things."

The team, from their place in the hospital waiting room, had been filling me in on each development happening with Mason and Horton. I didn't really care at this point, but it helped knowing they'd pay for their crimes against my family.

Rayne attempts to sit up, and I move out of her way so she can slowly prop herself against the pillows. Making sure she's comfortable, I eye her. "Can I get you something? Water, maybe? More pillows?"

She shakes her head but turns pleading eyes on me. I swear, I'd give her anything she wanted at this moment. "All I want is to see Decker."

Standing, I lean down and brush my lips against her forehead. "Then I'll be right back."

When I walk into the hospital waiting room, six sets of adult eyes turn to me, while Decker throws himself into my arms.

"Dad! Is Mom awake yet? Can I see her now?"

My heart clenches into a ball of emotion like it has every time he's called me Dad. Will it ever feel real, having this little boy as my own?

Kneeling down in front of him, my hands on his shoulders, I smile. "Yeah, bud. She's awake and she really wants to see you."

Standing and slinging my arm around Decker's shoulders, I look around the crowded waiting room. There are more people here than I expected to see. Berkeley, Dare's wife, sits beside him, her curly blond hair pulled up off her face. She blinks big brown eyes at me, concern marring her normally pretty face. Next to Grisham sits his fiancée, Greta. Her long, lithe frame is fitted into an uncomfortable-looking chair, her legs curled up beneath her. Her head rests on Grisham's shoulder, but as I scan the room she looks up at me. And then my eyes land on Jacob Owen, who I definitely didn't expect to see. Going rogue doesn't exactly send warm and fuzzy vibes to your boss.

Walking over to him, I offer a hand but he bypasses it and grabs me into a rough hug. "She okay?" His whisper is for me only.

Nodding, I pull away and offer him a chagrined smile. "We suspended?"

With a wry twist of his lips, he glances at the guys before meeting my gaze again. "We'll talk about that when we're all back home. But I definitely can't fault you for goin' after your family. Would have done the same damn thing." He glances down at Decker. "Looks like you. He seems like a really good kid, Teague."

Pride threatens to swallow me whole as I glance down at my son. He's looking up at me with nothing but trust on his face. Addressing the group, my voice is thick with all the emotions I've been holding back. "Thanks. All of you…for being here. For—" I choke off, scrubbing a hand down my face. Then I look each member of my team in the eyes in turn. "For all of it."

Ronin speaks up. "Get outta here. The little dude wants to see his mom." But there's nothing but sincerity and compassion in his eyes.

When Decker and I walk back into Rayne's hospital room, there's a doctor and a nurse with her. The doctor has a stethoscope over her heart while the nurse sits at the computer, typing away with busy fingers.

Decker runs to the bed. "Mom!"

Rayne pats the spot beside her. "Get up here, sweetheart."

He climbs up and the doctor moves out of the way so that she can hug her son. Straightening with a small smile, he glances at me.

It was hard when we first arrived and they were doing all of these tests on Rayne for me to get them to let me sit with her or to give me any information about her case. Apparently, "baby daddy" isn't on the approved list to receive patient information. But when I'd called Rayne's sister Olive in Paris, she'd given them hell over the phone, insisting that since she wasn't there to be with Rayne, they give me total access. And they'd caved.

"So your, um, Rayne here is going to be just fine. We were just waiting until she was awake to examine her. These tranquilizers, especially a heavy dose like she had, affect everyone differently. But she seems to be having no adverse reaction, except for a little weakness. There are no broken bones in her cheek, and she should recover just fine at home."

Rayne glances up at that. "You mean I can leave?"

The doctor nods. "I don't see why not. You were very lucky, Miss Alexander."

Midnight blue eyes, deeper than the sea, meet mine. There's something in them, something warm and intense, and it causes the inside of my chest to feel like it's caving in.

Lucky.

36

RAYNE

Ten Days Later

Yⁿ ou're both supposed to have your eyes closed. Are they closed?" I giggle as I walk backward in front of Decker, pulling his hands while he completes a zombie-walk down the upstairs hallway.

"Why do my eyes have to stay closed?" Decker's voice is full of delight. His long lashes flutter against his cheekbones and he squeezes my hands. His face is completely alight with thrilled anticipation.

"Because." Jeremy feigns gruffness. "It's a weekend of surprises, remember? Yours is today, your mom's is tomorrow."

He stands behind Decker, guiding his shoulders. "Just a few more steps."

I back into Decker's bedroom, my heart still leaping at the sight of everything we've done.

After taking a few days to recover from the ordeal in the

mountains, Decker went back to school and I went back to work at the start of the week. Today is Friday and Jeremy and I took the day off in order to decorate Decker's room.

My peace of mind was in rock-solid shape when, the day after we returned to Wilmington, we were informed that both Wagner Horton and Mason Teague were being brought up on multiple felony charges for their wrongdoings. And Jacob's connections at the FBI let him know that the federal government had enough evidence stacked against both men to make the charges stick.

Eventually, there would be trials for both of them, and we'd have to deal with reliving the experience again then. But until that day comes, I'm happy knowing that my family is safe.

An emergency meeting of the board at Teague Industries unseated Mason Teague as the CEO of the company, instead placing the current president of the corporation as the acting chief executive officer. There's been some shuffling of executives at the top level, and Jeremy was called in for the board meeting. When the board offered him a seat, he accepted. When I asked him why, his answer was simple:

"Just because my grandfather is an asshole and I want to see him live the rest of his days in prison doesn't mean the company should crumble. Peoples' jobs are at stake, good people, people who had no idea how despicable he'd become. If I can do something to help, I want to. Maybe putting on a suit and tie and heading to the office every day isn't in the cards for me, but I'd like to have a say in what goes on with the company that bears my name. My son's name. It could be his future, if that's what he wants. I don't hate the company, Rayne. If my grandfather had stepped up all those years ago and proven he cared about me more than what I could do for him, then maybe I would have actually wanted to learn the ropes at the company. Now, Decker has a choice. If he wants it, Teague Industries is his."

I'd squeezed him tight, trying to pour all of the love and respect I had for him in that moment into the fiercest embrace I could manage.

"Okay, bud...you ready?" Jeremy leans around Decker, his mouth curving into an enormous smile.

My heart falters for just a moment, watching him. Being in this house with Jeremy, spending time with him every day both at work and at home, falling into a routine of parenting together...it still blows my mind that we made it here. That after everything we endured in our past and over the last few weeks with Wagner Horton and Mason Teague, we ended up strong and resilient and together.

His eyes flick to mine, and the understanding I see there tells me that his thoughts are similar to mine. He turns and squeezes Decker's shoulders.

"This is your new room, Deck."

Decker's eyes fly open, and he pulls in a thrilled breath. He spins around slowly, and I follow suit, trying to see the room through his eyes for the first time.

Jeremy and I have painted the walls Carolina blue. There was a brick-red dresser and an entertainment console complete with the newest video game system. It was something I told Jeremy I'd never spent money on in the past, and he insisted on buying one that he and Decker could share. Jeremy handmade the headboard, a chalkboard framed with antique white wood. He'd drawn *X*s and *O*s all over the board, just like a football playbook.

The room is littered with Decker's stuff that arrived with the shipment of our things from Phoenix a few days ago. He had a box overflowing with his toys and stuffed animals, some of which I know he'll be outgrowing soon.

"Wow." When Decker's awed whisper reaches me, I focus my attention on my little boy standing in front of his dresser. He's holding up a framed picture. "Dad? Is this you?"

The utter reverence in his voice as he gazes at his father's high school football photo tells me something I already know to be true: Decker worships Jeremy. He finally has a father figure in his life, but not just any father figure. His dad. And Jeremy has become his hero.

He places the photo down and picks up another frame. The one with Jeremy and me snuggled together during our high school prom. Decker's eyes are still wide as he takes it all in.

My eyes well with sentimental tears, and I turn toward the window so I can let them fall. I listen as Jeremy shows Decker some of the sports-themed knickknacks that fill the room and how we've organized all of his clothes and shoes in his closet. I bite my lip on a smile when I hear him explain to Decker how we expect him to keep his room clean and take care of all of his things. Decker's serious "Yes, sir" in response almost pulls a sob from my chest.

"Hey, Deck. I think Night needs some more work on that trick you were trying to teach him. That dog isn't gonna learn to jump through a Hula-Hoop overnight. Why don't you take him into the backyard to work on it, and your mom and I will be out in just a minute."

"Okay!" Decker's arms wrap around my waist from behind, and I suck in a deep breath and squeeze his little hands as hard as I dare. "Thanks, Mom." His lips land on my back in a kiss before he dashes out of the room.

Then, bigger, stronger arms pull me against a broad, hard chest. I relax into Jeremy's grip and lay my head back against him.

"Everything okay?" He drops a kiss on my hair.

Breathing him in, his deep ocean-air scent, I nod and wipe my eyes. "It's just a lot sometimes. Things have worked out so beautifully for me and Decker, and he loves you so much. I…I don't know where we'd be without you. I'm thankful."

Jeremy turns me around to face him, and his eyes zero in on mine. "You and Decker belong to me. I'm not going anywhere, Rayne, and neither are you. This is our family. It took awhile to get here, but now we're here and I'm not wasting any time. You get that?"

Nodding, I try not to get lost in the depths of his jade-green eyes. When my tongue darts out to lick my lips, his gaze tracks the motion and go dark.

When he returns to my eyes, his hands move to my face, his thumbs stroking gently while his hands cup me like something breakable.

"I love you, Rayne. And it's not just because you've grown into this strong, amazing woman. And it's not because your beauty steals my fucking breath every time you walk into a room. It's sure as hell not because your sexy mouth needs to be washed out with soap. It's a combination of all of those things. It's the fact that I was made to love you."

Oh, God. I can hardly breathe through the lump forming in my throat. A big ball of teary emotions that I can't swallow and can't put into words. Except for the most important three.

"I love you, too."

His eyes flash with desire and love and need, and he dips his head low to kiss me. It's not a gentle kiss; it's rough and rugged and full of promise of all the things that are to come. It's a Jeremy kiss, and there's never going to be any other kind for me.

The following afternoon, Jeremy and I are getting the backyard ready for a barbecue while Decker and Night run around playing catch. Jeremy scrubs the grill while I add the brand-new cushions to the outdoor lounge and patio table set that Jeremy already had. The colors are bright and cheerful, the perfect addition to a backyard that Jeremy has already put his talented touch on.

With a happy sigh, I drop down onto a chaise lounge and close my eyes. A few minutes later, the lounger sinks under Jeremy's weight, and his ocean-spray scent washes over me.

"Hey." His deep, warm voice sends tingles of pleasure dancing all along my skin. Opening my eyes, Jeremy's face blocks out the sun, but it's a welcome interruption. He leans over me, two strong arms caging me in.

"Hey." I smile up at him. "Beautiful day."

"Mm-hmm. I think you should go upstairs and get ready for the barbecue." I gasp as his nose draws a path across my jaw.

His lips land lightly on mine before he pulls away.

I snuggle deeper into the lounger. "I have a little while yet."

He shakes his head, causing the bristly hair on his jaw to lightly scratch my face. "Come here, darlin."

He pulls me up off the lounger and then looks out into the yard where Decker and Night play. He gives a low whistle, and both boy and dog freeze. He waves a hand. Decker and Night race over to meet us.

"Is it time?" Decker's excited voice brings a smile to my lips.

"Someone's excited about the last barbecue of the season," I tease, ruffling my son's dark hair. It's getting long; usually I'd have taken him to get a cut by now. But I suspect he might want it to grow a little longer than usual, more like his dad's.

And that's more than okay with me.

Whipping a bandanna out of his pocket, Jeremy's entire face transforms into one of his larger-than-life smiles. "It's time, Deck." Crooking a finger at me, he holds out the bandanna. "Come here, Rayne."

"What the hell?"

Both Jeremy and Decker roll their eyes.

"Swear jar!" Decker tries to make a stern expression, but the happiness radiating out of him makes it difficult.

Jeremy just stands there, waiting, until I walk forward and stand expectantly in front of him. He wraps the bandanna around my head, covering my eyes completely.

"I told you this is a day of surprises," he whispers in my ear before I hear his steps back away. "Don't move, darlin."

I stand frozen in our backyard, trying my damnedest to

figure out what they're doing based on sounds, but it's like they've practiced whatever they're about to do and have got the process silently down to a science. I hear the birds chattering in the trees, I can feel the early fall breeze lingering on my skin. The jingle of Night's collar sounds not too far away, and a quiet, directive whisper from Jeremy reaches my ears, but none of that gives me a clue as to what's happening.

What have my boys been up to?

"Rayne..." I turn my head toward Jeremy's voice. He sounds like he's standing just to my right. "Even though I didn't know it, I've been waiting for you to walk back into my life since the day you left. I was getting everything ready for you...a career that could support a family, this house, a lifestyle that could include you and Decker thriving by my side. When you two finally arrived, it was the best day of my life. And now, it wouldn't be worth living without you. Either of you."

The backs of my eyes sting as I fight to keep the tears at bay. But the emotions curling in my chest, rising in my throat, they won't be denied. I love this man, and our son, and our brand-new life together. Everything I have right now is more than enough. More than I thought I would get from this life.

"Open your eyes, Rayne." Jeremy's voice, strong and brimming with love, comes from behind me.

I slide the bandanna up over my head and blink a few times to clear my vision against the now-harsh light of the afternoon. There's no one standing in front of me.

Scanning the yard, I find Decker first. He's kneeling down in the grass, his gorgeous smile nearly splitting his face in two. I smile back, and he points to the ground in front of him.

Where there are big, wooden letters painted white, spelling out one word.

WILL

My stomach flips over and I bring my hands to my mouth. They're trembling, but it's nothing comparing to the tremors in my heart.

Night barks, and I turn my head to find him on the opposite side of the yard. He's being a good dog, sitting exactly where his master told him to, in front of another word made from the white wooden letters. My hands fly to my mouth with a soft cry.

YOU

"Rayne."

Jeremy's voice, low and earnest, pulls me around. Turning to face the house behind me, he's also kneeling, right behind the last two words spelled with wooden letters. My eyes lock on his face. Serious. Strong. Intense love shining out of his eyes.

My hands still covering my mouth, my head already nodding before I read the words, my eyes dart down to the letters.

MARRY US?

When my eyes light on Jeremy again, there's a little white box in his hands. His hands, always so strong and steady and sure, are shaking just as badly as mine are.

"Say yes, Rayne. Say yes and our future starts right now." His voice is raw with emotion, thick with love.

Dropping to the ground with him, I rocket into his arms. He catches me, like I knew he would, and we both go down into the grass. My face is a mess of tears and laughter and a happiness I thought only heroines in movies and books got to experience.

"Yes!" I want to scream the word, but all that comes out is a raspy whisper. "Oh, my God! Yes."

Then Decker and Night have landed on top of us, and we're all a laughing, rolling mess of arms and legs and hugs on the ground. When the dust settles, and I really take a good look at what I'm getting out of this deal, I'm filled with the most peaceful sense of contentment I ever could have imagined.

Rolling onto his back on the grass, chest heaving to catch his breath, Decker glances at Jeremy. "She said yes, right, Dad?"

Jeremy clears his throat, rolls onto his side, and pulls me against him. "Yeah, Deck. She said yes."

I sniffle.

"So." Jeremy's voice is casual. "Why don't you go on upstairs and get ready for a wedding?"

Going still, I attempt to wrap my head around those words. "Wait…what?"

Standing, Jeremy reaches down to pull me to my feet. I might as well be floating on air, I can barely feel the ground. Jeremy glances at his watch.

"There's about two hours until our wedding. Give or take."

Mouth agape, I just stare at him. Now that I've said yes,

Jeremy doesn't have a care in the world. His face belies his control, although his eyes are sparkling with excitement.

"I don't have a dress!"

Really, Rayne? You get engaged five seconds ago and your fiancé, the father of your child, informs you that the wedding is today*, and the only thing you can think about is the damn dress?*

But I stand by my statement. "I don't have a dress" is code for: We aren't ready for anything remotely resembling a wedding.

Decker laughs, and Jeremy winds his arms around my waist and winks. "Head on upstairs to our room. I promise you, I've got this covered."

I look up into his eyes, utter disbelief filling me up. "You must have been pretty confident I'd say yes."

Dipping his head, he brushes his lips across mine twice. "Hopeful."

As hard as it is to turn away from them, I do and once my feet hit the wooden floor, I'm running. Breathless, happy, excited, I burst into our bedroom.

And pull to a stop in the doorway. My heart explodes.

"Olive!"

My sister, a blue-eyed, auburn-haired beauty, stands from the bed. "Well, hey. I heard you're getting married today." She gestures toward the ivory garment bag stretched across the bed. "Thought you might need a dress, so I brought one with me from Paris."

Now there's no possible way for me to control the sob that breaks free as I launch myself at her. We hold on tight, because it's been a year since Olive was last in Phoenix to visit Decker and me. So much has changed since then.

When we finally break apart, she pulls me to sit down beside her on the bed. Pulling her legs up under her, she grins.

My sister is my opposite. Reserved, demure, and driven by her career, she never has a hair out of place. She's flawless and in perfect control, because she's never been comfortable any other way. While I was the one who questioned our parents raising us so strictly, rebelling when I could, she catered to it and observed every rule with due diligence.

But one thing about us that never wavered? Our friendship. Our sisterhood. Olive is and always has been my best friend.

"You look gorgeous," I tell her. "All France-ey."

Her pert nose wrinkles. "France-ey? Is that a compliment?"

I nod. "Absolutely. Did you really bring me a dress from Paris?"

I glance at the garment bag again, curiosity and elation buzzing in my fingertips as I stroke the bag.

Her expression turns knowing and she brushes her long, sweeping bangs out of her eyes. "Jeremy called."

Narrowing my eyes at her smugness, I point a finger at her. "You got me a job at the place he worked on purpose."

She tries to fight her smile, but one corner of her mouth pulls up anyway. "It was time to stop the secrets. He needed to know what he was missing out on when it came to you and my perfect nephew. I just opened the door for you two. But I'm glad it ended up like this."

Worried eyes run the length of me before she takes my hands. "Are you okay? After everything that happened?"

Not even the gloom of what Wagner did to me can blacken this day. "I'm absolutely fine, Olive. I swear. I can't believe you're here! You're not supposed to be back for another month!"

A shadow crosses her face, obscuring her happiness for just a second before it's gone. "I decided to come home a little early. And I'm really happy to be here."

Studying her, I poke a little further. "Everything okay?"

Offering me a bright smile, she hops off the bed in one graceful movement and grabs the garment bag. "Ready to see your dress?"

I know my sister better than anyone. And even though she's going to try to keep everything pent up and controlled, something isn't right. I want to probe further, and I will, but it's my wedding day, apparently. So it's time to get ready.

There's a knock on the door, and Macy pokes her head around.

"Macy!" I rush toward her, my arms open.

After she hugs me, she pulls back and gives me a sunny smile. "I heard someone was getting married today."

My face threatens to split open from my continuous grin. "Jeremy called you?"

Macy's eyes crinkle at the corners as she smiles. "He sure did. And I wouldn't miss this for the world. God, you look happy, Rayne."

"Did you guys know that they surprised the shit out of me with this wedding?" I bounce on my toes as Olive unzips the garment bag.

"I did. And normally, I wouldn't have been able to get a

designer dress on such short notice. But I designed a château for Amelia Bourchard, so there are perks." Olive pulls out the most beautiful gown I've ever seen.

My sister inspects it. "It's perfect for a backyard wedding. Not too formal, but it's going to be so elegant on your long limbs. Let's do your hair and makeup first. Then we'll put it on."

Another soft knock sounds at the open bedroom door. I whirl around, ready to rip Jeremy a new one for peeking, but instead of Jeremy there're two unfamiliar women standing there.

"Hey, Berkeley!" Olive brushes past me, hangs the dress up on the bathroom door, and pulls the blonde into a hug. "I'm back!"

Berkeley, who I've only spoken to on the phone, pulls away and hold my sister at arm's length. "Hey! I didn't know you would be here. Greta and I wanted to see if Rayne needed help getting ready." She glances around Olive and gives me a warm, friendly smile. "Jeremy told the guys what was happening today, and Dare spilled the beans."

"Don't ever ask those guys to keep a secret that isn't top clearance. They're worthless." The tall, leggy brunette saunters toward me. Her face is beautiful and sweet. Her blue eyes sparkle as she holds out her hand. "I'm Greta, Grisham's fiancée. We've heard so much about you, and I can't believe the first time we get to meet you is the same day you're marrying Jeremy!"

Berkeley embraces me next and then holds me out in front of her as she scrutinizes my face. "God, you're gorgeous."

Greta interrupts. "Of course she is, who else could have reeled in Jeremy Teague but the drop-dead gorgeous mother of his kid?"

Olive rolls her eyes as Berkeley laughs. "Truth."

Releasing me, Berkeley opens the bag she brought with her. "A smoky eye for sure. Let's do this, ladies!"

Later, when I'm scrubbed, polished, made up, and wearing a beautiful Parisian gown, I glance at my reflection. The vision of the dress slams into me first. Long, flowing, and ivory-colored, the delicate spaghetti straps border a deep, plunging neckline. The natural waist is sheathed with a thin line of glittering, studded lace. The simplicity of the dress whispers beauty and grace, layers of chiffon flowing around my legs covering the dainty golden strappy heels on my feet.

"Wow." I try to breathe, turning slightly to admire the detailed back.

When I turn to face the girls, I'm greeted by four sets of shimmering eyes.

"Wow is right, little sister." Olive swipes at her eyes. "Now, let's go marry the man you love."

37

JEREMY

Scanning the yard to distract myself from my tied-up nerves, my voice thunders across the yard. "More flowers on the arch, please!"

A deep laugh from behind me pulls me around to face Ronin. "Something funny, Swagger?"

He sits sprawled in one of the white chairs the rental company arranged in the center of the backyard. The archway, covered in white gardenias already, stands proudly between the patio and the grass. That's where Rayne will enter, and I want her first view of our wedding to be perfect. Guests are beginning to arrive, even though I kept the guest list to a minimum. Close friends only, the people in our lives who could really appreciate all Rayne and I have gone through to get to this point.

Today, our family will unite for the first time. Three Teagues in this home, starting our lives together. And I don't want it to be anything less than amazing. For her.

"You." With a smirk, Ronin gestures around the backyard. Hanging lights, flowers everywhere, white Japanese lanterns ready to light the area when the sun sinks below the horizon. My backyard is transformed, and I can't wait for Rayne to see it. "Pulling an entire wedding out of your ass in a week? Never thought I'd see the day."

He stands, straightening the button-down I've asked all my brothers to wear as they stand by my side. "Happy looks good on you, Brains."

Slapping my hand, he pulls me into a one-armed hug.

"Can we get in on that, or is it for couples only?" Dare's voice booms through the yard as he strides toward us, carrying a brew. A grinning Grisham and a gruff-faced Jacob follow him closely. All are slated to be my groomsmen today.

Ronin slings a fisted arm around my neck, trying to choke me. "Find your own bro-mance, Wheels."

The laughter, the joy…it's all I've ever wanted. At one point in my life, I thought the only way I would get it was by living vicariously through my friends. Seeing them fall in love and get married one by one, while I sat back with the current flavor-of-the-week. But the second I saw Rayne sitting at that desk at the office, my entire outlook had changed.

And then, when I saw Decker and knew he was my son? The pieces of my future slid right into place like the most perfect puzzle.

The band, a steel drum quartet set up in the corner of the yard, strikes up, and everyone begins seating themselves. The atmosphere, casual and light, is exactly what Rayne would have wanted if she'd been able to plan this day. But knowing

Rayne, she's damn happy I took the burden off her plate.

Decker runs up to me from where he's been hanging out with his friend Jay. Night is close at his heels. I smile when I think about how fast my dog fell in love with the kid. Almost as fast as I had. Ruffling his hair, I pull him to my side. "Ready, bud?"

Decker looks up at me, his face unusually serious. "When you marry Mom, does it mean that we're a real family?"

His voice, tight with nervous concern and edged with barely-there hope, tugs painfully at my heart. "Absolutely. We're already a family, Deck. We're just making it official to-day in front of all our friends."

We walk down the aisle, toward the area in front of the seats where another archway, this one strewn with more gardenias and twinkling lights, stands waiting.

"Hey." Jacob leans over the row of men. "Mind if I walk out on my groomsman job? There's something more important I think I need to do."

My mouth drops open. "Seriously?"

He claps my shoulder with a reassuring twitch of his lips. "Trust me."

Since the answer to that is always yes, I give him a nod. He disappears into the house just as Macy appears on the patio. The band's music changes, and she steps forward with a big smile on her face.

Next, Olive appears. Her bouquet held at her chest, she strolls forward, smiling at the small gathering of guests as she goes. When she reaches the end of the aisle, she hugs Decker and gives me a huge smile. I return it, happy that I was able to get her here to share this day with her sister.

When I called Olive, she seemed all too eager to cut her business trip short. I don't know the reason why, but I'm happy she did. Rayne needed her sister here today.

There's movement out of the corner of my eyes, and when I glance down the line of groomsmen, I catch Ronin shifting his feet. His eyes are laser-focused on Olive. When he catches me staring, he shrugs and turns his attention back toward the patio.

The light, jubilant music changes once more to something more bound in the enormity of this day. The day that the family I didn't know I had until a month ago weaves a permanent place around my heart.

Everyone stands as the patio doors open, and a collective gasp sweeps over the guests. Rayne steps out onto the patio, her slender arm hooked through Jacob's strong one.

At the sight of her, I'm hit, the same way I would be if a bullet slammed into my chest. But instead of pain exploding inside me, it's an enormous balloon of pleasure that I don't think can be contained within my chest.

Just like always, it's her hair that I notice first. Dark, thick, and wound into an elaborate braid that hangs over one bare shoulder all the way past her breast. When her eyes catch mine, all the breath leaves me in one sweep, and I bite down hard on my lip to keep myself together.

I keep my gaze locked on hers, and it feels like there's a tether between us, drawing her closer as Jacob walks her down the aisle. When they reach the front, the minister asks Jacob if he gives her to me, and he answers with a solemn nod.

Then my hands are reaching for Rayne's and I pull her the rest of the way to the arch.

Staring at her gorgeous face, trying like hell to keep my eyes from dropping to her luscious curves that are damn near killing me in her dress, I commit myself to her. And I listen closely as she commits herself to me. All the rest is a complete blur until the minister informs me that I can kiss her because she's mine.

Mine. My wife. My son. My family.

Her arms go around my neck, and I lift her into my arms as I finally claim her pretty mouth.

I can't pull away, even when the applause, complete with whistles, starts. This is my wife. And it's been almost ten years in the making.

She giggles against my lips as she pulls back. When she realizes I've walked us back up the aisle and straight to the patio, her cheeks flush with pleasure. "What are you doing?"

Instead of answering, I turn with Rayne in my arms and address our guests. "Everyone can get the party started. We'll be back in a bit."

My groomsmen nearly double over with laughter and I watch as Ronin and Olive grab Decker. Then I'm inside my house with my bride in my arms and heading up the stairs.

Kicking the bedroom door closed behind us, I place Rayne on her feet and stare down at her.

Her eyes are shining as she stares right back. "Jer…"

With a groan, I slam my lips against hers. She answers by digging her fingers into my hair and nipping at my mouth with a fervent intensity.

Backing her toward the bed, we crash down on top of the covers. Pulling away from her lips long enough to kiss a path down her jawline, Rayne moans beneath me.

"Easy," she gasps. "This dress…is from…Paris."

Lifting my head, I let my gaze peruse her body, taking in the fact that one of her straps has fallen to one side. Dragging the other one down, I push the silky-soft fabric down to expose my wife's perfect set of tits. Licking a hot trail around one pebbly, dark nipple, I pull it into my mouth and suck.

Rayne's fingers tighten in my hair to the point of pain, but it's the kind of pain I'm starting to live for. Pulling one of her legs up and around my waist, I rock my aching, hard cock into her. Grinding against me, her moan almost drives me over the edge.

"Wife," I whisper. "Sorry I pulled you away from your wedding reception. I needed to be inside you." Switching to her other nipple, I bite down, smoothing out the sting with a caress of my tongue.

The skin of her bare thigh feels like satin against my fingers. As I stroke her heated skin, a scrap of lace against my fingers stills me.

Keeping my eyes on hers, I travel down her body, hiking her dress up around her hips so I can see the garter wrapping around her thigh.

"Fuck. That's the sexiest thing I've ever seen." I admire the white lace, and let my eyes sweep her toned leg down to the gold heels.

"Jeremy." Her voice is pleading, and my eyes flick back up to hers. "I need you…"

But she's my wife, and I already know what she needs. Reaching up, I grip the thin straps of her underwear, drag them down her legs, and discard them. I watch her, fascinated, as I trail my fingers up her thigh and through the soaking wet folds of her sex.

"Goddamn, darlin'. Wet as fuck. My wife wants me." Gravel in my voice, I let my tongue follow the path my fingers took.

At the first breath of my mouth against her pussy, she arches off the bed, and I grab her hips to still her while I lick a path around her clit. When I push two fingers inside her and draw them out slowly before plunging them back in, she cries out.

"Jeremy! Oh, God."

Swirling my tongue around the most sensitive part of her again and again, and finding a regular rhythm with my fingers, I'm torturing myself just as much as I'm pleasuring her. My cock strains against my pants, and the thought of sinking inside her turns my hands rough and needy.

When her walls start to quiver and clench around my fingers, I pull back and lick my lips. "Not yet, baby. Not until I'm inside you. Raw."

She gazes at me through heavily lidded lashes. "No condom?"

Going still, I gaze up at her with my hands still squeezing her hips and the taste of her lingering on my tongue. This is a big deal. I know she isn't on the pill. She told me that she's never had a reason to be, which only made me want to beat my chest with pride. "Is that okay with you?"

Standing, I unbuckle my belt and loosen my pants. Rayne scoots forward on the bed, making me smile at how mussed her hair is now. She begins to unbutton my shirt with swift fingers. When she's finished, I push my pants and boxer briefs down in one movement, toeing off my shoes and kicking the pants aside. As my erection finally springs free Rayne's eyes go dark with desire as she stares. Not bothering to pull off my open button-down, I gently push her back on the bed and hover over her.

"Okay with me? What if I get pregnant?" Her eyes search mine, nerves showing on her face as she pulls her bottom lip into her mouth.

Bending down to pull her lip into my own mouth, I suck on it until she moans. "Making a baby with you…getting to do it all right this time, from the beginning? God, Rayne…That sounds like the best fucking idea in the world."

Sliding her arms around my neck, she lifts her hips until the tip of my cock is pushing against her entrance. And where normally I would slam into her without pause, I take a second and breathe her in.

Her scent, always sweet floral mixed with the slightest hint of sassy spice, overwhelms me. Lowing my head to her chest, the powerful and rapid beating of her heart astounds me. And when I press my mouth to hers as I slowly press inside her, the connection of not just our bodies, but also our lives and our hearts and *fuck,* our souls.

I'm about to make love to Rayne for the first time as her husband, and I'm going to savor it like I never have before.

Her eyes wide open, staring into mine, our bodies closer than they've ever been, the expression in them tells me that she knows exactly what I'm thinking and feeling.

When I'm buried to the hilt, she wraps her legs around my waist, taking me even deeper into her heat, and we both groan with the pure bliss.

"You're amazing." My rough whisper blows across her lips, and her lips curve into a smile.

"I love you." Her simple words urge me to move faster, and I catch her gasp and kiss her. My tongue plunges into her mouth the same way my cock dives into her heat, deliberate and slow and loving.

When she tightens around me, her body pulsing and milking and quivering, my heart rate actually speeds up. Like I'm some teenage kid who's never done this before. The thought of pleasuring my wife, of making her come, of making her scream my name, is driving me over the edge and I can't hold back anymore. Pulling out of her, she whimpers in protest until I grasp the nape of her neck and pull her up until she's straddling my lap. Pressing her forehead against mine, she hovers above me, and my balls draw up tight with my impending release.

"Rayne," I choke out. "Ride me until you come, darlin'." Not knowing if I can hold out much longer, I lift her and set her down hard on my cock to get her started.

Not needing any more direction than that, my wife whips into action, riding me hard, her face lapsing into an expression of ecstasy that I can't stop watching. Her head falls back, her hands tangle in my hair, and her gorgeous tits bounce against my chest. I can feel the pressure building low in my gut, my abs tightening and my fingers digging into her hips.

"Oh, God!" she yells, and when she grinds into me, swiveling her hips as she comes apart, I can't hold out anymore.

"Fuck," I growl as I bury my head in her neck and shoot my release inside her.

Both of our bodies are slick with sweat, and I catch her as she starts to fall backward against the pillows. Following her down, I pull her to my chest and concentrate on taking deep breaths.

"Ohmygod, Jer…we just left our fucking wedding to have sex."

When I glance at her, I smirk to see her hands covering uncontrollable giggles.

"Wrong. I carried you out of our wedding so I could make love to my wife. Totally acceptable. Are you ready to go back?"

She rolls onto her stomach and props herself up on her elbows. My eyes stray to her full, heavy breasts, and I can't stop my finger from reaching out to stroke them.

Her eyes track my movements. "I love you, husband. I'm ready to go back if you promise me you're going to *make love to your wife* again later."

Staring up at the woman who now commands my world, I nod. "Absolutely."

Easiest fucking promise I've ever made.

Please turn the page for a preview of
the next book in the Rescue Ops series,

Promise to Defend.

Ronin

The sky above me is deep purple, especially beautiful tonight with the generous dotting of stars. There are no clouds to block the glittering specks of light overhead, and I appreciate the view more than I usually would.

Tonight is a celebration of love, something I avoid if I can.

The crisp North Carolina night hugs the wedding guests as they twirl around the dance floor or congregate at the tables, talking and laughing with one another like they don't have a care in the world. I spot the members of my team at Night Eagle Security gathered at one, and my gaze roams over the group as they burst into raucous laughter.

They're enjoying their night. The thought almost makes me smile.

As Jeremy Teague's best man, I've enjoyed myself, too. The process of watching him fall in love with his high school sweetheart all over again has been nothing but a pleasure. He never thought it would happen for him, thought he and Rayne were over a long time ago. When she strolled back into town with their eight-year-old son in tow, Jeremy about lost his mind.

I was proud of the way he stepped right into that father's role like it was easy. Like becoming a parent to a son you previously knew nothing about was a cakewalk. I knew it wasn't, but for him the choice was clear. He wanted that life with Rayne and Decker.

And now he has it.

My eyes find them, swaying on the dance floor. Rayne's head rests on Brains's—the nickname he earned as a gadgets guru on our private security team—shoulder while his hands wander up and down her back. It looks like they move as one unit, and I know that now everything will be different. She's his number one partner in life now, not me. And that's how it should be.

If I ever thought there was a chance I'd have it again myself, I'd take it.

But some people only get that kind of opportunity, that kind of pure, unequaled love, once in a lifetime.

I already had mine.

My gaze sweeps toward the sound of giggling, not far from the newlywed couple. I zero in on a flash of dark red hair pulled to the side, exposing a creamy expanse of graceful neck. Olive Alexander, Rayne's sister, twirls Decker around in a circle, and then ducks as he does the same for her. They're both grinning like mad, and her dark, midnight-blue eyes sparkle in the moonlight. White, glowing paper lanterns all around the yard mingle with the twinkling lights strung from the trees and the effect it has on Olive takes my fucking breath away.

I study the pair for a moment. Olive takes both of Decker's hands as the band launches into a lively tune and the silliness she gives him suits her. I've met Olive a handful of times, and even though her beauty always stunned me, I never took her for the laid-back, silly, hands-on-aunt type.

Apparently, I'd been wrong.

Two deep dimples appear in her cheeks as she drops her head back and laughs at something the kid did, and I find myself lost in a sea of thoughts. *How often does she smile like that? When will she be leaving to go back to Europe? Has she always had those goddamn dimples?*

"She's pretty." A soft, matter-of-fact voice reaches me, and I glance to the side and down to see that Sayward Diaz has crept up beside me.

I take her in, appreciating the utterly different way she's chosen to appear tonight. I've only ever seen Sayward in a pair of jeans and sneakers with a hoodie. Tonight she chose to forgo her usual uniform and wears a simple turquoise dress that sweeps the ground at her feet. Thin spaghetti straps arch over her shoulders, and the curves she apparently rocked underneath the jeans all this time are now on display as the dress hugs her body. The bright blue color sets off her skin tone that's so similar to mine, deep tan like toasted almonds. Her thick black hair is pulled off her face and tied into a loose knot at the nape of her neck.

"You look good tonight, Diaz." I catch her eye, making sure she knows I mean it.

Sayward acknowledges my compliment with a shrug. "I

know. Everyone is supposed to dress up for a wedding, right? I bought this today." She fingers the soft material of her dress, and I bite back a smile.

Social graces aren't really Sayward's strong suit. She's a legit computer hacker in her own right, and her skills can't be beat by anyone. As a recent consultant for NES, she has a special relationship with its owner and boss, Jacob Owen, that none of us are privy to. But she's easy to be around, and works her ass off, so I'd never complain about having her there.

"This is true." I raise my bourbon to my lips and sip, appreciating the fiery path it burns down my throat. "But all the same…you're rocking the shit outta that dress. Not every woman could."

Now her eyes meet mine, like she's only just figured out that I'm complimenting her. A small smile works its way onto her lips. "Thanks, Swagger."

Lifting my chin at her in acknowledgment of my own NES nickname, I indicate the table where our friends are sitting. "Shall we?"

I hold out my arm, and she looks at it for a second like she's wondering what to do with it before she finally slips her hand through and lets me lead her toward the table. I pull out a chair for her beside Dare Conners's wife, Berkeley, and take the empty one opposite Grisham Abbot. His fiancée, Greta, grins at me.

"You taking all of this in, Ronin?" her sweet voice asks.

Shrugging, I down the rest of my drink and contemplate getting back up for a refill. "It was a good wedding."

Berkeley leans over Dare to peer at me. "The boys of NES

are dropping like flies, Ronin. Don't tell me you never consider settling down."

Dare stares at her. "His nickname is *Swagger*."

I roll my eyes. "You know that has nothing to do with women."

No, I earned my nickname for the confidence I carry when making a man scream like a crying baby at my mercy. My claim to fame? All the ways I can torture a man without actually killing him. Because in interrogation, the goal is always to make the prisoner talk. If he's dead, he can't talk. I have a magic touch in this area. Something I'm proud of? Maybe not. But afterward, I'm able to walk with my head high because what I've done furthers the greater good. And that's something I can live with when my head hits the pillow each night.

Grisham, or Ghost as we call his stealthy ass, snorts. "Definitely has nothing to do with women."

My team's aware that I've already fallen. It's just not something we talk about, and that's my choice. It seems like a lifetime ago, now, but my heart went into the ground at the same time that my wife did.

Game over.

"I don't think that whole happily-ever-after shit is for me." I keep my voice low as I answer Berkeley's question, averting my gaze.

Inside, my chest tightens, the feeling of my heart squeezing dangerously tight overwhelming me. The emotion, the grief and fury that I thought I had recovered from a long time ago, resurface and threaten to pull me under.

Immediately, Berkeley's whiskey-colored eyes go all soft and gooey and her bottom lip disappears into her mouth. "You don't know that. Everyone deserves love, Ronin."

Shaking my head, I scan the ongoing party. If she thinks I deserve love, it's because she doesn't know the truth behind my story. I couldn't protect my wife the first time around. Pretty sure guys like me don't get a second shot. And I've accepted that.

I incline my head toward Brains and his brand-new wife, who are now standing beside a small table on the patio. Their faces are masks of utter concentration as they work together to guide a huge knife through a towering white cake. The crowd erupts in cheers when they succeed, and a photographer snaps their picture. I've never seen such a look of pure, unadulterated joy on my best friend's face. There's a peace about him he never had before.

I'm saved from having to answer Berkeley when Decker throws his little body into my side. "Uncle Ronin! You gonna eat cake?"

Looking at him, I'm pretty sure his cheeks might split open from the size of his smile. The kid just got everything every other child in the world wants. His mom and his dad together under one roof. Holding out my fist, he bumps it and then we blow it up.

"Cake? Heck yeah, it's a wedding, right? We gotta have cake."

Decker nods, serious as a lethal injection. "Yeah. We gotta have cake."

Olive saunters up behind him, leaning low over his shoulder to kiss his cheek. She pauses there, her deep, dark eyes meeting mine for a brief pause. I take the time to notice for the first time that there's a dusting of freckles, delicate and sparse, sprinkling her nose and cheeks. That, combined with the dimples, the huge, deep-set eyes, and the striking color of her hair, are enough to keep me locked in her stare.

Rising, she doesn't look away. "Hello, Ronin."

Olive's voice is a lot different from her sister's. Where Rayne has one of those throaty, sultry voices that screams sex appeal without even trying, Olive's voice is purer, sweeter. It makes me want to figure out all the ways I can dirty her up. I stand, holding Decker by the shoulders, and face her.

"Hey. Jeremy told me you'd be here for the wedding. How long you in town for?"

Her eyes go cloudy, and I zero in on her expression because something in it falters before she wraps it up tight and offers a strained smile. "Oh, um…I finished with the job in Paris a couple months ahead of schedule. My, uh, client…died. So, yeah. I'm back in Wilmington working out of our office here."

I know that Olive is an interior designer, and that the firm she works for has international clients. It's how she and Berkeley met, and how Rayne ended up working at Night Eagle when she arrived back in town. Beyond that, I don't know much of anything about Olive. There's something eating at her now, though. That much is obvious.

"I see." I nod, holding her gaze once more. But before I can get a read on her, she glances down at Decker.

"Ready for cake?"

He pumps his head up and down, turning toward me. "Let's go, Uncle Ronin."

Olive lifts her brows, her expression surprised. "He calls you Uncle Ronin?" she asks as we follow the little boy toward the patio.

I chuckle, rubbing the back of my neck with a hand. "Yeah. Brains's fault. I don't mind, though."

She frowns. "Brains?"

I smile down at her. The muscles it takes to do so feel unused, rusty. I've smiled at plenty of women before, just not women who affect me the way Olive seems to. And not with a smile as true as the one I'm using now. "Nickname. We all have one."

She nods, understanding dawning across her face. "It's a military thing."

"Yep."

Walking onto the patio, Decker rushes straight into Rayne's arms, and Jeremy edges toward me. We both watch as Decker stands between Rayne and Olive, both women showering the eight-year-old with loving attention. When Olive brushes a lock of his hair off his forehead, my chest pulls tight.

The fuck? It's the sentimentality of this day, drawing me in and fucking with my head. That's all it can be.

"I'm a lucky bastard." Jeremy folds his arms, and when I glance at him his eyes are locked on his family.

The family he never even knew he needed but is now willing to die to protect.

I watch them, too. My eyes keep straying to Olive, who looks so comfortable with Decker.

"You talked to her tonight?" Jeremy asks suddenly.

Glancing away from Olive, I find that he's staring directly at me. "Who? Olive?"

He nods, studying me. "Yeah."

Shaking my head, I look back at the two women and Decker. "Not really. Why?"

He turns away from the women, and I follow suit. Walking a few feet from the patio, he starts talking. "I don't know, man. She got into town last night. I picked her up from the airport, and...she was off. I mean, I don't know her that well, not since high school. But she seems...worried."

The protective instinct inside of me, the one that's lain dormant now for exactly seven years, lifts its head. "You ask her?"

He shakes his head slowly. "Didn't know how to. I mean, we knew each other back in high school because of Rayne, but we weren't close. And we certainly aren't best friends now. But she's my sister-in-law, and she means the world to Rayne. I want to know what's going on with her. I don't think she'd tell me if I asked."

"Why do you say that?"

He runs a hand through his long hair. "Olive is...capable. She likes to do everything herself. She likes to be in control. At least that's how Rayne tells it, and there was some of that back then, too. She wouldn't respond well if she thought I was stepping in where I don't belong, or trying to help her when she thinks she's got it handled."

I nod. I get that. Every vibe I've ever gotten off of Olive tells me she was independent as fuck. She's always well put-together, she drives a nice car, she owns her own house. And she has a successful career. So if she were in trouble, she wouldn't necessarily see it as fit to ask for help.

"What do you need?" My tone cautious, I wait for Jeremy to roll out whatever it is he's asking.

"Rayne and Decker and I are going to Aruba for a couple of weeks. You know that. I just want you to keep an eye on her, Swagger. Make sure she's okay. Shit, make plans with her if you have to. I just need to know that you'll be there if she needs you. Obviously if need be, we can be on the first flight back to Wilmington. You copy?"

Yeah, I copied. Jeremy's all about family, now that he has one, and he wants to protect Olive as a part of that family. As his best friend, I'm the first person he'd ask to make sure she's okay while he's away.

My eyes straying back to Olive as she takes a delicate bite of cake, that instinct inside of me to protect is now fully awake. Even if Olive wants me nowhere near whatever problem she's having, I'll be there. I'll step in whether she wants me to or not.

When her eyes meet mine, her fork freezes halfway to her mouth and a strong current of something I can't understand pulls taut between us. When the cake finally makes it to her mouth, I watch, fascinated, as she chews. Then she swallows, her slender throat moving with the action. Her tongue darts out to lick the stray pieces of sugar from her lips and my dick stirs in my pants. I want to lick those plump, succulent lips. And where the hell does that desire come from?

Maybe getting to the bottom of whatever bothers Olive Alexander won't be work, or just a favor for my best friend.

Maybe it'll even be fun.

About the Author

Diana Gardin is a wife of one and a mom of two. Writing is her second full-time job to that, and she loves it! Diana writes contemporary romance in the Young Adult and New Adult categories. She's also a former elementary schoolteacher. She loves steak, sugar cookies, and Coke and hates working out.

Learn more at:
 DianaGardin.com
 Twitter: @DianalynnGardin
 Facebook.com/AuthorDianaGardin

21982031735297

CPSIA information can be obtained
at www.ICGtesting.com
Printed in the USA
BVOW10s0928040817
491096BV00001B/9/P

9 781455 571543